Bad Moon

USA TODAY BESTSELLING AUTHOR

SHYLA COLT

Playlist

Delicate: Taylor Swift
Girls Like You: Maroon 5
High Hopes: Panic! At the Disco
…Ready For It?: Taylor Swift
Sorry Not Sorry: Demi Lovato
Look What You Made Me Do: Taylor Swift
My Blood: TWENTY ØNE PILØTS
Bad Moon Rising: Creedence Clearwater Revival
Gasoline: Halsey
Jumpsuit: TWENTY ØNE PILØTS

Pack: a group of wild animals, especially wolves, living and hunting together.

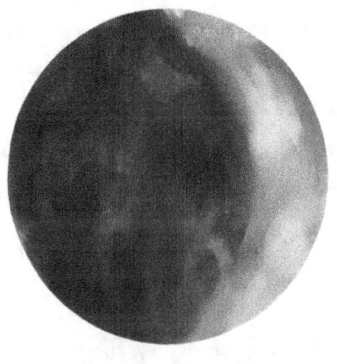

Chapter One

PACK IS PROTECTION, BELONGING, AND acceptance. They provide a home comprised of like-minded people willing to lay down their lives for one common goal—family. The driving desire to band together, watch each other's back, and defend against outsiders is instinctual and pure. Over time, even clean things can become corrupt. The White Creek wolves are being invaded by a cancerous growth, spreading through, decaying, destroying, and ravaging all in its wake.

Joss watched the white-robed pack members gather in front of the area where the Alpha, Ian Eberstark, would appear like royalty.

Too blind to see Ian and the White Creek compound for what they truly were, they looked to the older man for answers. He was charismatic and powerful. In his early fifties, he wore his thick salt and pepper hair pulled back from his face, showcasing a widow's peak. Thick brows framed his bright blue eyes. Sharp cheekbones were highlighted by a neatly kept beard and thin mutton chops. Without saying a word, his presence demanded respect. Six foot four, and muscular, he cut an impressive figure and stood above most in a crowd. Ian resembled a mountain man from times gone by. Perfect white teeth and warm brown eyes helped hide the cold, calculating, and narcissistic soul encased in the kindly packaging he presented.

You have no idea what darkness lurks in that man's heart. Disgusted, she turned away from the growing sea of white lemmings and eyeballed the twelve-foot-high corrugated iron privacy fence surrounding the compound. The shiny barrier was broken up by the honeyed spruce posts. Beyond that fence lie more than freedom.

It led to the outside world, normalcy, and the anonymity associated with not being known. Her heart rate increased. Longing pulled her along like a magnet. Helpless against the attraction, her feet guided her closer. Reaching out, she ran her fingertips over the smooth, cool surface. *It'd be so easy to slip away once the ceremony went into full swing. I could disappear into the night, leave everything, and never look back.* Closing her eyes, she imagined a life void of responsibility, familial ties, and lies.

The once pleasant scent of pine rose dispersed. Her stomach protested, rolling like a stormy sea. The clean scent that represented Christmas, hot chocolate, and presents in her youth had been bastardized. Warped and twisted by White Creek, the aroma became a symbol of an impending *ceremony.* Joss kept her back to the crowd, and pulled her hood down farther to hide her expression. Struggling to regain a blank façade, she breathed deeply. Angering the alpha lead to agony and humiliation.

Phantom pains shot through the faded scars on her back. Trapped by circumstances, her existence was likened to a rat in captivity, observed and used by scientists. She scanned the scene covertly over her shoulder. Fires flickered in the night, dancing wildly in the wind, their flames contained by hand built stone fire pits. Huddled together, the followers spoke in hushed voices. A wave of excitement swept through them, expanding as time slipped by. Their exuberance scented the air—a living, gut-wrenching thing she could almost see like an oily sheen that distorted her vision. People stood taller. Anticipation tinged their words. It looked like a fraternity or sorority event. *If only it were so harmless.*

She continued farther down the fence line, away from the others gathering in clumps. *Walk out and don't look back. You don't have to play this role any longer,* the rebellious voice inside of her urged her. Despite her misgivings, she pushed on, placing one foot in front of the other, feeling lighter with every step. Her heart slammed against her ribcage, echoing in her ears as she fell into tunnel vision. What would life be like free of White Creek's rules, secrets, and practices? She hadn't tasted that flavor of liberty since she was ten years old. At twenty-five, she was beyond ready to experience life on her own terms.

Images of a job in a quiet town by a lake where no one knew her danced in her head. Perhaps she could find a new pack or live solo? Being a lone wolf resonated strongly. *I've had enough togetherness to last a lifetime. At this point, I prefer wolves to werewolves.* For a moment, she allowed herself to forget about everyone who depended on her. An imaginary shiny, gold hoop hovered above her, glinting in a tantalizing manner. She wanted to grab it with both hands and bail.

Watching her new life play in her mind, she crept silently forward on bare feet. Thirty seconds later she was dipping into her bank account and purchasing a new apartment. A minute later, she was decorating and making friends with the quirky girl next door who had no clue she turned furry once a month. *I'm so close.*

"Headed somewhere, sister?"

The smug baritone acted like an icy bucket of reality delivered by an enemy. Pausing in mid-step, she steeled herself for the confrontation. Showing her stepbrother, Isiah, emotion equated to tossing gasoline into a fire and expecting it to die down. She turned to face him, coolly arching a brow.

"Did I miss the memo declaring traveling alone an illegal activity?"

His smirk drew attention to a plump lower lip and perfectly sculpted upper lip beneath his impeccably groomed close-cut beard. Soulful brown eyes glinted with mischief and menace. She couldn't deny his rugged beauty. Not with his square jawline, deep-set eyes, and spiky, dark brown hair that spilled across his broad brow. His refined, upturned nose added to an imagined elegance. He looked studious and sensitive. *Maybe, that's how he lures people into his web like a hungry spider. Thank God I know better.*

"No, but you had a look about you."

He stepped closer, breaching her personal space. She tensed. "I'm sure I don't know what you mean."

Leaning down, he whispered into her ear, "The one people get when they've had enough, and they're contemplating doing something stupid."

"You'd know that look well then, wouldn't you, *brother?*" she mocked, widening her eyes.

He chuckled. "I love it when you let the claws out." As his breath tickled the sensitive flesh of her ear, she fought to stave off her desire to shudder and move away. "You've got an endless supply of strength and courage hidden behind that demure persona you assume. I know it's not who you really are. I've seen that fire burning deep down over the years. No matter what Daddy does, he can't put it out completely." He chuckled. "It infuriates him. We share that honor." He inhaled deeply. "After all of this time, you *still* smell like honeysuckle and lavender. It makes me wonder if you *taste* sweet."

"Enough." She drew her boundary with the clipped word.

He pulled away, flashing her a wide grin. "Ah-ha There she is. The woman I can't wait to *bend* to my will."

She sneered, "You wish you held that type of power over me."

Sighing, he shook his head. "Why fight it so hard? We know how this will end, Joss. You've got the waning moon birthmark, and I have the waxing moon. Our destinies are entwined. We're children of the prophecy."

"Nowhere in that prediction, did it mention a requirement of romantic involvement." She clenched her jaw.

"But I want it," he whined, curling a lock of her thick, wavy, strawberry-blonde and auburn locks. "I always get what I want. Eventually."

"Indeed. It's why you have such poor character." She shook her head. "It's a shame really. Poor little spoiled rich boy has been deluded into thinking he runs things."

"You never let me get away with anything, do you?" He grinned widely as he beamed. "It's okay. I like that. I enjoy the fight."

"I won't even dignify this," she gestured between them with her pointer finger, "with anything that comes close to being described that way. You don't rate it." Acid dripped from her tongue. She wanted to burn him. To peel back the thick skin he wore and injure his pride.

"Ouch. Touchy words." He winced. "Except," he held up a finger, "we both know the pack's magic is the only thing keeping Step mommy alive and well. Is her only child truly going to leave her to fend for herself?" He clucked his tongue. "I wonder what she'd think, if she knew how *effortlessly* her own flesh and blood could abandon her."

"She's the Alpha's mate," she deadpanned, determined not to allow him to provoke her.

"No." His harsh tone caused her to flinch. "She's his *wife*." His voice turned into an arctic breeze. "There is *no* equality there. Your mother is weak-willed and frail." He scowled. "It's not a secret. A better woman than she is could be ruling at his side. Yet, Father has always insisted on her." He scratched his beard "Do you suppose that has to do with her daughter being the chosen one?"

The words were a direct hit, preying on her fears and the heavy weight that encircled her ankle, keeping her bound to the life she loathed.

"Who's to say he doesn't love her?" she asked with a flippant shrug of her shoulders.

"Love will never outweigh his vision for White Creek." He placed a hand over his heart. "Don't take my word for it. Leave and find out for yourself."

"Without her, you'd have no hold on me."

"Yes, but you're such a sweet, devoted daughter, aren't you?" He pinched her cheek. She nipped at his finger, and he laughed. "People will continually hold you back, Joss. You should remember that." His joyful countenance faltered. "I learned the hard way with my mother."

"What happened to your mother?" she whispered.

His toothy grin and dead eyes chilled the blood flowing through her veins. The mania was there for all to see. They didn't call Isiah Eberstark "stark raving mad" behind his back for nothing. The bottom dropped out of her belly. Fear crept in, pushing aside her boldness. Suddenly, she really didn't want to know the answer to that question.

"Smart girl." He caressed the side of her face with his knuckles. "Your time dodging me is running out. You're twenty-five. You know what's coming soon. Heat. Being Moon Maiden won't save you forever. The time for you to pick a mate is coming. How you've managed to avoid it for so long is a mystery." She stepped to the side, and he countered, pressing her body back against the gate. She could feel the long, lean length of him through her robe. His muscular frame dwarfed her own. Palms up, she pressed against his chest, forcing him back, regaining space between them. "You must realize by now, even if you tried to pick someone else," his voice dropped an octave, "I'd never allow it, Joss." Leaning in, he pressed his lips to her cheek.

"You're a repulsive tyrant."

"It's nice to know you've paid attention to me. I'm a man who was born to rule. Don't worry, little wolf. My time will soon be at hand." Her gut lurched. When he took over the pack, she'd lose all of her leverage. "Things are already in motion. Younger leadership is the next logical step. I wonder, would you deny our people, who've stood by us and waited patiently, with such inspirational devotion, that natural progression?" His voice was honeyed perfection, oozing over her ear as he spilled sweet words.

"You have a silver tongue."

"All the better to please you with." He waggled his eyebrows.

"It's never worked on me."

"You've never given me the chance to try." He nuzzled her forehead with the tip of his nose. On the outside looking in, they were having a *moment.* His pheromones swarmed her. Musk, vanilla, and dark spices blended together.

"And I *never* will."

"Hmmm. Never say never."

"Maiden. Beta." The reverent tone drew their attention to the pale woman who curtsied a few yards away.

"Adaline." Isiah turned on his megawatt smile. The thin, blonde blushed; her round cheeks turned red.

"Hello, Addie." Joss forced a smile. Addie beamed before she rushed off to join the group of girls watching the interaction with wide eyes. The gaggle of teens giggled as they moved toward the area where the ritual would soon take place.

Lambs being led to slaughter, each and every one. They swallowed the propaganda pushed by the Alpha hook, line, and sinker. *And I'm a willing accomplice who knows better. That makes me worse than all of them who believe blindly.*

She'd spent her tenth year watching her mother deteriorate as she slowly lost the battle with the cancer ravaging her body from the inside out. The chemotherapy stole her lustrous blonde hair, strength, and the weight that rounded her cheeks. She'd been a living skeleton clinging to life, without actually living. The Alpha fixed that. *How can I even consider returning her to that fate? It'd be a death sentence.* With her father six-feet deep, she owed it to him to look after her.

"Smile, precious, your mom is on her way over, and we wouldn't want to upset the queen." Isiah stepped away, wrapped an arm around her shoulders, and pulled her to his side. His charm ratcheted up to eleven as he morphed his body language. A chameleon, her step-brother was a master at being what others needed to feel comfortable.

"Mother," he said jovially.

"I should've known I'd find you two together." Her mother smiled. "Come. It's nearly time for us to begin."

Caught in the limelight once more, Joss put on her mask. She wiped the anger and frustration from her aura, and focused on exuding calm. Straightening her spine, she stood tall, falling in step with Isiah. They came to stand by the Alpha. Flanked by his betas, she should've felt protected. Instead, she silently suffocated.

"Tonight, we have much to celebrate. Odin has kept us safe for another season. Our harvests are plentiful, and the pack is strong. We all feel the tension rising. The time we've prepared for is coming soon. Have you heard the rumors swirling among the supernatural communities? They claim vampires are walking in the sun, wolves are able to change without the moon, and the witches wage their own internal wars." Murmurs of agreement mingled with gasps, and whispers coated with fear sprang up like stalks seeking the sun. "I don't take any pleasure in the plight of others," the Alpha said gravely. "Though it proves what we've always known. A war is coming. Today we pray for strength, understanding, and blessings as we move forward into the winter season."

The Alpha stepped back. Isiah removed his tentacle-like arm and took the drum from the beta, James. The hollowed-out log had deer hide stretched taut across the opening. Sinew thongs lashed the sides together. The drumstick was made from a branch from the same tree. The head of the stick was wrapped in deer hide filled with sheep's wool. White Creek took bits and pieces from multiple sources, most notably, however, was the Native Americans who lived off the land and used natural products. It fit with the prepper lifestyle the Alpha pushed.

The steady rhythm Isiah drummed, signaled the start of the ritual. Silence settled over the crowd as the followers formed a line.

"Maiden, take your place in the center of our circle. Use your influence to bend Odin's ear. Help us usher in a new season and ask for blessings."

Head held high, she walked to the center of the field lined with stones painted white and placed in a circular Nordic design. Sinking to the ground between two silver chalices, she tucked her legs under her, closed her eyes, and hummed. She rocked back and forth, descending deep into a trance-like state as she let everything else fall away. Drawing strength from the moon, she raised her arms above her head.

"We come to you humbled and grateful for your blessings, Odin. We ask that you smile on us once more as we gather the last of our harvest and prepare for the bitter winter months. Fortify our warriors. Make us sharp-minded and guide us where you will. We bring offerings of food and drink. Grant us this boon, if it is your will." Opening her eyes, she blinked rapidly to adjust to the brightness. Gathered around her with flaming torches, the members of the pack faced away from her. Rising, she picked up the chalices and began to travel in the divots created in the land, along the *path*. As she passed behind those who stood, each turned to *witness* her journey. Lowering their torches, they acknowledged her power and importance.

Their powers reached out and wrapped around her. Packs had their own brand of magic. They were, after all, magical beings at the core, despite their intense connection to nature. Ending her journey at the opening flanked by the Alpha and Isiah, she walked between the two of them. They escorted her to a set of steps carved from stone. Turning toward the group gathering, she held up the chalices as Isiah resumed his steady drumbeat. Once they were all lined up, she turned to stand by the statue of Odin with his wolves carved in Cedar.

Bowing low and reverently, she spilled a small bit of the fine whiskey at the base of the statue and straightened. The Alpha approached, taking the chalices from her, and finished pouring the offerings over the statue. Smoke rose up as if he'd extinguished a fire. He had the theatrics down, she'd give him that.

He turned dramatically. "Odin has heard us." Deafening cheers rose up.

She cringed internally. The Alpha stood taller as their hero worship inflated him. She ground her teeth, biting her tongue to keep from speaking out. *Look pretty, stay under the radar, and remember this will all be over soon.*

"Today we have much to celebrate. It's been revealed to me in dreams. My reign will be coming to an end."

Whispers rose. The scent of fear and apprehension soured the air. She wrinkled her nose. Bile crept up her throat like slimy slugs.

"I told you," Isiah whispered in her ear. The self-satisfied purr made her claws itch to be released. She wanted to rake her nails down his handsome face.

"Don't worry, my friends." He waved his hands in a downward motion. "This won't happen all at once! It'll be little by little. Isiah is a strong wolf who knows what needs to be done to survive the tough winter ahead. I will be elevating to my next position among us as Spiritual Advisor. You can come to me with your worries and concerns, and I'll continue to steer White Creek in the right direction."

Less work and more praise and worship for yourself. You'll let your little psycho do the dirty work because he enjoys it.

"This is all in preparation for the times to come. We will be even more vigilant than we were before. Now is the time for strength and bravery." He smiled, expertly steering them away from the source of their panic. "We all need to do our part, pull our weight, and ascend to the best version of ourselves for the pack."

She felt the Alpha's gaze lock onto her like lasers. *Message received, Alpha.*

He was done with her defiance. Most wolves her age were mated. Her position had protected her, until now. They were expected to keep the pack healthy. That meant breeding. Horror struck her. Did they expect her to lay down and start creating pack members with Isiah?

Isiah slithered his way beside her and kissed her cheek. It felt like a betrayal, a Judas kiss before she was bartered off for coin.

"Come, we will celebrate the changes together," Ian crowed, soaking up his final days as Alpha as the crowd moved forward like a wave.

Her mother preened. Joss wondered for the millionth time how much of her joy was authentic.

"Smile pretty, Moon Maiden, your adoring public approaches." The tentacle arm returned, wrapping around her waist and constricting like a snake.

"It was a beautiful ceremony, Moon Maiden." The elderly silver-haired woman patted her hand.

"Thank you, Mrs. Constance. I simply put the energy you lent me back into the environment."

"She's so gracious, Raymond. Won't she make a beautiful queen?" Mrs. Constance asked.

"I happen to agree with you," Isiah chimed in.

Constance patted Isiah's cheek. "So sweet. You've only had eyes for her all of this time."

"You should tell her that." He pressed his head against hers. "I don't think she believes me."

Raymond gave Isiah's shoulder a squeeze. "The good ones always give you a run for your money, son."

"I'll keep that in mind," Isiah said as the couple moved on.

"Look," he cooed, hugging her. "They think we're cute."

"There is no *we*," Joss whispered quietly out of the side of her mouth.

"That's not what they think, and we know how much perception shapes reality."

More well-wishers approached, preventing her from responding. They gushed over them, ingratiating themselves to Isiah, like wolves showing their soft bits in deference to his upcoming position. The line of people thinned as the party started. Beers were brought out, and music began to pour through the compound speakers.

He pulled her to him. "Which name do you like best, wifey ... mate, or maybe queen?"

"Fuck off, Stark," she said through her teeth.

He chuckled. "Oh, we'll do that, too." He licked his lips.

"Over my dead body."

"It'd be over your mother's actually."

She growled.

"Stop teasing one another, and mingle," the Alpha commanded.

Grateful to escape Isiah's clutches, she pulled from his lax grip, and wove her way deeper into the crowd, pausing to chat occasionally before she found her way away from the celebration toward the path that led to her home. The die was cast. She had to choose the moves that would guide her to freedom while keeping her sanity in check.

JOSS RAN HER FINGERS OVER the deep yellow, downy soft petals surrounding the dark brown center. Sunflowers were her favorite, and White Creek Country Store was known for its massive blooms. The fertile soil yielded monster stalks yearly, and people bought them by the bundle. The smooth butcher's block counter on the island was clean and ready to create upon. Its three shelves were stocked with floral foam, twine, butcher paper, and ribbons. They kept things rustic and simple, but it was no less beautiful. The superior quality of the flowers spoke for itself.

White Creek County Store was a haven. A safe place where she briefly escaped the madness that descended the moment she entered the compound. For at least eight hours, she was free to mingle with the outside world, and pretend to be one of them. Even more so, the floral station was a slice of heaven on earth. Buckets full of freshly cut flowers yielded a heady scent. Their bright splashes of colors never failed to improve her day.

Slowly positioning the sunflowers in their black display bucket, she milked the re-stock for all it was worth. Mingling with her co-workers wasn't high on her priority list. Here, she fled from the whispers and stares that dogged her every step since the ceremony weeks earlier. People waffled between kissing her rump and avoiding her like the plague. *This is what it feels like to be a pariah.*

"Are you done hiding among flora and fauna, Thumbelina?" The silky alto of her best friend, Brook, made her sigh. Joss met the steady light-brown gaze of her narrowed, wide-set eyes fringed with dark lashes. Arms crossed beneath her bosoms, and hip cocked, Brook embodied the word fierce. Her pointed toe black boot tapped against the wooden floor. Black skinny jeans hugged her lithe six-foot-one frame.

Joss shrugged and stepped away from the sunflowers. "The store needed restocking."

"For over two hours, though?" Brook replied with a deep frown.

"I stopped to help customers, too." The excuse sounded flimsy to her own ears. Regardless, she clung to it like a drowning victim clinging to a life preserver.

"Uh huh." Brook pursed her thin lips. "Well, it's just us now, Rapunzel, so you can climb down from your tower and be straight with me."

"I wasn't aware I was crooked," Joss mumbled.

"Cute, Joss. Real cute." Brook shook her head.

Joss's eyes darted around the tiny store in quest of a distraction. The six aisles were neatly arranged. Handmade jam and jelly jars lined the shelves, label out. The floor was clear of any debris and shone from a fresh coat of lemon-scented wood polish that filled the air. The clean smell blended with the odor of freshly brewed coffee, and her mouth watered.

"You've been busy."

"I have. Now, are you ready to talk about what's eating you alive? Or do we get to endure more uncomfortable silences and brooding? You're going to give your forehead wrinkles if you keep it up." Brook tapped her forehead.

Joss dropped her head and allowed her shoulders to slump. "Why voice what you already know?"

"Humor me."

"You heard the Alpha. He all but announced my betrothal to Isiah."

"Almost isn't the same as did, Joss," Brook said gently.

"In a normal, healthy, functioning world, yes. Not so much in White Creek." Joss held up a hand. "You know I'm right."

"Most are afraid of the impending change. People want to know where they stand. Stark hasn't fooled all of us. We see his love for cruelty and manipulation."

"And yet, they'd marry me off in a heartbeat to save their own hide."

"That's human nature, babe. They think you'll be able to temper that mean streak. You forget one important fact, though."

"What's that?" Joss asked glumly.

"You have to give consent. Nothing can happen otherwise."

She bit the inside of her lip.

"You're not thinking about saying yes, are you, Joss?" Brook asked, horrified.

"There's a lot more at stake than you realize, Brook. This is about so much more than just me." She exhaled.

"You'd die inside. That's all I need to know about this situation." Brook's outrage warmed her from the inside out. She'd found a true friend in the sassy pack member. The bell above the door rang. "We're finishing this talk later," Brook warned before turning to smile at the family coming in. "Welcome to White Creek Country Store. How can we help you today?" Brook asked.

Forty-five minutes away from the compound, this store was one of their many fronts. The small town saw them as a commune of hippies who strove to live off the land. While odd, they were deemed harmless.

The rumble of a truck pulling up outside signaled more to restock. Joss hurried out the front door, eager to do busy work that would keep her mind occupied. Isiah opened the passenger door. Her excitement wilted like a flower with no water and too much sun.

"Sissy," he cried, waving madly like a toddler who'd just learned the meaning of hello.

"Isiah," she said blandly.

He lifted the aviators and pushed them into his hair. "Long day?"

"It is now," she said sweetly.

"Careful," His eyes darkened with malice. A moment later he was grinning. His duality scared her most of all. He was unstable.

Shoving her resentment down, she straightened her shoulders and walked toward him, accepting his hug.

"Did you miss your big brother?" His breath blew her hair away from her face.

"The same as I always do."

"Such a clever little tongue. I can't wait to put it to better use." He squeezed her tighter than necessary, and then released her. "We brought you goodies."

"And I appreciate it." She watched as the stocky, russet-haired beta climbed down from the truck, and walked around to the back. "Hey, James."

"Hi, Joss. How's work been today?"

"Steady."

James grasped the hand, turned, and raised the liftgate.

"I'll get everything ready for you in the storage room," Joss said, swiftly excusing herself. She walked into the store stiffly with her heart lodged in her throat.

"What's going on?" Brook asked.

"Our delivery arrived along with the mayor of crazy town," Joss whispered.

Brook's jaw dropped. "Jesus, he doesn't quit, does he?"

"It's not like he's all there." Joss tapped her temple as she swept past Brook and into the back room of the store. Breaking down the few boxes left over from restock, she made a clear space for the new product. Isiah entered the back room alone and closed the door behind him.

"Where's James?" Joss asked.

"I asked him to give us a minute." He shrugged.

"Why?" she asked cautiously.

He shoved his hands in his front pockets. "'Cause I wanted to ask you something."

She studied him. He seemed jovial enough. The boyish grin turned his lips up at the corner, and his brown eyes sparkled with light-hearted humor. *This is good Isiah.*

"Okay?"

"Go on a date with me?"

"What?" She spun away from the table.

"A date. You, me, romantic setting." He rubbed the back of his neck.

Paralyzed by uncertainty, she studied him carefully. Was this a trick? Some test she needed to pass? "And if I say no?"

"I wouldn't." The steely tone silenced her sarcastic response. "Why do you continue to fight this? It's going to happen one way or another. Why not make it easier for us both?"

She swallowed, to moisten the desert-like cavern of her mouth. Her gut told her rejection now would be a bad idea. "When?"

He stood up straight. "I'm glad you reconsidered your position."

Like I have a choice?

"Do not read too much into this," she cautioned.

"I'll pick you up tonight at eight." He stepped closer. "I'm going to change your mind about me." He brushed a kiss onto her forehead and stepped away. A knock sounded at the door, and Isiah answered it.

"Let's get everything loaded in and leave this beautiful woman to her work." Isiah winked, and hell froze over.

Sickened by her choices, she worked mechanically, helping them settle the produce and dry goods before bidding them good-bye.

"Are you okay?" Brook appeared in the door frame soon after they departed.

She sighed. "I've officially hit rock bottom."

"What did he do?" Brook's eye flashed.

"Asked me on a date."

"Oh my God! You had me worried." Brook shoved her gently.

"I said yes."

"Why the hell would you do that?" Brook squawked

"Because I was afraid of what he'd do if I said no. God. I used to be so good at managing him. Now it's out of control." She spread her arms out, shrugging off her frustration.

"You need to choose a mate, Joss."

Joss balked at the word. "No."

"Then what?" Brook challenged. "Because you have to do something everyone will understand and respect. You know how the pack operates."

"So, I guess I'm screwed then." Joss wrapped her arms around herself.

"Stop. There are plenty of strong, attractive wolves capable and willing to provide for you. You're in a better position than any other she-wolf. You have your pick."

"None of them are for me," Joss insisted.

"Once you go into heat, you're going to lose the ability to choose with a clear mind. Why are you so stubborn?" Brook threw her hands in the air, letting them fall down and slap her thighs.

"Because none of the wolves are for me," she snapped

Brook jerked back. "And how do you know this?"

Joss glanced away.

"This is about *him*, isn't it? Your dream man?"

"I didn't say that." Joss had never been one for fairy tales and dreams of happily ever after, but the man she saw in her sleeping hours felt more real than anything else in her life ever had after her father's death. How could she feel so connected to a person she'd never met? She'd asked herself all of the questions. *What if he wasn't real? What if he was? Would they ever meet?* None of the answers ever deterred her.

Brook rolled her eyes. "You didn't have to."

"All I want is the ability to choose my own path. We all deserve that. I'm going to fight for it."

"Even if it's a fruitless endeavor?" Brook asked softly.

Joss balled her fists. "Especially then. If no one ever challenged the status quo, nothing would ever change." *Brook's right. I need to come up with a plan. It just won't look like anything she'd envision.* She wouldn't play by the rules when they were made by a fervent, self-inflated narcissist who had a messiah complex. Playing the game would buy her time. So, she'd go on the date, make nice, and find a way to ensure he'd never get his slippery hands on her.

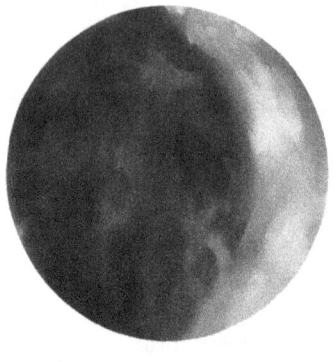

Chapter Two

Joss slipped knee-high black boots on over her black skinny jeans and stood from the bed. She moved into her bathroom and fluffed her curls. Light make-up enhanced her natural beauty and allowed her to look presentable without giving the impression that she'd *tried. Is this what I've been reduced to? Making deals with the devil and sacrificing my own life for my mother's?* Balling her fists, she forced herself to peer in the mirror.

She had her father's eyes and her mother's facial structure. Taller than her mother's five-foot-eight, she'd never reached her father's six-foot-two. With hair a few shades darker than her father's strawberry blonde, it struck the perfect balance between her mother's ash blonde and her father's bright red locks. Recognizing the pieces of her that came from her parents comforted her. It gave her something of her father she could hold on to and ensured she never forgot him, regardless of the years that passed.

There was a time when she'd been proud of the person she viewed in the mirror, and certain her father would be, too. Today, she saw an empty shell. Her reflection showed a woman who'd allowed herself to become a pawn. Ashamed, she peered away. Her refusal meant her mother's demise. What other choices could be made? *What about your own?*

There were a million ways to die. The passing away of the physical form was but one end. Her soul had been strangled and starved for years. Yet, somehow this felt like the final death rattle. Cavorting with the devil's minion of her own freewill. It was a surrender of sorts, ground lost that she might not be able to regain. This situation held no easy answers.

Gripping the edge of the sink, she bowed her head and drew on her reserves of strength. *It's one outing.* She could use it to do one of two things: show him how miserable life with her might be or try to appeal to what remained of his humanity.

Brook knocked on the door. "Are you ready or what?"

Pushing away from the counter, she retraced her steps and moved to open the door. "Or what," Joss replied glumly.

"Jesus, Joss. You look like you're going to a funeral, not a date."

"One should always be prepared," she said dryly.

Brook snickered. "Come on, add some color to it."

Begrudgingly, Joss walked over to the hook on the wall and added a heather gray cardigan with scalloped edges.

"I'll take what I can get." Brook rolled her eyes.

"I am not dressing up for him, Brook."

"No. But if you let him know he's gotten to you, he'll automatically have the upper hand."

Joss sighed. "You're right. I've never despised anyone the way I do him. It screws with my ability to keep my cool and see the big picture."

"Never let your guard down with Stark. He's a slippery eel with evil intentions. There are times when I've seen the ruin of our people in his eyes."

"So why do you stay?" Joss blurted the question that had been circling her brain for years.

"The same reason you do. Family, and the fact that we aren't meant to be lone creatures."

"There are other packs, Brook."

"Sure. But I don't know anything about them. I'm a creature of habit. I won't leave until it's absolutely necessary." Brook shrugged. "It's different for me. I blend into the background. You, he's gunning for."

"Maybe after tonight he'll stop." The words were empty. Joss knew he wouldn't. Isiah fixated. The more unattainable an item, the more obsessed he became with procuring it. Once she figured out exactly what role he wanted her to play, she might be able to negotiate. *I'll consider this an information extraction.*

She met Brook's gaze. "No," they said at the same time.

"Do I pass inspection?" Joss turned in a circle.

"You could wear a potato sack and do that. I'm more worried about where your head is currently." Brook placed her hands on her shoulders. "Are you ready for this?"

Joss cleared her throat. "This has been years in the making. I have the chance to throw down the gauntlet and try to establish battle lines."

Brook flashed her a sympathetic look. "I know this sucks, but I'll be honest, I'm glad to see you taking action."

Joss nodded, keeping the fact that he'd forced her hand with a threat to her mother under wraps. It was her burden to carry. Sharing it with Brook would change nothing, so she kept the truth to herself.

A knock sounded at the door.

"Speak of the devil," Brook whispered.

"Lock up when you leave?"

"Oh, I'm going nowhere. I want to make sure you get home, okay?" she said, speaking loudly for Isiah's benefit.

Joss grinned. "You're the best, you know that?" she asked sincerely.

Brook grinned. "Oh, I know, and I expect repayment. Pumpkin pancakes with homemade whip cream will do it."

"This Sunday. I promise." Joss hugged her quickly. 'Hang back, please,' Joss mouthed. She didn't want to pull Brook into Isiah's line of fire.

Brook sniffed but nodded before she made her way to the guest room. Squaring her shoulders, Joss strode to the front door. She opened the wooden rectangle, and her jaw dropped. Armed with a sheepish grin, a bouquet of deep purple chocolate sunflowers, dark pink Camille, and a giant 'She Said Yes' balloon in silver, he was painfully adorable. Disarmed by his thoughtful gestures, she struggled to regroup. She'd always loved balloons as a means to celebrate, and the flowers were her favorites.

"I'm sorry. Come on in." She stepped back.

"These are for you." He handed her his gifts.

"Thank you." She paused. "These are my favorite."

He smiled. "I've always paid attention to you, Joss. I know what makes you happy."

You bloody bastard. You're good at this. I almost believe you.

"Thank you for these. Give me a minute to put them in water, and then we can go."

"Of course. I'm glad you like them." He followed behind her at a reasonable distance. His gaze might bore into the back of her head, but he kept his hands to himself. *Are we playing at respectability tonight?* Cutting the stems at an angle, she placed them on the counter and grabbed the crystal vase from beneath the counter. "Are you going to tell me where we're going?" She turned on the water and filled the container.

"No. I think I'll let it be a surprise. Have you eaten?"

She shook her head, placed the colorful blooms in the vase, and tied the balloon around the cylinder. "Not yet."

"Good. You'll need your appetite.

Grabbing her small Pumpkin Spice latte shaped purse, she followed him out of the house, locking the door behind her. He held her hand, and her muscles tensed.

"You promised to give me a real chance, Joss. I've been well-behaved so far." She sensed an ellipsis behind the sentence, letting her know that could change.

Relenting, she forced her body to relax as he twined their fingers and guided her to his black SUV. He opened the door and helped her up into the passenger seat. When he closed the door, she took a shaky breath.

His behavior unnerved her. He slipped skins like a shapeshifter, embodying each personality so sincerely, you never knew which truly represented him or when he'd change. Unwilling to wake the slumbering beast, she gave a small smile. Climbing in, he returned the expression. *Now's the time to learn your enemy.*

❉ ❉

HE PULLED INTO A GRASSY field turned parking lot. Her lips twitched up. A brightly colored Ferris Wheel slowly rotated in the distance, illuminating the darkness. Well-lit booths and rides flashed and beckoned. The sweet smell of calorie-laden fried foods drifted through the car vents to greet them.

"You took me to a harvest festival?" It was the last thing she expected.

"I thought you'd appreciate it." He shrugged. The danger with him lay here. With his quick smile, warm eyes, and easy-going body language, he *appeared* harmless. If she wasn't on guard, she could easily forget what existed beneath the convincing façade. "Besides, I wanted to gorge myself on a funnel cake." He winked.

She laughed. Waiting, hands in her lap, she watched him walk around the side of the truck. Accepting his hand, she climbed down from the cab. When he wrapped an arm around her waist, she forced her body to remain lax. He stood a little taller and kept his hand in a respectful place as they walked through the Fall Festival Archway.

Whispers started and stopped the minute he stared the speaker down. There was a temptation when it came to dating a powerful man. The control they wielded over others was seductive. She bit her lip and ignored their judgment. This wasn't about them. People would talk no matter what she did.

"What do we do first?" he asked.

"If we're going to do swoopy rides, those before we eat anything."

"Swoopy?" He arched a brow.

She elbowed him playfully. "Spinning? Whirly?" She wrinkled her nose and pursed her lips. "You know what I mean."

He laughed. The rich baritone was pleasant. It amazed her just how damn appealing he could be when he wasn't monstrous. Guiding her to the small trailer that housed the registers, he bought them bracelets which allowed unlimited rides. His eyes lit with genuine amusement. Like rust stripped away to reveal a fresh layer, she caught a glimpse of child-like wonder and joy. Had he ever been like this, or was this too an act? He turned to her with a smile so wide she could've shoved a coat hanger in his mouth.

"Come on." Grabbing her hand, he tugged her to the Spider. The multi-armed black carts were trimmed in green neon lights. Moving in a circle, each cart rotated three-hundred and sixty degrees. Despite her predicament, her excitement level rose. Letting loose didn't happen much outside of the full moon when the wolf inside took over and thought became near impossible. The instinct to run, hunt, and be with pack prevailed over all other things.

The human remained in the backseat. It was an odd sensation she'd long grown used to. Raising on his tiptoes, Isiah all but did a dance as they waited for the carts to finish their round. She couldn't hold back the laughter

"What?" he asked. "I can smell your excitement, too."

"I can't remember the last time I saw you like this. Maybe when we went to Disney World when we were like thirteen?"

"You have to admit that was a bomb ass trip."

She held up her hands. "I do not deny that."

His face grew serious. "I show you what I want to. You haven't made your preferences secret, Joss. A man who doesn't protect himself from rejection and scorn is a fool. Tonight, you're open, so I'm returning the favor."

She turned his words over in her head like a worry stone. *Does he only give back what I send his way?* The thought made her gut ache. *Did I create this hostile environment? No, I'm cordial.* He forced her hand and pushed her into the standoffish fight or flight response. *Right?* She was Alice teetering on the edge of the rabbit hole, and he was all too eager to give her the final push she needed to tumble arse over kettle.

The line moved forward, and the passengers were exchanged for new riders. Yanked from her thoughts, she boarded with the overgrown man-child beside her, narrowly escaping the trap she'd nearly tumbled into.

The wind pulled at her hair, and she laughed as he lifted his hands, and threw himself into the ride, desperate for relief from the tension inside of her. The jovial emotions continued as they worked their way through the machines. She could play nice without falling under his spell.

A noisy growl from her belly led them to change course and arrive at the food carts.

"Is it possible to get one of everything?" she asked with a laugh.

"I'll get you whatever you want, J." His sweet tone made her antsy. He mimicked and mimed like a top-notch ventriloquist, but she wasn't sure it reached his heart. Half of the time she doubted the existence of a soul inside of him. "You deserve to be treated like a queen." He tugged a springy curl. "It's what you're destined to be."

"I don't want that," she replied automatically.

"That's the beauty of it. The best ones never do." He shook his head and blinked. "Order whatever you want. If you can't finish it, I will." He shrugged. Werewolves ate more than the average human. He'd have no problem delivering on his end of the deal.

Letting her stomach order for her, she ended up with a funnel cake piled with apple pie filling and whipped cream, two corn dogs, and freshly cut French fries. Some days it paid to have an insane metabolism. There were unexpected perks to being a shifter.

"I like a girl who isn't afraid to eat."

Rolling her eyes, she sank beside him on the bench. They ate in a comfortable silence that surprised her. It hadn't been the hellish experience she'd imagined.

"Okay. I can't eat another bite." She pushed the remnants of the funnel cake away.

"I'll handle the three bites left," he said dryly. She stuck her tongue out at him. "Careful. I might put that to better use."

She rolled her eyes.

He smirked and finished off the remainder of his fries and her funnel cake. "A gentleman knows when to pack it up, so I'll take you home." He stood, gathering their trash.

What new game are we playing tonight? She remained silent as they left, unsure of his next move. The ride was tense. The strains of popular music did nothing to soothe her.

He pulled into her driveway, cut the engine, and turned to face her. "Why'd you agree to this?" he asked earnestly.

"You know why," she responded quietly.

"Humor me."

"My mother."

"Hmm." He leaned back, resting his head on the seat. "It wasn't so bad, was it?"

"No," she answered honestly.

"We can play nice. Eventually, I think feelings will develop."

"Relationships aren't things that should be forced—"

"Mating isn't always about love. You know I'll be Alpha soon." He studied her for a heartbeat. "You have the power of an Alpha inside of you. You try to hide it," he sniffed the air, "but I can scent it on you."

"We don't know that," she protested, shaking her head.

He tsked. "Denial isn't a good look on anyone. Least of all someone as intelligent as you are, Joss."

"I haven't gone into heat yet. That in itself is an indication that things aren't right with me."

"No. I believe it's an indication of how damn stubborn you can be. Or maybe, you're just waiting for the right wolf to pluck you at peak ripeness." His tongue darted out to lick his lower lip.

Heat filled her cheeks. She looked away. "Don't flatter yourself."

"And we're back where we started. Why can't you let this happen?" His petulant tone signaled old Isiah's return was at hand.

"Because feelings aren't things that can be commanded, and deep down at the core, we're two completely different people—"

"Who want the same things." He held up a finger. "A good life for our people." He added a second finger as he checked off his list. "To be on top when things blow wide open, which we both know will happen. You can feel the difference in the magic the same as I. We're getting reports in from everywhere about wolves who shift without the full moon, and vampires who can stand the daylight. Things are changing. We need to be ready to defend and conquer."

"I'm not going to dispute that, but—"

He leaned closer. "But what?"

"I don't need to play the role of wife for any of that to be true."

"No, you need to perform that part because I will it." His words were razors.

She ground her teeth. "We don't always get what we want."

"The prophecy says we will succeed together or perish apart."

"I wasn't aware I had plans to go anywhere. I don't need to share your last name to be reliable."

"You think it's so simple? It's *never* that easy." His voice has softened when he states, "Everything always requires a sacrifice."

"Isiah?" *He knows something.*

He gripped the steering wheel until it creaked in protest. "I refuse to fail White Creek."

"Isiah!"

"The hourglass is running out of sand, Joss. Don't force my hand."

"Thank you for a not horrible evening," Joss interjected, eager to put distance between them.

"We could be like this all of the time," he said softly.

"Until I defy you, right?" she asked, clutching the door handle.

"I'm not a dictator. I don't require *total* obedience."

"Oh, right." She rotated her finger, adopting a high-pitched ditzy voice. "Just seventy-five percent."

"For you, I'd go sixty-forty."

Done with their conversation, she pushed the door open. He grabbed her wrist and squeezed. Cringing, she growled in the back of her throat.

"Tick tock, Joss."

Shaking free, she fled. Deluded like his father, he saw her as a means to an end, a part of taking the throne. He took the prophecy literally. The five lines she hated with her entire being began to play on a loop in her mind.

When powers change, and worlds collide
Together the waxing and waning moon will control the tide
They mark bearers determine the winning side.
Together they triumph, apart they perish
Their bond shall be among the rarest

❆ ❉

TAKING HER FINAL SIP OF coffee, Joss set down the white stoneware mug with the black rim and a wolf howling at the moon etched on the side. Brook leaned forward across the kitchen island. She was a comical sight in her oversized green, black, and blue flannel pants, White Creek tank top, and black silk hair scarf.

"Okay, I waited until you woke up and had your first cup of coffee. Spill your guts, woman."

Joss chuckled as she rubbed her heavy lids. "There's not much to tell really. It was actually kind of nice until he opened his mouth." Joss cringed and wrinkled her nose.

Brook reached across the table and laid the back of her hand on Joss's forehead. "Are you sick? Did he manage to brainwash you?"

"No." Joss swatted her hand away. "He took me to the harvest festival and we rode rides, played games, and ate until we were both stuffed."

"Are you changing your mind about him?" Brook asked softly.

"God no. He kept his psycho in check until he pulled into the driveway. It was a reminder of what he's capable of, and why he scares the holy hell out of me. Anyone who can change at the drop of a dime like that has serious issues. He's always playing a game only he has the rule book for. I'm not sure if he can actually feel or if he simply goes through the motions."

"You realize you're describing a sociopath, right?" Brook said.

"Oh, I'm well aware. I'm ninety-five percent sure that's exactly what he is, or some variation of. The things I saw growing up in a house with him …" A chill swept through her body.

"Like what?" Brook whispered, brown eyes the size of moons.

"Intense tantrums, manipulation, calculating moves, and rage accompanied with dead eyes. He's capable of great violence with no remorse afterward. It's not a good combination." *Tell her the truth.* The words lodged in her throat. He'd been hurt by the same hands. The cloying secrets wound themselves around her vocal cords. The withholding of food until they yielded to the Alpha's wishes and the way they were pushed past their breaking point with *special training.*

"No, it wouldn't be. Did he ever …" Brook trailed off and glanced away.

"Hurt me?" Joss guessed.

Brook nodded.

"No." *Our torturer wears the same face. Abuse was more than raising one's hand.* "The title's saved me even as it condemned to this existence." Joss's shoulder slumped.

"You hate being Moon Maiden that much?"

"It's become everything that matters. I know it seems like a grand honor, but it turns into your whole identity. What you think, feel, believe, or even *want* are irrelevant. You're a symbol, and your life is no longer your own. Suddenly, you're expected to shed your individuality to become a perfect being everyone can hang their hope on." Her lips curled up at the corners. "It effects everything I say, do, or wear. I'm trapped in a cage of someone else's making. There are mornings when it's all I can do to get out of bed and face the world." The words flow from her mouth like lava, burning her insides, and setting fire to the air around them.

Brook's brown eyes grew glossy. "I'm so sorry, Joss. I never realized."

"I know. I hid it from you. I didn't want you to see that side of my life when you gave me a sense of normalcy and belonging. Brook, you always saw past my title."

"I love you, J. You know that."

Joss reached across the table and squeezed her friend's hand. "I do know, and I love you more than I can put into words for that."

"Come on. Everything will seem better after breakfast. There has been enough brooding and dark recollections for now." Brook stood and walked to the pantry. "It wouldn't be a Brook and Joss sleepover without a breakfast skillet."

Joss snatched up the opportunity to shake the past off. "You're right." She stood and moved to the sink to wash her hands. "What's your poison this morning?"

"I think we should get back to basics and treat it like a massive breakfast burrito. Potatoes, bacon, and cheese topped with a bit of ketchup and syrup."

Joss's stomach growled. "That sounds so good."

"I'll wash and peel the potatoes if you fry up the bacon.?" Brook arched an eyebrow.

"Consider it done. I'm going to fire up the blue tooth speaker." Grabbing her MP3 player, Joss fired up her pop list. Bruno Mars came over the speakers, and they danced around the kitchen as they prepared breakfast. Nothing chased away bleak possibilities like a day with your best friend.

Belly full, she propped her bunny rabbit slippered feet on the table and pulled the pink chenille blanket up around her shoulders. The wood in the fireplace crackled, and Maroon Five crooned in the background about girls.

"You know you're running out of time, right?" Brook asked from her position on the opposite end of the couch.

"You sound a lot like Isiah right now," Joss grumbled.

"I hate to agree with a psycho, but in this, he's actually right. Why don't you take a mate?"

"For one thing, it shouldn't be a decision someone is forced into. That's asking for a disaster." *And I need to maintain control for as long as possible. I've experienced what happens firsthand when someone else dictates your every move.*

"Coulda, shoulda, woulda. You know the world we live in," Brook said.

"Yeah. Patriarchal and hypocritical?" Joss scoffed. "Don't pretend like you believe all of the shit the Alpha preaches here."

"No. But he does keep us safe," Brook admitted softly.

"Safety isn't a reason to shackle myself to a man I'm not interested in."

"That." Brook waved her index finger at her. "Why is that? There are plenty of eligible wolves in the pack."

Joss bowed her head.

"Admit it. This is about *him*, the man you see in your dreams. It's never stopped, has it?"

Joss shook her head. He was her shining light amidst the darkness. Her sanity saver when things were the bleakest. "No. It may sound silly and frivolous to you, but I know my mate isn't here in White Creek."

"J, you're twenty-five. It's time to admit Mr. Dream Man A. isn't real, or B. isn't coming for you."

Biting the inside of her cheek, Joss held her tongue. How could she explain to someone else what she didn't understand herself? "Dreams aside, it's impossible to create a relationship with a person who sees you as a holy relic."

"You have the mark of change, J. Nothing you do will change that," Brook said softly.

Joss dropped her feet to the floor and sat up straight. "I have a fluke. I'm not even from White Creek originally."

"Which makes you ending up here even more incredible. You have the old magic in you. We can all feel that."

"Please don't tell me you're subscribing to this, too, Brook. The lore has been twisted by one man to fit his own agenda."

"True as that is, that doesn't make everything false. The lore existed long before he created White Creek, and as out there as the Alpha might be, he's right about one thing … there's strength in numbers. The Alpha has protected our people. He created a safe haven during a time where we were viciously hunted down and destroyed." Brook cleared her throat and toyed with the hem of her tank top. "Do you know how my family came to be here?"

"No," Joss shook her head. It was forbidden to talk about life before White Creek.

"I coughed so hard, I woke myself up. The smell of smoke clung to my skin and made my lungs ache. The heat and clouded air made my eyes burn. I was terrified. Frozen in place. I clutched my bed sheets. My mom burst through the door and pulled me to the ground where the air was clean and cooler. I sucked it into my lungs. My stomach rebelled, and I puked my guts out right there in the hallway. My mother wiped my mouth off with her sleeve and forced me to move. I had a brother back then."

Joss gaped. Their family always seemed so close-knit, and happy.

Brook kept her gaze focused on her hands as she spoke in a shaky monotone. "He was a year younger than me. My father appeared with him in tow. Groggy, and sluggish, he looked ill. Like he'd already ingested more smoke than his small body could handle. We all made it out of the back door and straight into Armageddon. Fire-tipped arrows flew through the air, finding their targets in houses, and people." Her body shook. "I'll never forget the sounds of their screams or the sights of the flames swallowing the quiet village of shifters that had been our own home. An army of hunters slaughtered without discrimination. The elderly, young, and middle-aged were all executed. My father placed Camden into our mother's arms and told us to run for the woods. I ran as fast as I could. I hear Cam and my mother scream. I'll never forget that sound. Like a wounded animal." Brook wrapped her arms around her waist. "I saw the a-arrow. It was on fire; it was dipped in poison. His poor little body couldn't handle it. He turned blue and convulsed."

"Brook, please." Joss moved to place a hand on her shoulder. "You don't have to relive this."

"He didn't make it, and if it hadn't been for the Alpha showing up with reinforcements, the rest of my family would be dead." She cleared her throat. "He brought us to White Creek, gave us a second chance at life, and a safe place. So, no I don't buy into everything he's selling, but I owe him. I stay for a number of reasons." Brook cleared her throat.

Stunned by her friend's tale, she was humbled by the truth. She'd known tragedy, but nothing like this. Her father died unexpectedly, of natural causes. Even her mother's cancer paled in comparison. "I'm sorry, Brook."

"Don't be. I didn't tell you to play whose life was harder. I wanted you to understand where I was coming from. You have an aura of power and peace about you. Its why people look to you. Not simply because Alpha holds you up as some sort of fix all."

"I never wanted this."

"And yet it's been laid at your feet."

She sneered. "You sound like you're taking their side, Brook."

"No, I'm saying I understand why they'd place their faith in you. I'm your best friend. My job is to hold up a mirror and show you the truth, not lie. We both know you're different."

"Don't you think I'd know if I was special?"

"You're so busy being angry you miss what's in front of you. To hell with

Isiah and his madness. The pack needs you, which is why you need to have a plan in place."

"Like what?" Joss tossed her hands up into the air. "Want to hear why *I* stay? It's nowhere near as altruistic. If I say to hell with this cult, my mother dies. Pack magic neutralizes her cancer. You think I'm so giving. Well, you're wrong. I'm as selfish as they come," Joss snarled. A growl rumbled in her chest. Brook whimpered and dropped her gaze as she recognized the alpha wolf in front of her. "Oh, Jesus. I'm sorry, Brook. I didn't mean to do that."

Joss covered her face and wrestled the power she'd sent out back inside.

"Tell me again how you're normal, and there's nothing special about you," Brook croaked. Bent over, she breathed heavily. "This is only getting worse. You have the power of the alpha in you. We both know how rare that is for a woman. They can be mated to an alpha, but having a commanding force that strong all their own doesn't occur much. It's getting harder to control, isn't it?"

Joss nodded her head. "Yes, damn you." It took an absurd amount of energy to control the effects from the emotions constantly rolling through her.

"You're going to slip up at the wrong time, and it'll all fall down around you like a house of cards. Balancing on the tight rope is dangerous and temporary. You've been given a gift—"

"No," Joss barked. Spittle flew from her mouth. "This is no gift. It's a curse."

Brook shook her head. "Whatever you want to call it. However, it's your responsibility to wield it properly." She pointed. "You've been chosen."

"For what?" Joss rubbed the back of her neck. "I'm not good at this crap, Brook. I'm floundering and drowning."

Brook sighed. "You really aren't though. I understand you can't see the way the people look at you because you're on the inside of everything. Regardless of how you may actually feel, you frequently exude calm. Girl, your whole air is regal. Moon Princess is more than a title because you stepped into that role seamlessly. It's hard to remember a time when you weren't a part of White Creek. You balance us."

"And you believe all of these things because I have a waxing moon birth-mark?" Joss said skeptically. She pressed a hand to her side where the birthmark branded her. She'd peel the symbol from her flesh if it'd help. When she was younger, she'd tried to destroy it numerous times. Somehow, the bastard always healed perfectly.

"No. I have faith in the prophecy *and* your ability to fulfill it because of the incredible woman I've watched you mature into, and the things I see you do on a daily basis. A minute ago, you called my wolf without breaking a sweat and exerted your dominance. I'm no weak-willed pup. The mark is simply an outward symbol of rightness. You *are* the change bringer, Joss. The one who will usher us into a new era. One I believe we're ready for."

"If you're on board with the lore, do you feel I should mate with Isiah, too?"

"Oh hell no. I refute that assumption. There's always been a wrongness about Isiah. We don't call him stark raving mad for nothing. Every shining beacon of light has a shadow chasing it, trying to extinguish or dull its brilliance. He's the nemesis, not the partner. The Anti-Christ."

The words shake loose something inside of her. Joss gasped as visions of blood-soaked ground, fire, and chaos played on a loop in the back of her mind. Her gut clenched. An intense feeling of guilt and anguish wrapped around her, constricting like a boa. Her chest ached and bile crept its way up the back of her throat.

How can I leave him behind completely when we traveled through the same hell together? Am I so different? Look how I turned on my best friend in anger.

"Joss?"

She jerked and grasped Brook's hand. "I'm not sure what I saw, but I can't allow it to become our future." *Please let it be a warning.*

"Whatever you need to do, I'm with you." Brook squeezed her hand

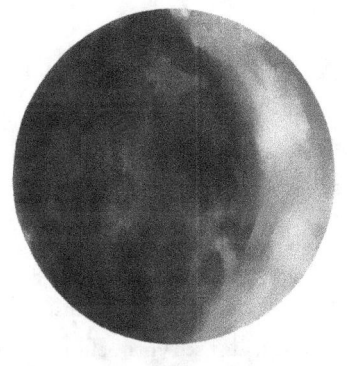

Chapter Three

A MAROON GLOBE HUNG OVERHEAD, like a fiery circle burned into the center of the sky. It cast an eerie red hue over the woods and the forested ground below. She moved toward the waterfall and surrounding lake that appeared to be full of diluted blood. Mesmerized by the rare phenomenon, she traveled away from the trees toward the water. A warm breeze blew thick hair around her face. She soaked in the balmy summer temperature and came to sit on the boulder.

The craggy surface of the round orb stood out, a lighter shade of red than the rest. *It feels good being out here immersed in nature and quiet.* A twig snapped in the distance. She jumped up and spun around. Her heart pounded.

A tall vampire with inky black hair that brushed his shoulders and smoldering, deep-set black eyes appeared.

"Kazimir." The fear dissolved instantly. Relief flooded her chest. It'd been so long since they last met, and she'd started to worry.

High cheekbones, impossibly dark eyes lashes, an angular chin, and a slender, upturned nose gave him the look of old royalty. Dusky rose cupid's bow lips curved upward into a wide grin.

"Joss."

She closed her eye and soaked his presence in. Her name turned into a sonnet when delivered from his elegant tongue. She rushed toward him. The scent of pine and fresh water was invaded by his rich, seductive smell. It reminded her of black silk sheets, moonlight, and wealth. Pausing inches away, she took him in.

"You came." It had been over a month since she saw him.

"I apologize, lovely. I was detained by circumstances beyond my control." His eyes drank her in as if he hadn't seen her before. "You're stunning." Cupping her face in his hands, he traced her cheekbones and lips with his fingertips.

"Kaz?" she whispered. Her cheeks flamed with heat. "I thought maybe you'd been in my head all along. But it's you."

"Yes." His eyes scanned her face, drinking her in like it's the first time he's ever seen her. "I remember everything now."

She frowned. There's something different about him. He felt more substantial than he ever had before. "You're different."

"I am awake."

"I don't understand." She shook her head.

"For the first time since we met, I am fully aware of you. Before I believed my kind did not dream. It was a lie. At least for you and I."

She took a step away from the gentle caress that muddled her brain.

"You are not happy?" The pain in his voice lanced her heart.

"I … I'm uncertain what you mean."

"I dreamt of you and interacted on a subconscious level before. From this day forward, I will remain fully present." He sank onto one knee.

Her heart jumped up in her throat. "What are you doing?" Her mouth went dry. *He can't propose, can he? What answer would I give him?*

"I am making you a vow, solynshka."

Despite the strangeness of the language, she understood it meant little sun. *How can I know this?*

"Surely you figured out that we are mates."

His voice in her mind made her jump. "How did you do that?"

"Things will fall in to place now. The way they should always have been once you came of age."

"No." She took a large step away. "You are a vampire."

"Yes."

She placed a hand on her chest. "I'm a wolf."

"And yet we've found one another despite the distance and energy required to do so."

She shook her head. "That's it. It's time for me to admit to myself, you aren't real. I have to get over this delusion." *Because the tragedy of you existing and me being unable to have you is far too much to bear.*

"I am not a figment of your imagination, and I will not be leaving. You are mine, Joss."

"No. I belong to myself." Being part of a mated pair ruined her mother, and turned her life into hell on earth. Her mother hadn't been able to function without her father. The dysfunction coupled with her illness landed them here at White Creek. The anger she hid spiked. Parents were supposed to protect their children. She refused to travel down the same path.

"For a long time, you were alone. Now we're starting a new journey *together.*" He floated forward, all grace and quick movements. She swallowed hard. He placed a slender finger under her chin, tilting her head up to meet his penetrating gaze. He was sin incarnate. "I've waited centuries for you. Nothing could force me to turn away from you."

She pressed her palms against his chest, desperate to place distance between them. "There's no other alternative, Kaz."

"Yes. There is. I am coming for you. We've much to discuss and decide together."

"No." Her voice cracked.

"You know what I am?" His power flared around him, nearly mesmerizing her.

"What?" she asked, dazzled by his intensity. "Of course."

"Then you must understand I am territorial. I'm coming to claim what is mine." His teeth lengthened. Chills ran down her spine. Her stomach clenched. "Allow me to demonstrate." His head moved toward her neck. She clutched the thick silk of his dark mane, and moved her head to the side, baring her neck in anticipation of the sweet torture to come.

A rapid pounding cop-knock jerked her from sleep.

His words, *"I'm coming for you,"* echoed in her head. Her brain and her body were at war. She wanted what he offered with everything in her being, regardless of the fear and complication that came with it. Groaning, she struggled to lift her heavy lids and rolled on to her side. The pounding continued.

Pushing herself into a sitting position, she swung her legs over the edge of the bed and stretched her arms above her head. The clock on her nightstand read fifteen minutes after midnight. She'd been asleep for a little over two hours. Rotating her neck, she forced her weary body from the queen-sized bed. Joss glanced back longingly at her down-feathered comforter with eyes full of regret, grabbed her oversized black robe covered in white polka dots with a kitten hood, and exited her room in a zombie shuffle.

Walking to her front door, she peered out of the peephole with sleep blurry vision. The sight of Isiah on her porch with his hands shoved in his pockets made her grunt. *Are you kidding me?*

"I know you're awake. I can hear you breathing, Joss."

Yanking open the door, she narrowed her gaze. "This better be good."

"It's beginning," he said cryptically

"What?" she snapped, unable to play games on so little sleep.

"Come see."

"No."

He huffed. "Come on."

"I'm not—"

He grabbed her hand and pulled her out onto the porch. After hastily closing the door behind her, she followed him down the driveway.

"Now look up."

Lifting her head back, she inhaled quickly. Long streaks of colorful light surrounded the perimeter.

"The energies are aligning. It won't be much longer before *everything* my father predicated comes to be."

Her muscles tensed. She balled her fists. Fight or flight instincts began to gather. *Is this the moment when he makes a move?* "Why does that statement sound like a threat?"

His regarded her silently. "Change is coming. Whether you wish it to or not. We're bound."

She bit the inside of her cheek.

"The birthmark and the fact that you came here of all places means something." He trailed his fingertips down the side of her cheek. "You're the only one who knows what I went through, Joss. We're survivors, you and I."

Her birthmark tingled. She placed her hand over it. "What are you doing?"

"Nothing. I meant it when I stated the energies are aligning. I feel it, too. I can smell you now." He sniffed. "Your body is changing, getting ready to bloom."

"I'm your mate," Kaz's voice whispered in her mind, grounding her against the pack magic Isiah wove. Was her body preparing to accept Kaz? Was that the real reason why she'd yet to experience her first heat? *I'm awake, and I'm coming for you.*

"We could be good together, Joss." Isiah's excited baritone returned her to the present. He grabbed her hand between his. "Imagine the power we could generate, and how we could rule. We'd be unstoppable. You're gentleness and grace. I'm the might and iron fist needed to keep unruly wolves in check." He held her hand up, placing their fingertips together. Sparks ignited. A current flowed between them. She could feel a link. "No one could hurt us again, or force us to do things against our will. It'd be the ultimate revenge."

The truth brought tears to her eyes. All of the avoidance of facts ended here. They were both a part of what was to come.

She pulled her hands back, hugging them to her chest. "We're brother and sister."

"In name only." He rolled his eyes. "Besides, I never saw you that way." He raked his gaze over her lewdly.

Her lip curled up in disgust. "This is wrong."

"No, it's not. You want to convince yourself of that because you're scared. You've always been so resistant." He shook his head. "It's what makes you irresistible, you know? The fact that you don't want the power you possess. You don't have to fight this. We're the same. The ones who were wronged, controlled, and manipulated." He cupped her face. "There's so much untapped potential."

She grabbed his hand and forced it down. "You can't make me do anything I don't want to. I get a choice in this matter. You can push, insist, and bully me all you want. We both know I don't break easily."

"Damnit, Joss," he screamed. She jumped back. "Why do you make me so angry? I want to make you my queen. To cherish you."

"And what about what I want, Isiah?"

"You've never been into anyone else. What are you waiting for? You know the pack duties, reproduction, and guidance to the younger members. You're starting to get long in the tooth. Even with your *special position*. Holding off on mating much longer won't be a possibility." He grinned. "Especially not with what I'm smelling."

"Even if you're right, I fail to see how it concerns you." She kept her tone even.

"I'm the best. The bringer of change deserves nothing less than an equal. They're all waiting for this to happen. Can't you hear the whispers? They know I want you."

"You can't always get what you want," she replied lamely. "If they're so observant, they've realized by now I'm not interested."

Isiah chuckled. "When has that ever mattered when it comes to building empires? You think they care so much about your feelings? They are sheep. They look to the Alpha to provide and protect. They don't want to think. Do you truly believe they had no clue what he was doing to us?" His words twisted her guts into knots. "If they could turn a blind eye to that, what do you suppose would happen if they understood the lack of union is threatening the balance?" He covered his mouth.

"You wouldn't dare." She thrust her chin out.

"Do you really want to find out?"

"There are plenty of wolves who would love to mate with you," she said exasperatedly.

"None of them are you."

"You have a serious problem, Isiah." Shaking her head, she pulled her robe closer.

He paused. "This isn't all about my own selfish desires you know. I've seen it."

"Seen what?"

"The future." He nodded his head. "A version of it. One I need to make that come to fruition."

"How?" She crossed her arms under her breasts.

"Kishi."

The name shocked her. "The lamia?" she spurted. "Why in the hell did you believe her? She speaks with a forked tongue, like most of her people. They tell you what you want to hear because it amuses them."

"People fear what they don't understand. Lamia are rare and nearly extinct."

"Yes, and she, in particular, is a mad one, who's been alone in her cave for too long. How could you trust her words?"

"She offers a glimpse into the future for those willing to take a risk. I'm no fool! She's been right many times before. I'll tell you a secret." His voice lowered. "Her powers are far beyond what anyone suspected. She's competent with magic."

"You break all of the rules, and answer to no one." She scowled. "How do you plan to lead?"

"As I see fit. There's always bumps in the road with shifts of powers. Can't you feel it?" He holds his hands up and slowly spins around. "That time we've all been on edge waiting for is coming."

"A war?" she guessed.

"A species war. Us versus them. I plan to make sure we end up on top." His eyes promised great violence. Cold that had nothing to do with the weather swept in and bypassed her soft robe.

"You're cold." The menace disappeared beneath the surface. "Let's get you back inside. I can't have you getting sick." The dual personalities had her always walking on eggshells. When he turned sixteen, the Alpha took him away for cleansing and brought him back changed. That trip broke an important part of his humanity. She grieved for the boy who'd once been her confidant.

"Thank you." She choked the words out and allowed him to guide her home. His warm hand burned through the material separating them. The announcement had made him more dangerous. He didn't bother trying to hide his infractions, and the entitlement ballooned. The truth in Brook's words delivered a roundhouse kick to her face. She needed an exit clause and a way to keep her mom alive.

❦ ❦

Joss stood outside of the cave entrance. The position of the archway entrance hid everything beyond from view. Her senses tingled. Magic aided the mysterious shadows. Her nerves exploded. Self-preservation told her to return the way she'd come. Her clothes were soaked with a light sheen of sweat from the long hike into the deep woods.

She ran through everything she knew about Kishi. Granted a safe haven on their land, she was known for her trickster ways, and they were cautioned against the danger they'd place themselves in trying to out-swindle the expert conwoman.

The lamia were nearly extinct, and the ones who remained struggled to create a sustainable living. Half human, half snake, the race couldn't hide in plain sight.

Embracing her fear, she stepped forward and crossed the threshold of magic and shadow, trusting her anxiety to keep her alert and help prevent stupid mistakes. She stumbled, stunned. A dark green, circular wooden door, reminiscent of a creation from a Hobbit village greeted her. Asian lettering drawn carefully in yellowed paint lined the edges. *It must be a spell.* Her skin prickled as she drew nearer.

A brass knob in the center of the door gave the dwelling a charming touch. Raising a shaking hand, she rapped on the door and braced herself for what would come. The hair-raising rattle of buttons greeted her through the thick door. She clutched the strap of her bag across her body and focused on breathing normally. The door creaked open to reveal the woman. Forcing her eyes to remain on her face, she met the odd pale green elliptical eyes similar to that of a cat. *She carries poison.*

"You are braver than I thought. I wasn't sure If you would arrive at my door or not." Kishi had a fluid movement, similar to a blade of grass swaying in the wind. A long, black dress covered her upper body and most of her ... tail? The reality of a snake combined with a woman was difficult to take in.

"I seek your knowledge, Kishi. If it pleases you, I'd like to speak with you."

"Such fine manners." Kishi nodded her approval. Her bronze skin and black hair reminded Joss of Egyptian queens from long ago. Thick, dark bangs were cut across her forehead. High cheekbones, and thin lips curved into a wicked smile that made her uneasy.

"Please come into my parlor." *Said the spider to the fly.* "It's so rare that I have visitors."

Kishi slithered her way inside, bidding her to follow with a wave of her slender hands. The walls were painted white, adding to the high ceiling effect. Colorful vases were arranged on the floor, and tasteful art hung on the walls. Thick, cream-colored Persian rugs with intricate patterns lined the floor. It was rustic luxury living.

"You expected me to live like a squatter?" Kishi asked with a smirk.

"To be honest, I hadn't thought too much on it."

"No, I don't suppose you would. Your Alpha pays handsomely to keep me here." The comment shocked her. *Why would Ian do that?* "I see I've surprised you. You better than most see things aren't what they seem in White Creek."

A square table was a whimsical mixture of roses and lace as multiple table-cloths were layered and carefully arranged to create a stunning background for a dainty cream-and-rose-colored tea set. A three-tier cake stand held scones, fresh fruit, and other pastries.

"You knew I was coming?" Joss marveled.

"I anticipated you were. The future is a constantly changing thing, impossible to pinpoint one-hundred percent of the time." Kishi shrugged. "Does Harvest Apple Spice sound okay?"

"Yes, please." Joss sank into a chair, placed her hands into her lap, and clung to the etiquette courses she's been enrolled in from the moment she came to live in White Creek. Everything people witnessed was a carefully constructed front.

Kishi didn't appear to be mentally unstable. Had this been another lie? She watched Kishi work in the kitchen visible via the open floor plan. She placed the shiny blue tea kettle onto the burner of the stainless-steel stove. Calling this cave a home didn't do it justice. This was a sanctuary tucked away inside of a stone fortress.

"I would appreciate it if you'd humor me. I don't get many opportunities for tea-time."

Joss nodded, trying to work her way through the thoughts spinning around her head in a wind tunnel.

"Biscuits?" Kishi appeared with a platter of lemon cookies.

"Oh. Yes, please." Joss took one daintily. The buttery flavor of the rich shell blended with the tart lemon filling. She hummed her approval.

"I'm glad you like them." Kishi smiled before moving to the kitchen and back at a speed that made her blink. A sugar bowl and creamer pitcher were set in the center of the table. "Cream and sugar?"

"Yes, please."

"How many lumps?"

"Two." The bizarre exchange threw her for a loop. The woman was cordial and almost grandmotherly. Her long, artistic fingers were graceful as she handled the dishes gently. French manicured nails with jewels caught the light. Was she playing a part or had Ian lied? Why would he keep her in the lap of luxury if he'd been *her* savior? The picture he painted didn't match the obvious arrangement.

The kettle whistled, and Kishi moved in her odd way toward the kitchen. Returning, she poured the tea into Joss's cup and then her own.

"You have questions?" Kishi asked.

"I do."

"Ask them." Kishi sat in the chair across from Joss and sipped her tea.

Stirring her spoon around in her teacup, Joss gathered her thoughts. "What does the Alpha pay you for?"

"That is the right question. Do you think his ability to control and predict comes naturally?" Kishi hummed.

"You," Joss whispered as puzzle pieces shifted into place. All of the things he'd said would come to pass. The way he stayed a step ahead of droughts and other natural occurrences. He'd gone to Kishi, wooed her, and set her up in a mini castle. The elaborate scheme made her horror grow. Ian was every inch the cold, calculated planner his son was.

"Why are you telling me this, Kishi?"

"Because you need all of the facts to deal with what's coming."

"You've seen things then?"

"I have, but it's more important that you experience it for yourself." She sipped her drink, peering over her cup at her.

"Is there anything I need to know now?"

Kishi narrowed her eyes. "You will come again soon and drink with me. We will speak again on things."

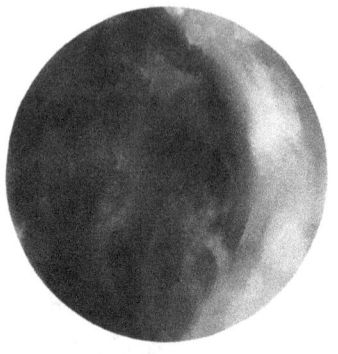

Chapter Four

JOSS APPROACHED THE RUSTIC LUXURY log cabin. A rectangle of large windows bisected by crisscrossed logs created smaller triangles that gave birth to a breathtaking focal point, set out front and center from the rest of the home. The open floor plan allowed anyone on the outside looking in to see the living room and dining area. It spoke of the power Ian wielded as Alpha. There was no fear of attack. He lived his life proudly out in the open. *And always on display.*

When she first arrived at eleven, the house felt like a grand manor home fit for lupine royalty. Two large wolf-themed totems rested on either side of the large, wooden door with a moon pattern burned into it. Intricately carved and colored in shades of black, white, and red, the totems told the story of the pack. *Or so Ian claimed.* It was the castle the king and queen presided in and ruled from.

Normally, she looked forward to her afternoon lunches on the back patio with her mother. Today, that wasn't the case. Uneasy from her talk with Kishi a few days earlier, she scanned the area for any sign of Isiah. His scent was imprinted on the grounds, but none were recent. Unlocking the door, she entered the building. The scent of smoky wood and the pumpkin spice air freshener her mother stockpiled once autumn arrived mixed with the sweeter female muskiness of her mother and dark spice of Ian.

"Mom," she called out.

"In the kitchen, baby." Her voice echoed in the cavernous space. Walking over the wooden floor, she found her mother arranging a cheese, cracker, and meat tray. The rainbow fruit platter with cream cheese and marshmallow fluff dip on the counter made her drool. It'd been a favorite since she was little.

"Are you trying to butter me up, Mother?" Joss teased.

"Wow. He wasn't lying." She placed her paring knife down on the large, rectangular cutting board.

"Who?" she asked, confused.

"Isiah. You're ready to blossom." Her mother beamed.

She sneered. "Mom." The thought of the charlatan discussing her hormones with her mother pissed her off.

"What? I've waited a long time for this." Her mother hurried around the counter. "It's an exciting time in a female wolf's life."

"It's open season on unwanted advances," Joss mumbled.

"No, honey. You have your pick."

"Not everyone wants a mate, Mom."

Her mother flinched. "You make it sounds like a filthy, four-letter word." She dropped her head. Pale blonde hair fell like a curtain, separating them even farther. Her thin frame was accentuated in her high-waisted jeans, with a white T-shirt, and red and black checkered plaid shirt on top. Despite the magic preventing the cancer from ravaging her, she always seemed right on the verge of relapse. It was like the power could keep the inevitable at bay, but it couldn't restore her hardiness.

"It's not where my head is. I don't knock others for their beliefs and practices, but this isn't Victorian times. It's not my time to come out at social season and seek a husband. I refuse to be offered up like a prize mare everyone wants to breed."

"Joss." Red splotches appeared along her mother's angular jawline. She tilted her pointy chin down and shook her head.

"Are we going to pretend like all of this is normal?"

"Wolves mate—"

"What goes on here is not natural," Joss snarled. The time for tiptoeing around the topic had passed.

"I've been waiting for this moment to arrive. I did my best to do right by you, though truthfully there weren't many options available to me. I'm sorry I couldn't be the strong example of a woman you deserved. When your father had his heart attack, I was caught off guard. I'd never imagined a life without him. Stone was young and in his prime. I hadn't sensed anything through our bond, or his scent that signaled anything was amiss. Grief and guilt are a hell of a combination to deal with, and I was a suddenly a single parent with no support on top of it. It's not an excuse, mind you." She held up her hand, staving off Joss's response. "Merely an explanation." She glanced around. "Let's take our food outside and finish this conversation there."

"Mom." *Really?*

Her mother's brow furrowed, and Joss instantly recognized the no-nonsense expression. Always one to pick her battles, Joss grabbed the fruit tray, a pitcher of fresh sangria, and followed her out to the stone grotto without saying another word. The manmade waterfall, built-in hot tub, and pool area were a work of art. Setting their food on the dark wicker table, Joss sank onto the soft, black cushion that formed to her rear. Her mother followed suit with the cheese tray and two glasses, then filled their glasses to the top with the alcohol and fruit medley.

Her mother angled her body toward her and grabbed her drink. She swirled the liquid rapidly. The clink of the ice did nothing to break the tension. "The cancer was a cheap shot when I was already down. I'm still ashamed when I look at the way our roles so swiftly reversed. I should have been taking care of you, not the other way around. You've always been so much like your father, strong, independent, and ready to take on the world. I'm less adaptive. I hit the limit of what I could handle far too soon, and for that, I sincerely apologize. It's pitiful how long it's taken me to speak these words out loud." She exhaled and gripped the handle of her glass tighter. "Cowardice is a state of being I can no longer stomach. You should have better. Your father must be rolling over in his grave." She sucked down half of the drink, cringing as if her head ached. "Your father's death took a spark from me I never got back. The chemo had me on my last leg." Her mother grabbed her hand. "Don't allow my piss poor showing as a mate and a mother be a reason to stop you from finding love, building a family, and living your best life."

"Maybe my best life doesn't include a family or a live-in love."

"Joss. You can't mean that," her mother said, stricken.

"I don't know how I feel. How could I when I'm constantly told what to do, how to act, and where my future lies? I can't breathe here. The walls are closing in, eyes are constantly watching me, and I'm held up to impossible standards."

"I know you don't understand." The anguish in her mother's shaky voice created a physical ache.

"I don't! Please break it down for me. You can't love him. Not like you did Daddy. So, why did you drag me away from everything and everyone I knew to join this cult? Because we both know that's *exactly* what this is."

Her mother straightened and glanced over her shoulder. "Lower your voice," she whispered.

"Or what?"

"Speaking against White Creek on this property is a recipe for disaster." Her mother wrung her hands.

The fear leaking from her mother startled her. "Has he hurt you?" she whispered, balling her hands into fists. "'Cause I'll kill the arrogant bastard."

"No," her mother croaked. "He's never done anything of the sort. I've seen what happens to others who oppose the beliefs we live by. To control this many wolves takes an iron grip that borders on cruelty. I understand that. You've always been given more leniency because of your title. Ian's shielded you and kept you safe."

"*Are you justifying what goes on here?*" *Are you truly ignorant to the things he did? Didn't you see I wasn't thriving?* She swallowed the internal screams back down.

"No, I'm trying to protect you." The desperation soured Joss's stomach.

"What aren't you telling me?" She searched her mother's face in an attempt to understand the guilt twisting her features into a painful expression.

"You were always meant for more, Joss."

She huffed. *Not this shit again.* "Everyone's mother thinks that. It's part of the job description."

"No." Her mother gripped her wrist tightly.

She winced. "Mom—"

"There are things I need to tell you. Secrets I can no longer keep. Reasons why I've made the choices I have." Her eyes were wide and haunted. "I prayed you'd assimilate and all of this could be avoided."

"What are you talking about, Mom?"

"Your father and I were both foster children."

"I knew that already."

"That means we taught each other everything we knew about being a shifter growing up. Finding one another was a one-in-a-million chance that saved us both. The family we had wasn't bad, but to say they didn't get us would be an understatement. Wolves, gone on hormones, experiencing their first shifts alone without the guidance of an elder. It was an intense, dangerous, and painful time, physically and emotionally. We had to be so careful to keep our distance from humans. If they knew what we were, we'd have ended up in a lab. So, when we hit eighteen, we left. We had enough money to buy a decent car, and travel to a small town to work. We existed that way for a time, traveling, seeing the United States and holding down whatever jobs we could."

"It sounds exciting." It was a rare thing, seeing her mother this happy. Her skin all but glowed, and her eyes sparkled.

Her mother laughed weakly. "Oh, it was. Every month was an adventure. We always had enough space to run nearby, and we were free." Her mother looked up toward the sky, and for a moment she saw the once radiant woman who existed B.D.D.—Before Dad Died. "It was the best time, Joss. I wouldn't trade it for anything."

Sharing the new-to-her memories warmed her heart, and gave her hope. The person who raised her was still alive and kicking.

"Low on money, we holed up in a tiny town in the middle of nowhere. We were working at a bar when we met the Lobos. What appeared to be an Outlaw Biker Club was a hell of a lot more."

"Wolves?" Joss asked.

Her mother nodded. "Once they caught our scent, they took us on and taught us everything we needed to know. It was incredible. Neither of us had ever belonged to a pack. We were like babes in adult bodies. How could we walk away?"

"Wait. You rode with a biker gang?"

"They're a club, and yes. They weren't saints. Their dealings were shady, and their lives were wild. We were sucked into the madness." Her eyes lit up. "It was a whirlwind of crazy. I loved it. There's an addictive quality to that kind of danger. Life lived on your own term pleases the wolves inside of us." Leaning in, Joss nodded, eager for more morsels of her parents' past. "We were already outsiders. It wasn't a big stretch to cross the line between what was legal and what wasn't when it came with family."

"It sounds amazing. What happened? Why didn't I grow up with them?"

"We were happy for a long time with the Lobos. Then I got pregnant."

"Was that against the rules?" Joss asked, baffled.

"No. They welcomed the new blood. Cubs are a precious to a pack. Without births packs die. Your father was over the moon. I was scared. What did we know about being parents? He convinced me it was more important that we knew what we didn't want to be like." She chuckled. "Stone always had a way of making me feel like I could do anything. Once I conquered most of my nerves, I caught his joy."

Joss shook her head. "If you were so happy, why hide all of this from me? Why leave at all?"

"When they saw your birthmark, the Alpha was spooked. We didn't understand. Unlike them, we hadn't grown up learning the lore. The whispers began immediately. The familial vibe evaporated like water on a hot day. What once felt like the ultimate freedom became a prison. Eyes were constantly trained on us. We were never left alone for long periods of time. Soon the Alpha came to our home. It was a relief. Finally, we'd be put back in the loop. He came in with his usual confident swagger and easy smile that set us at ease. The beer flowed between him and your father, and we had a fine meal of beef stew and fresh bread. You slept like an angel through it all in your swing. After we dined, he asked to hold you. Seeing the burly man cradle you in the crook of his arm and smile down at you melted my heart. I guess that made it easier to break when he told us you needed to be killed. You were a danger to their way of life." Her voice cracked.

Joss stared at her mother, horrified.

"You see, the Lobos have a well-kept secret. They've learned to shift without the aid of the moon, and they weren't about to let a slip of a girl come along and wield a power that would make her entire species bend the knee." She grimaced. "We asked the Alpha for one last night with you. To say good-bye. He granted our wish. We took all we could carry, every bit of money we'd stashed, and left through the forest. We got as far away as we could, stopped only to procure a new identity, and continued on, never looking back. We changed our last name to Weber and found a small town to raise you in. We did all we could to make sure you had a normal childhood."

"How could you keep this from me?" Joss jumped to her feet. The betrayal stung like a thousand bee-stings. A torrential downpour of varied emotions hit her full force. Anger, sadness, confusion, and understanding melded together, blurring her ability to think straight. The blood drained from her mother's face.

"How could I not?" She stood in front of Joss, waving her hands about wildly. "Don't you see? We still ended up here. Your father's death drew that point home. The universe demands certain things. She's a callous bitch who'll stop at nothing to collect. This way you're in a position of power. You have a pack who'll die for you, and while you'll be restricted, you'll be alive."

"Why do you keep saying that?"

"Healthy wolves do not drop dead of a heart attack, and my cancer cinched the deal for me. We are being haunted, hunted, targeted. Give it whatever name you will."

"This is ignorant insanity. Plenty of people experience tragedy," Joss yelled.

"Not us. Not like this, so close to the onset of *your* puberty. I had to find a place with enough power to keep you safe. Don't you see?" Her mother grasped Joss's face desperately. "I heard rumors about White Creek. It was never about me being healed."

"And dating Ian was a part of your brilliant plan?" she scoffed.

"It provided security and allowed me to have a voice in what happened with you. Your birthmark granted us an audience, and shortly after we came to live here with an understanding between us that grew to more."

Joss gripped her mother's hands and pulled them from her face. "I can't except this."

"The truth isn't always pretty." Her mother chewed on her bottom lip. "I am your mother. I will always love you, and do whatever it takes to provide and protect. You might not agree with my choices, but they were the best ones I could make at the time." She held her head higher, like a queen.

She had to respect her honesty and grit.

"You should've told me this long before."

"Perhaps. I had hoped things would turn out differently, and I would not have cause to."

"I've stayed here for you, Mom. Knowing you placed me here to play the role of a false goddess prophet infuriates me." Anger sealed her lips shut.

"Tell me what you would have done in my place, daughter. 'Cause I saw no other way out." Her mother's shoulders slumped. "If you want to blame me, feel free to do so. I can't change the past."

"No, but you sure could hide it."

They stood inches away, but an ocean might as well have sprung up between them. The sound of the front door opening sent them both into motion.

"Are my girls out here?" Ian called.

"I was just leaving," Joss replied, pivoting before he could reach them. Let her mother explain why she hadn't touched any of her food. She was good at making things up after all.

�֍ ֍

THE HIKE INTO THE WOODS and the cool weather did nothing to curb her anger. Joss pushed her legs to the limit, stepping over tree roots, and setting a brisk pace. The muscles in her legs burned, and her heart rate spiked as she began an almost jog through the steep and overgrown terrain. The woods were home. The smell of moss and leaves in various states of decay and wood called to the animal leashed inside. Today, she didn't want to be a human. Too much pain waited for her in the two-legged form. Her skin itched with the desire to shift.

Hopping over a log, she tapped into the restless she-wolf pacing inside of her and clawing to get out. The wind battered her face, and her heart lightened slightly as she hit her stride. Her sneakers pounded against the earth, and her nails lengthened and sharpened, catching the bark of a tree as she leapt over fallen, rotted-out trunks. The makeshift obstacle course gave her something to focus on.

"Slow down, Wonder Woman. Us mere mortals aren't full of Amazon juice and anger." Brook's unsteady breathing made Joss draw up short. She brought her canter to a brisk walk and peered over her shoulder.

"I'm sorry, Brook." Joss lifted her gaze, finally registering the burnt orange, scarlet, and gold leaves on the trees. The colorful burst contrasted the bleak sky, clinging to the last vestiges of fall before the winter months set in and stripped the land bare as everything slumbered or died in hopes of a spring rebirth.

"You're fit to be tied. I knew when you asked me to head to the falls it was serious." Brook bent over, placed her hands on her knees, and took a moment to catch her breath. "I'll be honest. Your kind of freaking me out right now."

Joss sighed. "Join the club. I don't recognize myself in the mirror a lot these days."

"Did you and Isiah get into a fight?" Brook asked softly.

She shook her head. "I wish that was what caused this."

"Joss?"

"I had it out with my mom … Or I attempted to. In the end, I'm the one who got the rude awakening."

"Oh, crap." Brook placed a hand on Joss's shoulder.

"Come on, let's walk the rest of the way to the falls. I needed this trek to formulate my words and burn off the worst of my rage. Among other things, she tried to push her mating agenda." Joss sneered. "I lost it, Brook. She's supposed to love me unconditionally and support me and *my* desires. I've lingered here for her. Before we joined the pack, she nearly died from cancer."

Brook gasped. "Is that why you're here when you don't believe?"

"Yes. I mean, what would you choose between your happiness and your mother's life? It felt like a small price to pay up until recently. It was all built up. A dam broke, and I couldn't hold back the floodgates. I read her the riot act and told her this was a modern day and age, and I would choose. I'm so sick of having my life dictated by others." Her throat dried out as they reached the bank and the waterfall came into view. The white water cascaded over the cliffs, creating a stunning curtain.

Tall pines surrounded the area, creating a private, lush green paradise. The sound of the rushing water prevented anyone from overhearing a conversation.

It was extreme, but this was the only place she felt capable of completely relaxing. Looking upon the natural splendor, she prepared to spill her guts.

"From the minute I was born, this tattoo has been fucking me. My last name isn't even my own. I was too pissed to stop and find out what it had been originally. My parents had to flee in the middle of the night because of their pack. The wolves they trusted most in the entire world, wanted to kill me on sight because of a few lines of dark skin and an ancient prophecy that may or may not have referred to me at all. They left it all behind and rebuilt a life based on lies."

"They did it to protect you."

"Yes, when I was younger. What about now? I'm twenty-five. I should've heard the truth ages ago." The anger bubbled up like water boiling in a pot.

"You're right. Your mother should have come clean. I wonder how one tells their child that, though."

"She doesn't think my father's death was due to natural causes." Joss blurted out the words.

"What are you talking about?"

"A wolf in his prime suffering from a sudden heart attack with no warning?"

"I thought the doctors said they didn't see any signs of foul play," Brook said.

"You and I know there are ways to harm another that can't be traced by any human means, and if the caster is good enough, they'd be exempt from magical means of dedication."

Brook's mouth dropped open. "You think someone murdered him?"

"I think the coincidences that occurred and brought us here are beginning to look suspicious, and I have no doubt this group will stop at nothing to get what they believe they need to make their fantasy scenario come true."

Brook whistled. "That's a heavy accusation, Joss."

"Yet, there it is on the table where it'll stay. Why wouldn't she try to find out what actually happened to my father?"

"Drawing attention to herself would, in turn, lead people to you."

"Damnit, stop being reasonable, Brook." Her voice was an octave too low. "I am done pretending to be a sheep when I'm a wolf." Her voice rang out, clear and powerful. "If I'm a freak, it's time to embrace all that comes with it." Facts ripped away the wall of ignorance, and truth delivered a heavy blow. *Maybe my life was never my own.*

"Wow," Brook whispered. "That's what I've been waiting for."

"What are you talking about?"

"This moment. The one where you got fed up and came into your own. This is the woman I always knew lurked inside of you, wrapped up in white robes, lashed down by rules and familial obligations. If nothing else, this situation has loosed you."

"I'm not feeling the Polly Anna vibe right now, Brook."

She smiled sadly. "I know. We never understand the hardships even as they shape and form us into the people we need to be. Believe me, I understand that."

"Everything I thought I knew was a lie. How do I move forward from that?" Joss's anxiety spiked. "I can't un-know it. I wish to God I could."

Brook shook her head; her best friend had run out of pearls of wisdom to give. Joss's nostrils flared. The itch returned to her skin full force. She snorted, forcing puffs of air out of her nostrils. Rolling her shoulders, she felt her spine stiffen. She coughed as her voice box shifted.

"I know this is a lot to take in, babe. But you need you calm down."

She heard the worry in her friend's voice, but she couldn't stop the downward spiral. Anger rose up hot and ravenous. It incinerated the common sense and compassion she was known for. Heat emanated from her pores.

An entire life built on lies, tailor-made to keep her docile and managed. *When did I become a tool instead of a person? I'm a chess piece moved in a long game.* Kept blind and imprisoned in an ivory tower by loyalty.

She began to shed her clothing. *I'll show them all how done I am with rules.* Connecting with the companion who'd always weathered the storms with her, she stopped fighting the urge to change. Muscles contracted, and tendons snapped as her bones reshaped and fur replaced skin. Dropping onto all fours, she threw her muzzle back and howled before she left her stunned friend behind. She'd changed in the middle of the day with the full moon weeks away. Things would never be the same.

Exhausted, she stopped by the Sacred Dancing Lake. The Blackfeet Tribe believed the mountain peaks were the backbone of the world. They often climbed the mountain, collecting berries, herbs, and plants for food and medicine. Admiring the impressive mountain range in the distance and the placid water, she could understand their train of thought. If the spirits of the ancestors were to gather anywhere, this peaceful place would be a prime location.

Collapsing on her belly, she rested her head on her paws. Missing her father was a condition that never healed, and was prone to flares. His presence always made her feel safe.

She longed for him now with an acuteness that made his loss feel fresh all over again. Saline obscured her vision. Whimpers spilled from her throat. Tiny white flakes of frozen water began to drift down. Watching them dance, she let her mind rest as they melted harmlessly on her thick fur. In the distance, a cluster of snowflakes, whirl together. Energy pulsed in the air. Apprehensive, she rose to her feet. As she sniffed the area, she caught an impossible scent. Dancing back on her hind legs, she saw a misty white fog blowing in toward the mainland.

Her heart knocked in her chest as a tornado of snow flurries took on a shape. She knew that stance, those broad shoulders, and long legs. *Am I hallucinating?* Had she just been pushed over the edge and fallen headlong into a mental breakdown? The image blurred, and in its place was that of a familiar four-legged form. Backing up, she prepared to run when the *vision* solidified and took on color. The russet and brown wolf stole her ability to move from her.

Dad?

Golden eyes full of affection and power met her own. She held her breath as the wolf padded over and she looked down in deference to his dominance. He nuzzled her muzzle, and she offered her neck. *This isn't possible.* The words repeated in her brain on a loop.

"*My little wolf. You've had to deal with so much on your own, but I'm here now.*"

Giving in to her desires, she returned his affection with gentle nips. Whatever this might be, she'd fully bask in the presence of her father, and deal with the fallout later. *Daddy.* Playful licks and nuzzles drove home the fact that he was corporal as they roughhoused. Time seemed to stand still as the two reconnected.

"*Daddy, I don't know what to do. Please, help me.*" She communicated with him through the mental link all family members possessed.

"*Do what you were born to do.*" Her father's vagueness confused her.

"*I don't know what that is, Dad.*"

"*The right thing, little wolf. Not the easy route, or the one that feels like an obligation. Make choices you can live with because they resonate with your soul and your gut.*" He nudged her face with his muzzle. "*I'm sorry I can't offer you more. You will never have a simple life. Fate dealt you a wicked hand. One, I know you're strong enough and smart enough to play the game well. It may not seem like it, but you were sent here for a reason. White Creek hasn't gotten much right, but they weren't wrong about you. It's no secret the balance has been shifted. As much as our species like to believe the vampires and witches are rivals completely separate from ourselves, we aren't. It's why we're all failing to thrive, and the darkness is beginning to overpower the light. We're on the verge of discovery. In an age of social media where telephones have cameras capable of high-resolution videos and photos, rogue brethren are a serious danger. Across the board, the rules we've been bound by are bending. The cracks are forming, and all too soon, our foundations will break, unless we do something about it.*"

"What do you mean by something, Dad?" She sat back on her haunches, watching him pace back and forth as he spoke.

"Together we will see the world burn, or watch it be healed. The original bloodlines must reunite to repair the damage done."

"How am I going to accomplish that?" she asked.

"You're going to need help, little wolf."

"From who?" Everyone here felt indebted to the Alpha.

"The ancient wolves who've long retreated and washed their hands of the modern world. They have watched and waited for a sign."

"I think we'd know if there were wolves here."

"Not these wolves. They were here long before we were thought of. Let me tell you the Blackfoot legend of the Wolfman."

Blackfoot Mythology

The Wolf Man

There was once a man who had two bad wives. They had no shame. The man thought if he moved away where there were no other people, he might teach these women to become good, so he moved his lodge away off on the prairie. Near where they camped was a high butte, and every evening about sundown, the man would go up on top of it, and look all over the country to see where the buffalo were feeding, and if any enemies were approaching. There was a buffalo skull on the hill, which he used to sit on.

"This is very lonesome," said one woman to the other, one day. "We have no one to talk with nor to visit."

"Let us kill our husband," said the other. "Then we will go back to our relations and have a good time."

Early in the morning, the man went out to hunt, and as soon as he was out of sight, his wives went up on top of the butte. There they dug a deep pit, and covered it over with light sticks, grass, and dirt, and placed the buffalo skull on top.

In the afternoon they saw their husband coming home, loaded down with meat he had killed. So they hurried to cook for him. After eating, he went up on the butte and sat down on the skull. The slender sticks gave way, and he fell into the pit. His wives were watching him, and when they saw him disappear, they took down the lodge, packed everything on the dog travois, and moved off, going toward the main camp. When they got near it, they began to cry and mourn so that the people could hear them.

"Why is this?" they were asked. "Why are you mourning? Where is your husband?"

"He is dead," they replied. "Five days ago he went out to hunt, and he never came back." And they cried and mourned again.

When the man fell into the pit, he was hurt. After a while, he tried to get out, but he was so badly bruised he could not climb up. A wolf, traveling along, came to the pit and saw him, and pitied him. 'Ah-h-w-o-o-o-o! Ah-h-w-o-o-o-o!' he howled, and when the other wolves heard him, they all came running to see what was the matter. There came also many coyotes, badgers, and kit-foxes.

"In this hole," said the wolf, "is my find. Here is a fallen-in man. Let us dig him out, and we will have him for our brother."

They all thought the wolf spoke well, and began to dig. In a little while, they had a hole close to the man. Then the wolf who found him said, "Hold on, I want to speak a few words to you." All of the animals listening, he continued, "We will all have this man for our brother, but I found him, so I think he ought to live with us big wolves."

All of the others said that this was okay, so the wolf went into the hole, and tearing down the rest of the dirt, dragged the almost dead man out. They gave him a kidney to eat, and when he was able to walk a little, the big wolves took him to their home. Here there was a very old, blind wolf, who had powerful medicine. He cured the man and made his head and hands look like those of a wolf. The rest of his body was not changed.

In those days the people used to make holes in the pis'kun walls and set snares, and when wolves and other animals came to steal meat, they were caught by the neck. One night the wolves all went down to the pis'kun to steal meat, and when they got close to it, the man-wolf said, "Stand here a little while. I will go down and fix the places, so you will not be caught." He went on and sprung all of the snares; then he went back and called the wolves and others—the coyotes, badgers, and foxes—and they all went in the pis'kun and feasted, and took meat to carry home.

In the morning the people were surprised to find the meat gone, and their nooses all drawn out. They wondered how it could have been done. For many nights the nooses were drawn and the meat stolen. But once, when the wolves went there to steal, they found only the meat of a scabby bull, and the man-wolf was angry. He cried out, "Bad-you-give-us-o-o-o! Bad-you-give-us-o-o-o!" The people heard him and said: "It is a man-wolf who has done all of this. We will catch him." So they put pemmican and nice back fat in the pis'kun, and many hid close by. After dark, the wolves came again, and when the man-wolf saw the good food, he ran to it and began eating. Then the people all rushed in and caught him with ropes and took him to a lodge. When they got inside to the light of the fire, they knew at once who it was. They said, "This is the man who was lost."

"No," replied the man, "I was not lost. My wives tried to kill me. They dug a deep hole, and I fell into it, and I was hurt so badly that I could not get out. Luckily, the wolves took pity on me and helped me, or I would have died there." When the people heard this, they were angry, and they told the man to do something.

"You say well," he agreed. "I give those women to the I-kun-uh'-kah-tsi; they know what to do."

After that night the two women were never seen again.

She moved back, digesting the tale. "This is where the pack came from?"

"Yes. They've had enough of cruelty. If you could gain their ear and trust, you'd be a force to reckon with."

"*Why me?*"

"*Who else?*" Her father's automatic response sobered her.

"*How will I find them?*"

"*Purify your body, clear your mind, and show respect to the spirits. You can do this, Joss. I'm proud of you. Despite the adversity, you've grown up well. You protected and cared for your mother. It's no longer you task. Tell your mother she will always be my moon, and I her wolf.*" The words carried a weight she couldn't understand. How could he remain so dedicated to her when she hadn't even tried to avenge him?

"*What happened to you, Dad?*"

"*You're not ready to know yet. I have to go, and so do you.*" He backed up, fading in the snow he'd originally formed from.

Heeding her father's words, she turned and took off for home. The sun had set an hour earlier, and she had no idea how long she'd spent with her father. Time seemed to move differently when they interacted.

Torches flickered in the hands of people clustered into groups. Floodlights punched wide holes in the darkness. She loped through them, ignoring their alarmed cries and shouts of relief.

"The Moon Maiden turned without the full moon." The voices became a buzz. *Things are changing. The end time is near.*

"It's begun," Isiah yelled, raising his arms in the air. The screech of an owl in the distance felt like a herald of the death of White Creeks' ignorant innocence.

⁂

HER MOTHER SWEPT OUT INTO the crowd, clutching her scarlet half cape to her thin frame.

"*What were you thinking?*" The words had a bite. Anger raced down their mental link. She winced, not used to her mother's anger or aggression.

"*Dad said you will always be the moon and he, your wolf.*"

The blood evacuated her mother's face swiftly. "*What did you just say?*"

Joss lifted her head. *"You heard me."*

"I realize you're upset, but this is beyond cruel." Her mother clutched her neck.

"I bring you truth. How could I have known that phrase meant anything?"

Her mother shook her head. *"After all this time …"*

"He doesn't blame you for anything. I do."

Her mother stumbled back, eyes wide, and mouth agape.

"We should get her inside." The Alpha's voice was steel stretched over barbed wire. He was furious.

She bowed her head in submission. But her heart protested the action. Their relationship was wrong. He wasn't an Alpha she loved, respected, admired, and trusted. He was the warden who held the keys to her cell. The unhealthy arrangement had eaten away at her soul, weakened and depressed her. Starting today, she took her power back by any means necessary, and at any cost. She couldn't lead on her knees, and she owed the members she'd helped keep here—virtually enslaved—a way out. If they choose it. She owed them this much.

Head jammed to the max with facts, musings, plans, and realizations, she hardly registered the walk to the wooden mansion.

"What the hell were you thinking?" His voice never rose, but the rage behind every word was palatable.

Her ears turned down, and her shoulders slumped back.

"Change." When she resisted the urge to obey, his nostrils flared.

"Perhaps she can't, Father. You seem to believe her change was intentional," Isiah said.

The Alpha turned from her. "What do you mean?"

"The change may have come on her spontaneously. None of us has ever experienced a shift outside of the lunar pattern. The call might have brought her to her knees. Should we punish her for what's beyond her control?" Isiah tilted his head.

Joss glanced back and forth between the two men. Ian frowned.

"You deal with her then. Dorothy." Her mother jumped and rushed to follow him as he stalked off.

Isiah knelt. "You've gotten yourself into a mess, little sister." The mocking tone earned her yip. Isiah chuckled. "And she's found a backbone." He stroked her back. "What happened to you out there in those woods, hmm? I've felt an otherworldly presence before, but it's never shown itself to me." His fingers felt good behind her ear. Narrowing her eyes, she refused to relax. "I can't help but wonder if you've aligned yourself with this power."

She growled.

"Would you rather I let the Alpha deal with you?" He removed his hand and met her gaze.

She sniffed. He had her between a rock and a hard place, his favorite position to maneuver her into.

"Smart girl. You and I have much to talk about. You accelerated my time schedule."

Her ears perked up. *What is he talking about?*

"I wasn't expecting to see outward signs of transformation so soon. It's okay. I've prepared for this, and it's one step closer to our union."

She stepped away.

"People saw you travel through the town as a wolf, others will hear about it shortly. You'll be the talk of the town by mid-morning. People fear what they can't understand or control. Keeping the peace requires a certain finesse and reassurance. We wouldn't want the locals to panic, would we?"

Her stomach knotted. *"Control how?"*

Isiah shuddered. "I love the feel of you in my mind. Regulating the information and showing them we have a plan and a direction. Because this is all a part of a strategy. Together, we'll usher in a new era. Surely the ability to change without the moon will be necessary to win the war on its way. Why else would evolution occur so spontaneously?" The smugness insinuated he knew more than he let on.

"What do you know?"

"What are you willing to give for the information?"

"What do you want?"

"Your cooperation when I announce our union."

"Fuck off."

He chuckled. "We both know it's been leading to this."

"I'm not that desperate."

"But you will be. I'm going to enjoy watching you break down and ask me for help, Jossy. Until then, I'll protect you from Father. Call it a gesture of good-will between us. I want to help you and make things good between us. We've been through too much to remain at odds."

"Then stop trying to chain me to you."

"Silly girl. Haven't you realized by now, our births did that? I'm playing the role assigned to me. You've spent your entire life resisting it, waiting for a chance to escape an inevitable situation. I used to be like you until I came to understand that would never work. Tell me what your real apprehension with us mating is."

"It doesn't feel right. I don't see you that way, Isiah. I never have. At best, you're a brother-like figure. I can't imagine being intimate with you."

"Sweet, naïve Joss. That's the price of sitting on the throne. Sacrifice, loss of choice, and acting for the greater good. You're under the impression that I have a crush on you. Don't get me wrong, you're gorgeous. I lucked out in that department." He gripped the scruff of her neck. "But what I truly crave is your power." His eyes flashed amber. "No one, you included, is going to take away my opportunity to rule."

"You don't need me for that."

"Unfortunately, for you, you're the only one who believes that." He placed a sweet kiss on her crown and stood. "Come. Let's work out the details. Things will be so much better when we have a plan and a script."

She dug her back paws into the dirt and stiffened.

"Oh, those are the games you want to play?" In a lightning-fast maneuver, he grabbed her scruff and lifted her from the ground. His strength stole her breath away. "You aren't the only one finding new strengths and talents. Some of us keep our secrets until they're worth revealing."

His words terrified her. *How much is he hiding?* She'd never find out if she continued her open opposition. Her gut told her the time for rebellion had yet to arrive. Her ego told the wise voice to piss off. Warring with herself, she missed the trip to his house farther on the property. The golden boy had moved out, but only just so. He opened the door and dropped her to her feet. She landed spryly on all fours and hopped back, barking.

"Are you ready to change yet?" He locked the door behind them and moved to the kitchen. "I'll go get your clothing."

Wary, she watched him disappear down the hallway. He seemed more at ease here away from prying eyes. He returned with a pair of gray sweatpants and a black Henley. Wolves weren't prone to shyness, but the thought of being so vulnerable alone with him made her balk.

"I'll go to the kitchen and make us some hot chocolate. I know how you like yours." He always reminded her of their connection. As if the good times in the past could make up for the monster he'd become. Life with a loose cannon was like walking a tightrope—one misstep and she'd stumble and tumble to the ground below where no net waited to catch her. Grabbing the clothing clothes with her teeth, she pulled them from the arm of the couch and took them to the bathroom. Breathing deeply, she focused on calming her nerves and connecting with her humanity.

She slammed to the ground as her body contorted and muscles crackled as tendons realigned. Her vision doubled, and she grew light-headed. Breathing hard, she gave herself a moment to adapt to the conversion. She rose on shaky legs, then slowly slipped her legs into the soft pants. After pulling the shirt over her head, she peered in the mirror at her wild hair. Turning on the faucet, she used the water to tame her mane and gathered her thoughts. He was baiting her, giving her just enough detail to pique her curiosity. *He's willing to talk. Get what you can out of him, and use it.*

The weight of the innocent members enthralled by the false environment she helped create nearly pulled her down. *Hold steady, girl. You've got work to do.* Her father's words played in her head as she straightened and walked out of the restroom with her head held high. *A true queen doesn't cower in the face of adversary.*

"I see you've come to play." Isiah lifted his mug in a toast.

"It's not a game."

"Life is but a game and we the players."

"Don't wax poetic on me, Stark."

His smile faltered. "You're the only one who could get away with saying that to my face."

She took the hot chocolate with the peppermint stick, whipped cream, and creamer. "Hmmm." She took a sip and smirked. "I know."

"You did more than change outwardly tonight." He studied her with a small smile. "You smell differently, and your mannerisms are different."

"Maybe I'm just done hiding."

"Is that it? I'm not so sure." He took a sip of his hot chocolate.

"You said you wanted to talk." She peered at him over the stack of whipped cream.

"This doesn't have to be the torture chamber you're making it out to be. You know I'd never lay a hand on you."

"There are worst things than physical abuse, Isiah. Don't play coy now."

"And the hunter becomes the huntress," he all but purred.

"I'm not hunting you. I think we've both established I'd rather be left alone."

"We'll come out naturally, being seen together, holding hands, kisses—"

"On the cheek. Seen no more than three times a week on a more personal level." She wasn't going to make this arrangement easy for him.

"Why the sudden agreement?" he asked abruptly.

"If I can't alter my fate, I'm damn sure going to have a hand in shaping it."
She leaned against the counter, crossing her legs at the ankle.

"You look good in my clothes in my kitchen."

"Don't mistake my agreement to work with you for anything other than it is, Isiah," she said sternly.

"I won't. For now."

She rolled her eyes. "At least you're honest."

"We'll be together for a lifetime. Trust needs exist between us."

She jumped on the opening he presented. "Then tell me what you were hinting at earlier."

"I've looked outside of this pack. We're going to need allies. I worked hard to *procure* them over the years. I'm not taking over the job as Alpha for no reason. I possess the connections and strength needed to win. Father is no longer in his prime. It's no secret some of his practices are outdated. He recognizes the fact that I'll be the tougher Alpha. Remember, Daddy dearest is all about the greater good." The bitterness in his tone made her ache for him. Ian had always been hardest on his son. Rarely giving praise, he constantly demanded an impossible level of perfection at all times. The dressing down, harsh words, and heavy-handed handling meant to push Isiah to be *tough* helped mold a sociopath.

"I thought we didn't trust outsiders."

"No man is an island. White Creek isn't exempt from that rule. You fight fire with fire. We need vampires, other packs, and witches on our side to win."

"You're going to upset a lot of people," she observed. His thoughts were sound, the way he went about achieving them was the fucked-up part.

"I'll be the Alpha. Whatever comes out of my mouth will be magical. It's like a unicorn … even their shit is rainbow-colored, and smells like fruit."

She spit out her frothy drink and laughed.

He grinned. "I like it better when you're happy. I've come to count on that from you even when you're angry with me. Growing up, you and Dorothy were my anchors. Those never-changing people who didn't expect more than I could deliver."

"Siah." The childhood nickname was out before she could stop it. "You can rule your way. You don't have to follow your father's vision." She reached out to the little boy who'd made her laugh after her father's death, and never minded when she tagged along with him and his friends.

"Just like you, I'm trapped by the role I have to play, Joss." He smiled at her sadly. The sorrow was gone in the blink of an eye by a too wide grin and strain around the eyes. "Enough of the trip down memory lane. How shall we come out?"

Lose a battle to win the war. She repeated the chant in her head to combat the intense wave of defeat that battered at her psyche.

JOSS OPENED THE DOOR TO find her distraught best friend on the front porch. Her eyes were wide, and her usually perfect coif was frizzy and mused. Brook pulled her thick tresses back into a messy bun. Her neon pink pajama pants with unicorns on them were covered by an oversized gray sweater that said 'Sleep' across the chest; both were deeply creased with wrinkles. She'd literally stumbled from bed to come here the minute she'd hung up the phone. The Alpha had prevented Joss from contacting anyone or going anywhere other than the main house for a week.

Buffed, waxed, polished, and damn near interrogated, she was groomed insistently about what to say and how to act when they reintroduced her to society. Food was withheld, and she was constantly placed in the sauna to *cleanse* herself. *More like weakened to make more susceptible to suggestion and cohesion.* She felt like a specimen. A creation invented in the laboratory that they were preparing to release into society.

Biting her tongue, she'd remained quiet and pliant while she silently ragged on the inside. At the moment, she was walking on a razor's edge with the Alpha. He watched her every move carefully and questioned her motives, coaching, berating, and correcting every time she gave a response he deemed unsatisfactory. The sympathetic glances from Isiah stung. He remembered all too well what this was like. Could she blame him for being twisted? Even now her muscles clenched and her stomach spasmed as she remembered the *treatment*.

"Where the hell have you been?" Brook shouted as she stepped into the house.

Joss held a finger up to her lips, closed the door.

"Are you kidding me right now?" Brook huffed.

"Shh." Joss jerked her thumb down the hallway. Brook scowled as she followed behind her. They entered the den, and Joss turned on a twenty-one pilots record. Cranking up the volume, she rushed back to the kitchen, turned on the dishwasher, and started the washing machine.

"Joss!"

"I want to make sure our conversation is private." Her paranoia was at a fevered pitch.

"You are scaring the hell out of me." Brook grabbed Joss's arm and stopped her in the middle of the hall. "No one would tell me where you went or if you were okay. I've been worried sick. My sleep has been shit all week. I've dropped five pounds. Everyone had a different theory about how you changed, and why you disappeared. None of them were reassuring. I'm done waiting to hear answers."

"I know." Joss covered Brook's hand. "And I am sorry. But it was taken out of my hands." Joss gestured toward her room with her head. "Come on. Let's go to my room, and I'll tell you everything."

Brook ground her teeth.

"I promise."

"What happened, Joss?" Brook asked softly as she followed her into the large room.

"I made a deal with the devil, that's what." Joss closed the door to her bedroom, and they collapsed on the sofa that was set against the wall. The light streaming into the pale blue bedroom from the bay window with a view of the forest did nothing to lighten the mood.

"Start talking, woman," Brook growled in the back of her throat.

"Everything I tell you has to stay between us."

"Like you had to give *me* a disclaimer."

"I know. I'm just reeling. After I ran, I ended up at the lake. It started to snow, and my father appeared in wolf form."

"Are you sure it was him?" The disbelief oozing from Brook's stiff, closed-off body language was nearly offensive.

"He spoke to me through our familial bond. Who else could do that?"

"You had a lot going on that day, Joss. I don't want you to let a delusion dictate—"

"It wasn't in my head," Joss insisted. "He gave me the information I needed, and a message for my mother she clearly understood. The land is special. There are more things on heaven and earth."

"Psst. I'm not Horatio, and you aren't Shakespeare." Brook placed her hands on her hips.

"No, but the Native American lore originated for a reason. There's a pack out there now, an old pack of ancient descent."

Brook's brow furrowed. "We're the only one in this area. You know that."

"Do I?" Joss cocked her head to the side. "Do *you*? Think about it. If you had that much power, would it be impossible to hide your presence?"

"I suppose it wouldn't. But why the hell would you?" Brook asked.

"The Native Americans dealings with new people weren't exactly ideal. Think about the way Alpha acts about the *outside* and his paranoia is unmitigated in comparison to anything the Native American pack may feel."

"How is it possible though?" Brook marveled.

"We're made of magic and hide in plain sight. Is it shocking to know there's more out there we've yet to uncover? My father told me, the wolves are displeased with what's happening. The deterioration of our magic and the laws that have guided us disturb them. He thinks they might be persuaded to get back in the game."

"Okay, this is all great in theory, but realistically, how in the hell do you plan to do that?" Brook sucked her teeth.

"Well, I'd have to find them first. But they see my birthmark as a long-awaited sign."

Brook puckered her lips. "Oh, really? They do?" She raised her voice a few octaves, mockingly.

"Shut it," Joss mumbled. "Do you know the Blackfoot legend of the Wolf Man?"

"Where the two wives try to murder the husband by making him fall into a pit?" Brook's brow wrinkled.

"That's the one." Joss nodded. "It's more than lore."

"The thought of them lurking in the woods watching us undetected all of this time is terrifying. I mean, none of us have sensed them." Brook shuddered.

"It speaks to their power. We need them on our side if we're going to come out on top."

"You're really going to look for them?" Brook toyed with the hem of her sweater.

Joss rubbed the back of her neck. "I have to. Isiah has who knows how many allies waiting in the wings."

"He told you this?" Brook asked skeptically.

"Once I agreed to play the part of smitten, soon-to-be girlfriend, he couldn't share enough."

"You didn't." The horror in Brook's voice embarrassed her.

"I had to. He saved my ass with the Alpha who was none too happy about my jaunt through the town as a wolf. I've spent a week being reamed out and coordinating plans. If it wasn't for Isiah, I'm sure he would've forced me to go into reconciliation."

Brook cringed. The intense retraining program to right wrongs was notorious for its awfulness.

"Alpha doesn't like having his thunder stolen," Joss said sullenly.

"This is madness."

"You wanted me to bring change. You can't change your mind because you don't approve of my tactics." Joss folded her arm under her breasts.

"Why now?" Brook asked.

"I feel it here." She placed a hand on her stomach. "And waiting is a non-option. I can only pretend with Isiah for so long before reality expects us to take bigger moves."

"Why would *he* agree to this?" Brook questioned.

"I thought about that. I believe it's to keep face. He can only take so much rejection and save face. Right now, he needs to look strong for the others. A rocky transfer of power could destroy everything that's been built. They need to have confidence in him."

"And you? What do you get out of this mess?" Brook gestured with her hands.

"I get more time and an inside look at what's happening behind the scenes. The system is broken. These are the fracture lines before the big break. If we don't stop it, I feel like it'll be like Humpty Dump syndrome. There'll be no putting anything back together again."

Brook shook her head. "You're playing a dangerous game."

"It's the only move left on the board." Joss toyed with the ends of her ponytail.

"What can I do to help?" Brook sighed.

"Help me figure out how to find this pack and keep me sane."

"Well, when you're asking for so little," Brook drawled sarcastically.

Joss shoved her playfully, relieved that the tension had lightened. She was on board, even if she was skeptical.

"Thank you. I've started doing research about the Native Americans who lived here, and the legend itself, but I'm not sure what I'm looking for."

"And Isiah?"

"Is planning on taking me for coffee after the big meeting everyone will gather for tomorrow afternoon."

"Are they going to talk about your shift?"

Joss nodded. "And what it means for our people. It's a spin job, but we both know the Alpha is as slick as an oil spill."

"All of this insanity aside, are you okay?" Brook grabbed her hands.

"I'm numb. It's all happening so fast. I can barely catch my breath before I'm pulled under again."

Brook squeezed her hand. "I'm here. Let me help."

"Can we take a break from all of this and just be us?" Joss's voice was small and shaky. Tomorrow her entire life would be turned upside down. Today, she wanted to burrow deep into normalcy.

Getting up, Brook tugged her hands. "Come on, we'll bake brownies, drink White Russians, and I'll tell you about the last date I went on."

"Have I heard this story?" Joss asked, rising to follow her friend.

"No. Your life got infinitely more interesting, and it completely slipped my mind during our last conversations."

Joss snickered. "I'm terribly sorry about that."

"Me too. I have some serious horror story moments I needed to hash over with my best friend."

"Trust me when I say I'm all ears now." She wiggled her ears, and Brook giggled. Humor was a release they both needed. Brook linked their arms. Soaking up the silent support and acceptance from her best friend, she put the rest of her worries on the back burner. They'd be there waiting for her to pick up tomorrow.

"Who was your victim … I mean date?"

Brook gasped. "For shame, Joss Weber. You shut your mouth. Any wolf would be lucky to have me."

"Oh, I agree. It's just their ability to handle you that makes a match difficult."

"Well, you're not wrong there." Brook gave her the side-eye. "Don't get me wrong. There are some great guys in the pack."

"But you can bulldoze them with your eyes closed, and you'll never be truly attracted to that particular personality type?" Joss supplied.

"Ugh. Exactly. I mean, I can do easygoing, but I need a man who has the ability to stand up to me and tell me to slow my roll. You know? A best friend and a boyfriend all in one?"

"And yet you were trying to pawn them off on me."

Brook sniffed. "Who knew what you liked? If it's not your dream lover, you're not interested."

"He's not my lover."

"Yet."

"So now you believe he exists?" Joss asked, exasperation evident in her voice.

"I think you do," Brook replied elusively.

"Oh no, this is all or nothing, sister." Joss slipped her arm free and grabbed the Kahlúa from the fridge while Brook freed the vodka from the cabinet.

"Are you still dreaming about him?"

Joss grabbed two tumblers and paused. She hadn't told her friend about the strange way the dreams had changed. Filling the tumblers with crushed ice from the fridge, she wrestled with her desire to keep things to herself. "It's different now."

"What is?" Brook asked, measuring out the vodka with a metal jigger.

"My time with Kaz. It feels more realistic. He said things have changed."

"Is that new for him?" Brook asked

"Very."

Brook continued to mix the drinks. "Hmm."

"He said he's coming for me."

The glass slipped from Brook's hand and landed on the marble counter, the sound of shattering glass reverberating through the room. "Why the hell are you just now telling me this?"

Joss bent down and grabbed the dust pan and broom from the cabinet under the sink. As she cleaned, she replied, "Well, you said it was all in my head."

"And if it's not, and he randomly shows up?" Brook waved her hands wildly.

"Then it'd be long overdue. Don't you think?" Joss shrugged.

"How are you so laid back?"

"I've seen him my entire life, Brook. It'd be nice to know he's not simply a figment of my imagination." Gripping the edge of the counter, she bowed her head. How could she explain the feeling of disconnection she experienced between waking and sleep when she thought of Kazimir?

"People, in reality, are rarely what they appear to be from a distance," Brook cautioned.

"I know that. Don't judge me harshly. I just … I need this moment to happen." She pushed away from the counter. "I'm tired of being in limbo. For better or worse, this needs to play out."

"Okay then." Brook slid the drink toward her. "You look like you need this."

Joss took a sip of the sweet beverage and let the taste dance over her tongue. "I've had my head buried in the sand like an ostrich. I'm ready to bring it all out into the open." The time for secrets and silence had passed. "Fear will no longer be the one in the driver's seat." She knew better than to tempt fate. Even as the words left her mouth, she regretted them.

Chapter Five

THIS TIME, SHE CAME TO Kishi's prepared. Knocking softly on the door, she balanced her handmade lemon biscuits. The thin cookies were golden brown and held the perfect snap when you bit into them. She knew because she'd made three batches before declaring them fit to gift to the lamia. If you were trying to woo someone with food, nothing short of spectacular would do. She'd spread a thin layer of white icing to add a hint of sweetness to the tart lemon flavor. *Who says watching baking shows doesn't pay off?*

The lamia opened the door and grinned. She was dressed to kill in a jade silk dress with a deep V-neck that highlighted her décolletage and kissed the ground. She never got the sense that Kishi was ashamed of her lower half, but she didn't put it on display either.

"You are a fast learner," she purred. "Come in, my new friend. Please, set your gifts on the table."

Moving into the sumptuous space, she did as she was told.

"You have a different look about you today. There is more fight and knowing. Things have been revealed to you, yes? How has it changed you?"

"It's been freeing? I guess when you have nothing left to lose, what can hold you back?"

"Hmm." Kishi nodded. "The darkness conceals and traps. Letting light in doesn't always mean it will be an uplifting experience. Merely one full of truth. You have to remember that the truth is a mighty sword that can be devastating when wielded correctly."

"People have to be willing to see the truth first." Joss sighed when she thought of the people salivating as they bought into the Alpha's every word.

"Sometimes, they need a mirror held up in front of their faces. Like you."

"You think I was blind?" Joss asked.

"No, I think you needed to see the entire story to be able to act accordingly." The kettle whistled. "Tea's ready."

"You knew I was coming." Joss would never get used to her knowing.

"My blessing and curse." Kishi shrugged as she slithered away. The tip of her tail rattled as she used it like a ruder to steer. "You came bearing gifts, so the first question is on me."

"How do I find the pack?"

"You've been a busy bee. I think I continue to underestimate you. Isiah's suffocating shadow made it hard to see you for who you really are."

"What does that mean?"

Kishi clicked her tongue. "The first one was a freebie." She poured the tea, remembering Joss's preference of two sugar cubes and a heavy-handed dollop of cream.

"What is it you want?" Joss asked cautiously. She wasn't foolish enough to believe the lamia wanted to be friends. Her presence broke up Kishi's daily monotony, nothing more.

"I need you to research something for me."

"That's it?" Joss said incredulously.

Kishi smirked. "Before you agree to this, know that it won't be an easy search, and I would swear you to secrecy in the old way."

"What do you consider the old way?"

"A blood oath."

Her eyes bulged.

"I hold my secrets close to my chest, dear. If I choose to share, you'd best believe I'm covering my tail." She rattled the buttons on the end of her tail and winked.

"I won't agree blindly."

"And I won't share without that oath," Kishi countered.

Joss sighed. *If the mountain won't come to Muhammad.* "Is it illegal?"

"No."

"Then why do you say it's hard?" she probed.

"Because not all secrets reveal themselves to me so easily."

"But you have the sight."

"And yet when it comes to matters concerning me, I am blind. Nature always demands her balance."

"Is there a time limit?" Joss asked, trying to get the parameters.

"No. The oath will make sure you hold up your end of the bargain, regardless of how long it takes."

"You can't give me anything else?" She studied Kishi, who perched on the chair across from her and sipped her tea.

"It won't harm you in any way. It's more of a mystery waiting to be solved. A past so old, people have begun to believe it was fiction. That I am unreal." Her gaze moved to the wall behind Joss's shoulder, but she knew from the removed expression, the older woman saw something that wasn't actually there.

"If I agree to do this, what do I get in return?" Joss was prepared to be shrewd.

"My services rendered. No more hoops, or bartering."

Whatever this was, it meant a great deal to her. Having Kishi on her side could make a world of difference.

"Let's make the oath."

Kishi set her cup onto the saucer. "If you're sure. It takes a person who's fully committed to undergo this ritual."

"I'm all in. I won't renege on my word."

"Very well then. Come." She set her tea down and stood. Slowly, she made her way out of the dining area and farther into her room. They moved out of the living area and deeper to the cavern. Stalagmites hung down. She entered another area, covered in salt. Himalayan salt stones covered the wall and granulated salt.

"This is my salt room."

"What does it do?"

"It brings peace, and helps cleanse impurities and negative energy. Pharmaceutical grade salt is ground up and diffused into the air. It helps focus energy for ceremonies as well."

Joss nodded, still amazed at the incredible space created inside of the mountain.

"Sit by the altar, and I'll get everything we'll need."

Sitting on the ground, beside the altar, she watched as Kishi retrieved a silver goblet, silver handled knife, and a strange metal bowl with a thick, fat, wooden roller half painted black.

Lining everything up on the altar, Kishi moved to the wooden bowl to light incense. Humming in the back of her throat, she gave off an odd hissing sound, which seemed to hypnotize like a cobra. She ran the stick on the inside of the bowl. A harmonic hum filled the room. She sang in what Joss believed to be Chinese, though she wasn't knowledgeable enough to decipher a dialect.

Electricity swept through the woman, followed by a cool wind, that chilled her skin and blew the curls away from her face. Despite the miniature hurricane, Kishi was unruffled. Her skin glowed with an inner light. Her dark hair billowed around her like a dark cloud, and her eyes glowed with power. Her tail rattled in time with her chanting.

"What are you doing?"

"I'm asking the gods of old to serve as our witnesses. On this day we create a bond until our vow is met."

"Are you going to explain what exactly you want me to do?"

"The first step is to be bound by secrecy." Kishi sliced her palm. The bright red liquid slowly welled up from the slash. She held it over the silver chalice. "I shall keep our vow wrapped in secrecy and help you in exchange for the search for my lost love."

Joss's jaw dropped.

Kishi handed her the knife. "Now you."

Joss made a small cut, and dripped her blood into the silver chalice, adorned with carvings of warriors. It looked old and practically hummed with power.

"Repeat the words."

"I shall keep our vow wrapped in secrecy and search for your lost love in exchange for information and assistance."

"Good." Kishi nodded her approval. She lifted the chalice and began to chant again. The smoke drifting up from the incense swirled wildly, forming a large snake made of white smoke. Kishi leaned back on her heels and sighed. "It's done."

"Who am I looking for, Kishi?"

She shook her head. "I don't know."

"Why can't you tell me?"

"Because it's my punishment for wanting what I knew I couldn't have and making a holy man fall for me. I'm older than you can comprehend. Sonnets, stories, and plays have been written about my tragic tale of what never would be. I retreated for a time, distracted myself with mischief, and more lives than any one person should experience, but always it comes back to him."

"Who?" she asked, intrigued by the complete change in the icy woman with the polite façade.

"Jizi Zhao."

She chose her words carefully. "Was he *like* you?"

Kishi smiled sadly. "No. He was completely human. A good, sweet man, who saw behind this odd form to the woman beneath."

"Then how do you expect me to find him?"

"Every now and then I can feel him. I am certain he's been reborn in this lifetime."

"And what if he's some ten-year-old boy in California?" Joss pressed the issue, not about to deliver a helpless babe into the lair of a monster.

"Then I will wait, and come to him when the time is right."

"That's incredibly creepy." The words were out before she could tamper them.

"Your job is to find him, not to judge." Her words cut like razor wire.

Joss held her hands up. "Fine. I'm not sure how to go about this though."

"That's up to you to figure out." Kishi fixed her eyes on her, and the temperature in the room dropped.

"Tell me what I want to know, give me the last known location of Jizi, and I'll get started today."

"Ask your question."

"How do I find the pack?"

"You don't. They will find you if you put yourself in the proper state."

"And how do I do that?"

"You need to go on a vision quest."

"I'm not a Native American, Kishi."

"You don't need to be to tune into yourself, and the spirits around you. Start researching the process, and we'll work on meditation. Show them you respect their beliefs and aren't a White Creek sheep."

"Are you giving me homework?"

"Yes, little one. Respect goes a long way, and you've got the history of the past attached to you. It's long and painful, and when they look at you, they won't be able to help but see that. The past always affects the present whether or not we want to admit." Her voice suggested she spoke from firsthand knowledge.

Joss glanced down at her watch. "Crap. I have to go. We have a town meeting today."

"I'd like to be a fly on the wall. You riled them all up, coming into town like that."

Joss didn't bother to ask her how she knew.

"It wasn't intentional. If I had thought it through, I wouldn't have made such a dramatic entrance."

"Always follow your instincts, Joss." She rose, leading her out of the peaceful space. "I'll keep our blood in a vial. Think of it as a physical contract for our agreement."

"Is there anything I should know about today?" Joss asked as she followed her through her home toward the front door.

"Let things play out naturally. Observe, and bide your time waiting for an opening. You'll know it when you see it."

Joss's shoulders slumped. "So, more of the same?"

"Remember, you're playing the long game. That takes patience, cunning, and acting skills. I know you possess all three. Don't overplay your hand now when things are getting critical. Once you show your cards, there's nothing left to bargain with." They reached the front door and paused. "What about Isiah?"

"You won't like what I have to say, but the two of you are connected and inexplicably bound." Her eyes glazed over and she stared at a fixed point beyond Joss's vision. "His future shifts constantly. I can't see where he's headed. There is good left in him. If you look. He's drawn to you for reasons he doesn't want to admit to himself. You remind him of the better parts of his life. You've got a bright spirit. It beckons him, and so he tries to keep you close, but in the end, he suffocates."

"Understatement," she mumbled. The revelation only complicated things further. It was easier to think of him as the unredeemable enemy, but he was just as caught up in the cogs of the machine as she.

"Remember what I said about the truth. Choose your moments wisely. There's more resting on your shoulders than you can imagine."

"What do you mean?"

"Go, you don't want to be late. The Alpha is growing impatient as each day passes."

Joss stepped from the house feeling manipulated but knowing she was right.

❀ ❀

LARGE OAK TABLES WITH THE pack symbol carved in the middle were packed with bodies. The sour scent of anxiety tinged with fright battled with the smell of freshly baked loaves of banana, pumpkin, regular, and zucchini bread. An assortment of scones broke up the breads while staying in the same wheelhouse. The Alpha took the phrase breaking bread literally.

Joss stepped closer to Isiah, grateful for his ability to make others look elsewhere as she waited in the wings for the Alpha to speak. Isiah wrapped an arm around her shoulders, and she thought of Kishi's words. Was this part of his act, or a glimmer of the good inside of him? *Does it matter?* She needed him. Her stomach lurched. She hated being the center of attention, and this was only going to put her front and center in front of prying eyes seeking answers and reassurance.

She tugged on the bottom of the soft, white cashmere sweater her mother paired with white pants that stopped at her ankles. The four-inch nude heels made her ankles weep. Her curls had been straightened, and her locks were brushed 'til they shone and tucked demurely behind her ears. She looked like a carbon copy of her mother. In the worst possible way. It was a subtle hint toward her future position. *I might do the song and dance they've planned out, but I'm in charge of my mind and my future for the first time since I set foot on this godforsaken land.*

Her mother was in queen mode. Head held high, hair polished to a high gloss, and stacked to God with body, she balanced expertly on her red-soled black Christian Louboutin heels. Black slacks paired with a cream-colored button-down T-shirt and a fake smile made her the perfect accessory. The Alpha placed a large hand on her hip, and they stepped out. The whispers turned to applause and cheers and whistles.

After a few moments, they settled down.

"My friends, it's so good to be under one roof again breaking bread. I know there's been unrest and questions. I'm here to answer them all. We witnessed a miracle a week ago when our very own Moon Maiden changed without the moon. It's an omen. Everything we've worked so hard to prepare for will be coming to pass soon. The old ways are shifting."

The tittering of warbling voices rose up like a disgruntled crowd about to turn.

"Fear not. This is what we want. It proves we were correct all along. We plan on increasing our training, gathering, and sending out scouts to see where others in the supernatural community stand. It's important to know our enemies, so we can stay ahead of them."

"Where's the Maiden?" a voice called.

"Well, she's been feeling a bit shy. You know our beauty doesn't like to be the center of attention. An admirable trait in one who holds so much power, don't you think?"

"Yes." The quick agreement made her face flame.

"They love you." Isiah twined their fingers and lifted her hand to his lips.

"The love the idea of me," she whispered.

"No." Isiah shook his head. "You're the real deal. You care because it's the right thing to do, and your heart is built that way. There's no try with you. It's simply being. Remember that."

"It's going to be a busy time full of growth. We need to pull together now and have patience. If you see something out of the ordinary, speak up. If you feel the call of the moon, come to me or one of the Betas so we can assist you," the Alpha stated.

Brainwash you and control your thoughts and actions to turn you into an example we can present to the masses to show them everything is all right and we are the ones steering the vehicle. Never mind that our course is headed straight through the center of crazy town with the final destination straight off a cliff. There would be no race war of epic proportions. It would boil down to good against evil, and she wasn't convinced White Creek would be on the right side.

"Now it's my pleasure to present to you the *future* of the White Creek pack."

"That's our cue, beautiful. Pretend you enjoy spending time with me." Isiah planted a kiss on her cheek and gently tugged her toward the door that led out into the dining area. He gave her hand a quick squeeze and gifted her with a dazzling smile. She heard others gasp at their interactions. It was clear things were not as they once were.

Forcing her lips to curl up at the corners, she slid back into her old ill-fitting skin. Bright smile, vapid eyes, and demure body language. She leaned heavily on Isiah, as if drawing strength from him. He led her to stand beside the Alpha who watched her every move. Her sudden power acceleration made him nervous. The merriment was thunderous. People whistled, stomped their feet, and howled. She didn't have to fake the blush that tinted her cheeks, visibly heating her face, neck, and the tips of her ears. A present from her red-haired father.

The Alpha raised a hand and silence fell over the crowd. She glanced at Isiah who gestured for her to speak first.

She cleared her throat and stepped up. "I want to thank you all for your kindness and concern over the past week. I was caught off guard by the sudden shift. When I sought out the calm of nature and reconnection of self, I got a lot more than I bargained for." Laughter rang out, and she smiled bashfully. "My family has been helping me adjust and fully comprehend what occurred. We believe it's the natural step in evolution. That Odin has truly gifted us for our vigilant and faithful service and sacrifices to him. I urge you to check your hearts and houses to make sure they're ready for what we know is coming." The words were bitter in her mouth.

"Can I be done yet?" She glanced at Isiah who nodded and stepped up.

"Our Maiden is resilient and gracious. She'll continue with her schedule as usual, but we'll be keeping a closer eye on her. One must always protect what's most precious to them." Jaws dropped as they looked from him to her. He hadn't let go of her hand, and she kept her body language accepting of his obvious interest. Her stomach ached. *How much longer can I do this?* The desire to run and leave everything behind was high. What would it be like blend into a town, and become just another face making a living?

A wave of reassurance washed over her. She felt the presence from her dream. Pulling the supporting energy close to her heart, she breathed deeply. *Is he closer?* Even now he could be in town. The thought thrilled her.

"My father and I will begin to plan the transfer of power ceremony. We ask that you bear with us. We want to make things move as smoothly as possible, but there are always kinks to iron out when a new Alpha takes over. I have large shoes to fill, but I believe I'm up to it. I hope you agree. I have White Creek's best interest at heart, and I have no problem doing what's necessary to keep us all safe, and comfortable. Your well-being and happiness is of the utmost importance to me." Relief spread through the crowd like an audible exhale. They were eating up every word he served them and asking for a second helping. "On that note, I bid you all enjoy your food and fellowship." Isiah raised his hand, and a slow clap caught spark, spreading around the room like wildfire.

The age of Stark is upon us.

He led her into the crowd, and she was engulfed with well-wishers expressing their concern and relief as they vied for her attention. She did her best to address each question thrown her way with an acknowledgment. Isiah was smooth, soothing fears, turning on the charm, and diverting attention from her to himself. If it was for her benefit or his own, she couldn't say. Maintaining the contact between them, he kept an arm around her waist, on her hips, or slung across her shoulders. It made her skin crawl. Crowded, and run down from the game of pretend, she longed to escape. Unable to handle the close range, she stepped away.

"If you'll excuse me. I'll be right back." Isiah arched an eyebrow. '*Bathroom,*' she mouthed. He nodded his head, and she kept her gait slow and steady as she wove through the crowd, smiling and nodding her head at people. The minute she entered the empty hallway that led to the bathroom, she ran. Her heels clicked on the wood as she reached the back door. Yanking the wooden door open, she slipped out into the crisp autumn day. Inhaling, she bowed her head as her heart struggled to exit her chest.

"*Be calm. Do you need me?*"

The voice, which only spoke to her in dreams, jolted her.

"*Kaz?*"

"*Do you need me?*"

"How can I hear you? Where are you?"

"*Close. I can come to you now.*"

"No!" Her pack would descend like rabid beasts. "*I'm at a pack event.*"

"*Ahh. You are well though?*"

"Physically? Yes. Mentally, I'm exhausted."

"*I want to see you tonight.*"

Her throat went dry. He was here. Finally, after all of this time. Excitement quickly replaced everything else. She threw caution and doubt to the wind. They needed this.

"Yes. When and where?"

The pure joy she felt sliced through the darkness surrounding her like a beam from a lighthouse cutting through thick fog.

"*You tell me.*" His voice held dry humor.

"*The Sacred Dancing Lake at midnight.*"

"*I'll be there, and I suggest you be there, too, solynshka. Lest I come looking for you.*"

She held the fact that they'd be together tonight close to her heart. "*I will be.*"

"*Are you better now?*"

"Yes. Thank you."

"*Always, moye Serdste.*"

He retreated from the link, but his presence remained close by. *Is he monitoring me for signs of distress?* She'd never had someone looking out for her this way. She'd always been the protector. This was foreign territory. He wrapped around her like a hug. Closing her eyes, she allowed herself to return the mental embrace. Her knees weakened under the onslaught of passion and protectiveness she sensed. How could a man occupy the title stranger and best friend at the same time? What would it be like once they shared the same space? Butterflies tickled her belly.

The cold feeling of dread faded, and gave way to excitement. Flushed for a different reason, she moved back to the building. The door opened, and Brook slipped out.

"I thought I'd find you here."

"I needed a minute."

Brook walked over to join her. "They kind of descended on you like piranhas."

"I anticipated it."

"I only knew because I know you so well. To everyone else, you were perfectly poised, polite, and elegant. Everything a future queen should be."

"Ugh. Don't make me vomit."

Brook giggled. "It looked like Stark was behaving himself."

"He's been scarily helpful."

"Well, he's getting what he wants now. So why wouldn't he be?" Brook asked.

Her tongue tingled with the urge to share her meeting. Joss had just opened her mouth to speak when she spotted Isiah making his way down the hall toward him.

"Speak of the devil, and he shall appear." Joss nodded toward the brunette.

"Doesn't want you out of view, does he?" Brook asked.

'*No,*' she mouthed.

Isiah opened the door. "Bathroom?"

"I couldn't exactly say I need to get some air before I scream." Joss shrugged.

"Brook," Isiah nodded.

"Isiah," Brook replied, refusing to budge.

Joss glanced down and smiled at her friend's pluck.

"I figure you've had her to yourself long enough. I needed to get some bestie time in."

"I thought you did that last night," Isiah replied casually.

Joss tensed. "Are you spying on me?"

"There's very little that goes on we don't know about at White Creek."

"And somehow that's even creepier," Brook said, stepping closer.

Isiah glanced from Brook to Joss. "Between us isn't a position you want to take, Brook."

Joss stiffened and stepped in front of her friend. "That sounded like a threat, Isiah. But it couldn't be because I know you're not stupid enough to come for someone I hold dear and expect to like the results."

"I'm stating a fact, Joss," he said calmly.

"We'll see about that." Joss balled her fists.

"Come, Father, wants us to lead a toast." The mention of the Alpha took away her options.

Gritting her teeth, she turned her attention to Brook. "I'll call you when I get home tonight." She willed her to understand she needed to talk to her.

Brook nodded. "I've got no plans, so I'll be there."

Refusing to let Isiah think he had all of the power, she turned back toward him. "Lead on."

"We're presenting a united front, remember?" He held out his hand.

"Not if you continue to make power plays. We're supposed to be in this together. That means meeting in the middle. Do you even remember what that's like?" Taking his hand, she froze him out. He tightened his grip. Ignoring the twinge of pain, she refused to respond. He thrived on responses. Mentally, her mind began a count down until midnight.

Chapter Six

"ARE YOU SURE THIS IS safe?"

"Yes," she lied convincingly.

Brook frowned. "I'm not so sure."

"He's been in my head for years, Brook. We both deserve this moment."

"And if he's a psycho who plays minds games?" Brook placed her hands on her hips.

"I don't think life would saddle me with two of those," Joss said dryly.

Brook's worried her bottom lip. "It's not funny. You're all dressed up and glowing. I've never seen you like this. Knowing it's for some strange vampire unsettles me."

"He's not strange to me. I could never explain to you how well I know him. Years of intimate conversations without the boundaries of normalcy, politeness, or embarrassment. In our dreams, we're free to be ourselves, one-hundred percent. He's seen me at my very worst. Right after my father died, and my mother became sick, he was the shoulder I leaned on. It was him, my mother, and I. You want me to discount all of that because your opinion of what I should do differs? It's not going to happen. I have my own doubts and some reservations. I don't expect everything to fall into place like some magical fairytale."

"I'm not sure that's true. Your face lights up when you talk about Kaz. It always has. I'm afraid of what meeting him will do if he's not what you expected," Brook remarked earnestly.

"For once, I'm taking a risk. Don't try to talk me down from it." Joss placed her hand on her shoulder. "I'm past due for some serious rebelling. Let me rebel yell, mama Brook."

Brook rolled her eyes. "Is this how you usually feel about me and my choices?"

"Yeppp." Joss popped her p. "Now tell me I'm pretty, help me fluff my hair, and sneak the hell out of here without being dedicated. I'm nervous enough on my own. I can't take your anxiety onto my shoulders, too."

"Okay." Brook took a deep breath. "First of all, you're stunning." Her black tights were tucked into a pair of black, steel-toed boots with a breathable interior. A black Henley stopped at mid-thigh. The thick material would keep her warm, and keep her from becoming shapeless. She wore a light coat of makeup and cherry Chapstick. It was a careful balance of details and not trying too hard. "Secondly, I think we should give you a thick French braid. Your curls are distinctive. A braid hidden under a hat would be smart."

"You're right."

"Sit and let me work my magic." Brook patted the back of the chair. As she finger-combed Joss's hair, she asked, "What did you tell captain crazy about tonight?"

"That we were going to be catching up, and I needed at least a day off from him."

"Jesus. You guys are like a divorced couple trying to get along for the kids."

"No, to be divorced you had to at least love one another enough to be married first," Joss quickly corrected her.

"Oh. You two would be an arranged marriage for sure."

"Let's be honest, that's what we *are*," she said sarcastically.

"How far are you going to take this act?" The guitar riff heavy nineties playlist created a safe space where they could speak their mind.

"I don't know," Joss answered honestly.

"You'd better start trying to figure it. Because I can tell you right now, Stark doesn't know when to quit or have a normal stopping point. He's the type who'd take you with him over the cliff, so you better know when to bail out."

Brook's words rang with truth. Ice formed in her veins. *I passed the point of no return a long time ago, my friend.* Keeping the thought to herself, she clung to the emotions Kaz brought to life. In the fathomless darkness, he stood as a lighthouse, guiding her through rough waters fraught with craggy rocks. She trusted in his ability to keep her from harm, regardless of everything else she was uncertain about.

"I've waited forever to do this prep with you. All of the other dates felt like you humoring the poor boy who gathered up enough courage to ask you out."

She grimaced. "I mean, basically that's what it was."

"Be honest with me. Are you in love with this vampire?"

"I don't know, Brook. I went from thinking he might not be real, to knowing he had to be, and now I just want to be in his presence and feel things out. It's like being in a long-term, long-distance relationship, without meeting the other person."

"The fact that you called it a relationship says a lot, Joss."

"What else can you call the bond you have with the person you've continuously spilled your guts to?" Embarrassment crept over her like a fine mist. Dropping her gaze, she studied the beige carpet. "We've been two people whispering to one another in the dark. Now we're going to turn on the light switch and hope each of us likes what we see."

"With you, there's nothing to dislike, Joss. You've got this. I mean, the man came from who knows where to see you. I don't like the thought of you going alone, though."

Joss tapped her temple. "You'll be a call away."

"If he hurts you, I'm going to hunt him down," Brook promised.

"He won't."

"Look at you. Seriously, you can't help but defend him, can you?" Brook marveled.

"He would do the same for me," Joss said smoothly.

"I hope so."

"It's like the pack bond, Brook."

"Maybe he's your—"

"Don't say it. Please," Joss pleaded. Her heart raced, and her body vibrated with nerves.

"You're right. I'm not the one you need to hear that from." Brook squeezed her shoulder. "You're all done. Let's get you to your clandestine meeting."

Joss rolled her eyes, but couldn't keep the smile from her lips. Adding a black hat to her ensemble, she moved to the back of the house, facing the woods. Sending out her senses, she searched the area for the presence of wolves. They were gathered in the front of her home, where they had the record player going, and Brook making drinks in the kitchen. Their energy level was low. They were tired and relaxed. She quietly opened the door she'd left unlocked, and slipped outside and into the woods without notice.

Borrowing from her inner wolf, she sped through the forest at a clip no human could produce. The hairs on her body rose as she entered the sacred space. She could feel the years of history and magic emanating from the land. The barrier between the past and present felt thinner in this sacred place. The Native Americans believed it was a central point in the universe. She was inclined to believe them. Studying the history of the Blackfoot Indians, she'd learned more about their beliefs and how they connected to the land she'd been living on for years.

Feeling Kazimir approach, she turned away from the water. Her breath froze in her throat when he came into view. Tall, slender, and pale, his warm brown eyes were fringed with dark lashes. His thick, dark hair brushed his shoulders, and his thin, pink lips curled up into a smile that made her belly drop into her boots in the best possible ways. His high cheekbones, strong jawline, and angular chin created a face made for paintings. Her fingers itched to touch him. Inches away from her, he stopped. For the first time in years, she felt whole. Basking in the feeling of completion, her lids grew heavy. She swayed forward slightly as she drank him in from beneath her lashes. Like magnets, they were pulled closer until they were mere inches apart.

"Hi," she whispered, feeling shy.

"Hello, Joss." His deep voice sent a chill up her spine. Strong, yet soft—when it came to her, he'd always made her feel completely protected. "May I touch you?"

She nodded, unable to speak around the lump in her throat. Wrapping his arms around her waist, he pulled her body to his. She wound her arms around his neck, then rested her head on his shoulder, perfectly content in the shelter of his arms. He rocked them both slightly side to side as they simply existed together in the expanse of a perfect moment.

"You're not cold."

He chuckled. "And you feel like a miniature sun."

"Wolves run hot."

He shrugged. "Vampires run lukewarm."

"Good to know." She burrowed her face into his soft, worn leather jacket, inhaling his citrus and bergamot scent. "You smell good."

"So do you … like an expensive caramel coffee. I can smell your strength and sweetness."

"You sound like you want to eat me, Kazimir."

He groaned. "Say it again."

"Kazimir," she whispered.

He wrapped her hair around his fist and pulled her head back to look up at him.

"You're perfection."

She licked her lips. "This is insane."

"No, this is right. Had I known, I never would've left you alone for so long."

His words thawed the ice that had formed inside of her chest, separating her from most people.

"Don't say things like that."

"Why? I mean them. You've been neglected and used. That stops tonight."

"I—"

"Never should have been made to be a parent when you were only a child. You deserve far better than the position of the false goddess they forced you into. I will make sure you never have to do anything you don't want to again." The prettied words made her dizzy. He felt intensely for *her*, Joss Aryn Weber. She couldn't remember the last time she'd experienced that. Everything had been tied into White Creek for so long; it overtook her own personal identity.

The fire burning in the depths of his dark gaze reinforced the truth behind his words.

"Kazimir."

"Surely you must know by now what you are to me."

"We're strangers who have a deep bond, and—"

"No. We haven't met in person before today, but you could never be a stranger to me. You're my mate."

Her soul sang at the word.

"No." She shook her head. "You're a vampire, and I'm a werewolf."

"And yet we both know things are strange lately. It's part of why it took me so long to come to you. There are unsettling things happening in the vampire community. But that can wait. I will not allow anything to intrude on our time together. Walk with me?" He pulled back, linking their fingers. She let him guide her to walk around the lake.

The awkwardness she expected never came. "I'm not sure how to feel about this."

"About what?"

"Us."

The corners of his lips curved down. "Why?"

"I don't want a mate."

He stopped abruptly, and she stumbled. "Give me a reason why what is between us should not be celebrated."

"I've seen what it does to people." Her mind wandered to her mother.

"We are not your parents, Joss."

"They didn't think they would be like that either," she said pointedly.

"We know one another in an intimate manner most will never experience. Don't you think I know you by now? Just as you know me."

"No, we know aspects of another. It's not the same. I mean, we were asleep for Pete's sake." She was grasping at straws.

He never wavered. "You know me better than any other person walking this earth. How many siblings did I have?"

"Six," she answered quietly.

"What was my youngest sister's name?"

"Fanya. What does this prove? They're facts," she said, ignoring the warmth growing in her chest.

"They are my history. The one thing most vampires guard with their lives or try to forget. I handed it to you on a silver platter. Don't cheapen what we've created together."

"How can you be so damn certain?" she snapped.

"You called me back from the edge. It was you who kept me sane when the sickness fell upon me. My people are slowly losing their mind, and falling prey to a disease that mimics the desire to go to ground and rest their weary minds and hearts. Only, they never make it, because the process happens too rapidly. There's no time to plan or think clearly before they become slobbering, savage beasts, glutting themselves on blood, risking us all, and stopping only when they're put down."

"Kaz." She gripped his arms. "Is that why you went silent?" The thought of losing him to this wasting disease that ended with insanity, blood, and death made her nauseous.

"Yes."

She cupped his face and studied him intently. "But you're okay now?"

"Yes, solynshka. See how impassioned you became at the thought of my peril?" He arched a wing brow.

"I care about you!"

He placed a hand on the small of her back and pulled her close. "This is not the way friends behave." His lips ghosted over hers. "Or do I have someone to be worried about?"

The brief contact tied her tongue. She wanted to wipe the cocky smirk from his lips. Pushing her hips into his, she watched his eyes widen and his nostrils flare.

"I'm trying to be the gentleman you believe me to be. You shouldn't tempt fate."

"Are you saying you aren't that man?" she asked curiously.

"I'm not a good person generally speaking. I've too much blood on my hands. But for you? I'll try." His honesty endeared him even further.

"There's too much kindness in your gaze for that to be true." She lost herself in the abyss of his dark gaze.

"Is it so bad, being my mate?"

My worry isn't for me. It's for you. "My future isn't promised."

His face hardened, and his eyes glowed red. "I'd destroy the entire world to see you safe."

The matter-of-fact statement stunned her. "Kazimir."

"You are my priority. I care not what happens to this world any longer. For you alone will I fight."

"You can't say things like that."

"Why?"

"One person can never be worth more than the entire world."

"And yet, to me you are." He squeezed her hip with his left hand. "You've been fed so many lies you don't see how truly priceless you are. I'll fix that." He leaned in closer. "I'm going to start with a kiss."

Leaning her head back, she met him halfway on tiptoe. There was no closing of eyes. They watched one another as they fed from slightly parted lips—each afraid the other would disappear and the entire evening would be another dream. She moaned softly, and he slipped his tongue in, moving his head to deepen the kiss. Their tongues glided together in an elegant dance. Her toes curled in her boots, and she gripped the lapels of his leather jacket as she tried to get closer. Her lungs screamed for air, and she turned her face away breathing heavily. His muscles were tense under the hands that rested against his back.

Pulling back, she saw his eyes had turned crimson. "Your eyes …"

"Change when I'm emotional." He licked his lips, and she saw a hint of fang peeking out from his upper lip.

"Can I touch them?" She gestured toward a fang.

"You can touch any part of me you like."

She ran the pad of her pointer finger up and down the smooth, white tooth. Fascinated by the sharp point, she ran the pad of her thumb over it. It pricked her finger, and she jerked. His nose twitched and inhaled. "Your blood smells like caramelized sugar, like the perfect crust on a Crème Brûlée."

Before she could stop herself, she was painting his lips with her blood.

"Are you testing me?" he whispered.

"Maybe."

He held himself stiffly, never letting his eye stray from her face. "I can be patient and wait if it's what you wish. I've had centuries to develop control. I also learned persistence. I'm a man who gets what he wants." The words were different coming from his mouth. They drugged her like good whiskey, frazzling her brain.

"Do you want to taste me, Kazimir?" she asked daringly.

"Every part, but none until you tell me it's okay."

"Open," she demanded.

His lips parted. She pressed her thumb inside. He moaned and sucked gently. The wound closed, and she removed her digit.

"You're even more delicious than I imagined."

Heat pooled in her belly.

A twig snapped in the distance. They startled.

"Rabbit." They laughed as the tension dissipated.

She sighed. "It's getting late. I can't stay away much longer."

"Why?" He tentatively nudged their link. "Show me."

Relaxing, she allowed him to enter her mind and replayed the last few weeks.

"I'll snap his neck," Kazimir whispered.

"Who?"

"Father and son. I've yet to decide who deserves to go first."

"You can't do that. I don't have what I need."

"That's part of the reason I'm here, Joss. I didn't come alone."

"What?" She stepped back, and his arms tightened around her.

"I'm alone *now*, but I have companions I'm traveling with. You'll want to hear what they have to say. Everything happening is connected. My people getting sick and falling into blood lust, yours changing without the moon. It's the work of spell unraveling."

"A spell?"

"The ones that separated us from the humans long before the title *human race* existed."

"Wait." She jerked back. "You're saying we were all created from the same magic?"

"When the people who would become known as humans left the cave dwellings, we remained in the darkness and became something else entirely. We were feared, hunted when seen, and trapped in caves by our *different* qualities.

Then one day, we were offered a choice by a magic wielder. Perhaps one of the first of their kind."

"That would make us all distant descendants," she marveled.

"It makes all of the bickering and posturing seem trivial, does it not?"

"If that's our origin and lineage, when did the desperation and hate begin?"

"A very power-hungry Shaman tried to recreate the spell for himself and weakened the integrity. To fix it those of the lines he stole from must come together and recast."

"What did he steal, Kazimir?"

"Livers, blood, and hearts. He gorged himself on all three, and nature saw fit to punish him. The balance is meant to be maintained. Too much one way and it all falls apart."

"Is there a specific reason you're telling me this?"

"You are one of those descendants, Joss. The last one we need."

Of course. She stumbled back, disgusted. Her eyes blurred with the tears she fought to hold back. "I would've helped you regardless. You didn't have to launch an elaborate ruse—"

He gripped her face gently. "Don't even suggest it. I never imagined you'd be such a coward. At the core of your being, you know my feelings for you are true. Finding offense when there is none is a low blow." His words stung. "It doesn't matter. I assure you I am more stubborn than you. I will outlast your doubt, anger, and desire to run. We *are* mates. It's a fact, not an opinion. Denying it will only make us miserable and distracted. Neither of us has the time or the luxury for that."

"I have a duty to my pack, and apparently the rest of the supernatural world at large."

"You won't always." He released his hold. "Besides, I am here to help you with that. I'll escort you home, and we'll meet again on the morrow. You can speak with Nakeeta and Crewe. Like us, they're an *unusual* pairing. He's a vampire and she's a witch."

Her eyebrows rose toward the sky. "But they hate each other."

"I assure you, Crewe and Keeta don't. They're almost sickening really."

She snickered. "This is too bizarre. I have to be dreaming."

"If we are, I hope we never wake up." He kissed her temple. "I'll walk you as far as I can without them catching my scent. For now, I'll play your game."

She bit the inside of her lip. How could she be upset with him for putting her first? It tapped into a part of her she'd closed off to mask the pain she felt at always being last on everyone's the list of priorities unless it served their needs.

"When and where shall we meet tomorrow?"

"I have to work from open at seven in the morning until three o'clock," she said.

"Three thirty then. Where?"

Trying to dissuade him would be useless. "The town library. I need to do some research. We can kill two birds with one stone, and hopefully, none will be the wiser."

"I'll have Nakeeta mask my scent."

They reached the mid-point in the woods, and she stopped. "I should go alone from here." Her shoulders slumped, and the heaviness she'd left behind returned.

"I'm a call away."

Images of his pale flesh ripped by canine teeth as a wolf pile descended up on him flashed in her mind. "This is an extremely dangerous situation for you, Kazimir. If the pack discovers you and your friends are here—"

"Nothing short of death will keep me from you again. You're mated to a very old man. I believe you'll find I'm not so easily killed." His roguish grin made her smile.

She sobered quickly. "I can't be responsible for your death."

"You're the only reason I'm alive right now." He leaned down and stole the protest from her mouth with a sweet kiss. "Go, we'll speak more tomorrow."

Floating away on a cloud, she listened. The hour grew later, and she didn't want to get them caught. Dazed, she slipped back into the house, careful not to rouse the wolves sleeping on the job. Once inside, she locked the door.

"You took your sweet time, didn't you?" Brook hissed.

"Jesus." Joss grabbed her chest. "You almost gave me a heart attack."

"Good! I was ready to come out there and find you."

"Why? How long was I gone?" She searched the house for a clock.

"It's four o'clock in the morning, Joss." Brook crossed her arms under her chest and frowned. In her fluffy pink robe, black flannel pants with hearts, and a black satin hair cap, she looked every inch an angry mother who'd caught her teenage daughter sneaking back into the house.

She wrestled down a snicker to keep from riling Brook further.

"Whoa. I'm fine. It didn't seem like that much time passed."

"And you're okay?"

Joss smiled goofily. "So okay."

The tension melted from Brook's body. "Tell me everything!"

She laughed as they walked over to the couch and she spilled her guts. For a moment, she almost felt normal. When she ignored the nagging voice in the back of her mind that couldn't stop thinking about everything to come, Kazimir scolded her gently, *Enjoy your evening, solynshka.*

Even now he was in the wings, ready to slip in even if only to ease her pain. Unlike other bonds, this didn't feel intrusive.

"Is this where I say yes, sir?"

"Only if you're sure you're ready to deal with the consequences of that action." The warning tone made heat pool in her belly.

"Like that idea?" he asked.

"I'll let you know after we test it out."

"Temptress." He retreated.

"What just happened?" Brook asked.

"Kazimir," she replied distantly as she returned to the present.

"You're speaking in your minds now?" Brook whispered. "That takes a true bond and trust. My God. He truly is your mate. That's why no one else ever appealed to you."

"What are you talking about?"

"How could anyone stir your emotions when you spend every night with the man you're meant to be with?" Brook pressed a hand to her heart. "You're like a romance novel come to life. The werewolf and the vampire."

Uncomfortable, Joss shifted on the couch. "Now who's reading too much into things?"

"I don't think I am. Why are you so resistant to it?"

"Forgive me, I'm at my max for dealing with complicated situations, currently."

"If you could see yourself from my point of view, you'd know why it's not necessary. You're shining like a polished diamond. That's enough for me to get behind it."

The sincerity in her best friend's words chipped away at the wall of denial crumbling around her. *What do I do if he is my mate?* Interspecies relationships weren't a thing she knew about. *You'd better learn fast,* her conscience whispered back.

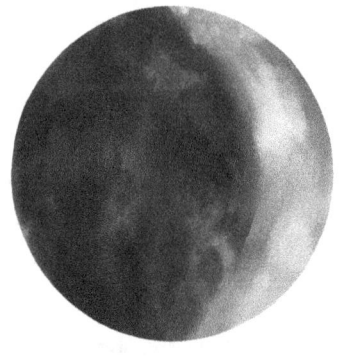

Chapter Seven

SHE CLUTCHED HER MUG OF coffee in her hands like a talisman from the exhaustion, counting on it to make her made her lids feel less superglued shut. The soft sounds of snoring coming from her room made her smile. At least one of them would be well rested today. They'd stayed up until sunrise quietly whispering to each other like teenagers. The heat warmed her through as the tiny brown beans ground to perfection began to do their job and infuse her with energy. Leaning against the counter, she watched the world outside. Fall leaves drifted to the ground, and the sunlight shone down through the clouds. The sight of her mother's silver SUV made her tense.

Draining the last drops of her coffee, she went for a refill. *I'm going to need another cup to handle this.* After pouring liberal amounts of pumpkin spice creamer into her mug, she added coffee and stirred. Her mother parked and climbed from the car in a pair of fitted jeans, and a white T-shirt covered by a pink and white long-sleeved flannel. She was dressed casually enough, but her harried step and rigid posture pointed to something being wrong. They hadn't had a real conversation since their blow out.

She walked to the door and opened it before she could knock and disturb Brook. "Hey. Brook is still asleep. We had a late night."

"Oh." Her mother blinked. "Good morning." The tentative smile on her mother's thin lips broke her heart. Things had never been this awkward between them before.

"Come in." Joss stepped back reluctantly. "I have to work this morning."

"I know. I couldn't leave things the way they were any longer. I tried to give us both time." Her mother laced her fingers and let them hang down in front of her.

"I haven't changed my mind about anything." The words were severe but heartfelt.

Her mother winced. "I wouldn't expect you to. I can see your point of view, Joss. I just ask that you try to see mine."

"You were the adult. I spent too much time playing parent long after your cancer went into remission. I never should've assumed that much duty. The guilt and burden of responsibility for your continued well-being has eaten away at me for years. It pecked away at my soul, little by little like a ravenous corvid."

"I didn't know." Her mother placed a hand over her chest and grimaced.

"How could you not, Mother?" Joss asked incredulously.

She shook her head. "Maybe I didn't want to. I knew you weren't one-hundred percent invested, but here we're safe and taken care of."

"As long as we stay in line. You present White Creek as a utopia. It's not," she snarled.

Her mother's eyes widened. "It has its faults."

"Too many, Mom."

Her mother dropped her gaze. "Perhaps."

"Are you telling me you had no idea what he did to me and Siah on those weekend cleansing trips? That you didn't see the hunger or exhaustion as he continued to push us past our breaking points?"

"Ian's been correct about many things. But he's not infallible," her mother said, avoiding an answer.

Because he has an inside tip thanks to Iamia. "I guess your silence says everything. How do you suppose he managed to do that, Mom?"

"You're there for the rituals the same as I am. I didn't come here to fight with you, Joss."

"Why did you come?" Joss cocked her hip.

"To tell you it's okay to let go."

Joss scrunched her nose. "Let go of what?"

"Everything holding you back. Your words have haunted me. You feel responsible for my well-being. That's not your job."

"Mom—"

Her mother held up a hand. "No, hear me out. I'm sorry for being blind to your needs. Life knocked me down and carved my heart out with a blunt object. It was easier to hide after that. I fell into the habit of not seeing. We never switched back to our proper roles after that. Not fully. In that, I'll admit I dropped the ball. I won't continue to do so. If I am what tethers you here, allow me to be the one to cut the strings."

Because it's so simple? "Mom. We're talking life and death."

"You know as well as I do, we all pass through this world one day. I always knew you were intended for greater things. I thought I was helping you achieve that. Hearing that I've done otherwise guts me. I see the power struggle between you and Isiah. And no, I don't buy your supposed relationship for one moment. I won't be a bargaining tool." Her mother lifted her chin.

"You expect me to walk away and leave you here to fend for yourself? If you think for one second, I could condemn you to death without batting an eyelash, you don't know me well at all."

"I do. That's why I'm here. I've dreamt of your father every night since you delivered his message."

Joss stood up straight. "What did he say?"

"Things I needed to hear," her mother said elusively.

"I thought we were done hiding things from each other?"

"There are things that should remain between a husband and wife. Yes, you're twenty-five, but you're still *our* child." The power behind her mother's words was a warning to drop it. She knew the tone well from her youth.

"Yes, ma'am," she replied automatically.

Raising her head, her mother nodded. "What do I need to do to make this right?"

"Mom, I'm not sure you can. We can move past this, but I'll never forget all of the choices you've taken away from me."

"I don't accept that."

"Well, you don't have a choice." *Just like I didn't.*

"Are you trying to hurt me on purpose?" Her voice warbled.

"No. I'm trying to process. Why can't you understand that?"

"Because this isn't like you." Her mother shook her head.

"Yes, it is. This is me, Mother. Not the perfect daughter who hides everything going on behind your back because she doesn't want to upset you or rock the boat. I'm fighting for my life."

"No one here is out to kill you, Joss. That's the whole point of being here."

Joss's eyes welled with tears. "And yet, a life that I have no control over would slay me just the same."

"I can't watch you die," her mother croaked.

"Now you know the burden I've carried all these years," Joss said coldly.

Her mother's jaw dropped.

"You want honesty, here it is. I'm done watching the world go by while I remain in a holding pattern. I don't blame you for the things I've chosen to do, Mom. I didn't have the full picture, but they were my choices. So, I can accept that. No one forced me to put you first. This is me informing you that time has passed. I hope you're right about Ian. I really do. I hope he loves and protects you from anything that comes your way." Her voice cracked. *You are not responsible for the actions of others.* She chanted the words, trying to believe them. "But I can no longer take ownership over the fallout that might happen."

"Do you think I wanted you to?" her mother whispered.

"I don't know anymore," Joss admitted weakly.

"I'm going to show you how wrong you are about me." Her mother lifted her chin. "Wait and see."

"I really hope you do, Mom. At the moment, I've got a shift to get ready to work, and my boss is a real stickler about being on time and setting an example."

Her mother flinched, knowing her boss was Ian. "Okay." The hitch in her mother's voice was painful.

Joss turned away, unable to witness the hurt on her face. *I'm allowed to feel the way I feel.* Protecting her space emotionally and physically was the first step to real independence. At twenty-five, she'd lived for everyone except herself. *And now it might be too little too late.*

"I'll let you finish getting ready." Her mother's hollow tone nearly brought her to her knees. Steeling herself against her natural reaction to comfort and fix, she reminded herself it was time to separate herself and stand tall on her own. She followed her mother back to the door. No words were spoken as she left. Locking the door, Joss rested her head against the wooden surface.

"*You're distressed.*" The sleep laden voice made her smile.

"*Mother-daughter drama. Sleep. You should be resting.*"

"*I should be tending to my mate. As I am.*"

"*How are you even awake?*"

His laughter echoed in her ears. "*I told you, little wolf, I'm old.*"

Kazimir's presence receded, and she moved to shower and dress for the day. He was another issue she didn't have the brain power or physical strength to deal with.

THE BELL ABOVE THE DOOR jangled violently. The door slammed against the wall. Rachel flinched beside her. The teenaged brunette whimpered in the back of her throat. The color left her round face, and her dark blue eyes threatened to bulge from her skull. The stench of fear rolled off her in thick waves. Isiah was in full beast mode. A vein bulged in the side of his forehead, and his nostrils flared. His eyes were narrowed slits locked onto her face. Dressed from head to toe in black, he looked like a dispatcher of death, come to collect a soul.

"Rach. Why don't you take your break?"

"O-okay, Joss." She all but ran to the backroom like the devil himself was on her heels. *Maybe he is.*

"Can I help you, Isiah?" she asked coolly.

He threw his head back and laughed. "Can you help me?"

"No? You just came here to throw a tantrum? Well, it's a place of business, so I'd suggest you take your meltdown elsewhere."

He rushed her, getting just inches from her face. "You'd better watch how you speak to me."

"I've done nothing except speak the truth."

"Did you think I wouldn't find out?"

She swallowed hard. *Does he know about Kaz?* "You'll have to be a bit more specific."

He snarled, leaning farther into her space. "You think you're so clever, don't you?"

She forced herself to remain calm. He lived for the response. "Maybe?"

"Stirring up your mother."

She laughed, dizzy with relief. "You know, not everything is about you, Stark."

His eyes widened.

"Mothers and daughters fight."

He shook his head, his brow furrowed. "Not you two."

"Oh, believe me, we were long overdue." The words were as bitter as a fresh batch of salt and vinegar chips.

"If you think upsetting her and sending her running to my father for comfort will thwart me in any way … I know you still care about her. You wouldn't abandon her so heartlessly."

"Might I?" She smirked. "Do you know my character well enough to make that statement?"

"You will not renege on your end of our bargain." His jaw clenched.

"I never said I was. You come in here like a bull who's seen a red flag because me my mother and I are on the outs? It doesn't look good for you."

He tensed. "I want to remind you of everything you have to lose. I will crush anything that stands in my way."

"And we're all well aware of it. I don't need you constantly lording over me like a movie villain."

He rocked back on his heels like he'd been physically hit. "You're different."

"I'm tired." She sighed. "Why do you have to hold on so tightly to things until you suffocate them?"

"Ruling isn't so black and white. You'll learn that." He shoved his hands into the pockets of his peacoat.

"I disagree. Followers don't need to be bullied and beaten into submission."

"You're too gentle. It holds you back." He shook his head sadly.

"No, it's what makes us human."

"We aren't human, Joss. Maybe you ought to remember that." The anger flowed from his body little by little and his face smoothed over as his posture grew relaxed.

"We are partially human. No matter how much we connect to the wolf, Isiah. Maybe you're the one who's forgotten that."

His jaw clenched. "You're starting to make noticeable waves."

"If you expect me to lead, my position will be beside you, never cowering beneath you."

He arched a thick brow. "This is you rising to the occasion."

"You've shown me time and time again, weaknesses are open spots left for others to use against us. Perhaps I'm simply preparing myself for what's to come."

His lips curled upward. "You're learning." He nodded his approval.

"So you know, there are different ways to do things, too."

He glanced away before meeting her gaze. She angled her body, and they stood like opponents ready for battle. Neither backed down from the other. Strange energy buzzed to life. She pushed at it, and he did the same. The energy recoiled and threw them in opposite directions. Stunned, she stumbled back. *What the hell was that?*

"What just happened?"

"I don't know." Her birthmark tingled. Pulling up her sweater, she gasped at the white glow of the waning moon.

Isiah yanked up his shirt. "Look." The waxing moon pulsed a dark black against his skin. Joss gasped. "Light and dark. Yin and yang." He grinned. "This is proof we belong together.

No.

"It's more than a romantic notion. It's the feminine and masculine. The two energies that make up a whole."

"I'm a wolf. I love the chase, Joss."

An intense sense of wrongness had her swallowing down bile. Things had changed overnight. *Because you've met your mate.*

The idea of another male too close or intimate was abhorrent. Stepping away, she held out her palms. "Stop."

He moved forward and paused as he hit resistance. Throwing back his head, he chuckled. "Now we have an interesting development." His eyes glowed amber, and he hummed. He was a hunter who'd caught her scent.

A growl rumbled in her throat, surprising them both.

"Are you going to show me your claws now, she-wolf?"

"We had a deal, remember?" The words extinguished the visible lust in his gaze.

"So we did. Make sure you're holding up your end of the bargain."

"I'm not the one threatening the arrangement right now." She glanced around at the public place pointedly.

Clearing his throat, he straightened.

She stepped forward. "When are we going to try things my way?" She placed her hands on his shoulders. "Everything doesn't require conquering." The energies between them flowed smoothly. He gasped. "This is about balance. One cannot bulldoze the other. It's about meeting in the middle. Can't you feel that?"

"When have I ever been good at compromise?" he asked softly.

"New leadership means new rules, and developing your own style. You're not locked into anything."

He peered down at her. "Do you honestly believe that?"

"I wouldn't say if it I didn't." She squeezed his shoulders. "Maybe you're right, and we're meant to do this together."

"But not romantically?"

She bit her bottom lip. "Do you really care if that aspect is a part of things?"

The jingle of the front door interrupted his response.

A family of three townspeople smiled at them. Mom, Dad, and the tiny tot were adorable and exactly the interruption she needed.

"Welcome," Joss said, giving them a responding grin. "Is there anything we can help you find?"

"We're just here to stock up on some of your delicious apple butter."

"Excellent. Let me know if I can help you in any way."

"Will do," the dad said with a nod of his long golden-haired head. The baby's tiny golden-brown curls were a combination of his slender blonde mama's and dad.

"We'll talk more about this tonight."

"No. I already have plans. I need to do some research."

He snickered. "Coming from anyone else, I'd think you were lying. Tomorrow, then. Brunch?"

"Fine."

"I'll pick you up around eleven."

"I'll be ready."

He kissed her forehead. "I'm hard on you because I care so much. We need to make this work for us."

I think you have faith in that. She nodded to keep from setting him off once more. Watching him walk away, she closed her eyes and willed herself to keep it together. It was like holding a ticking time bomb she knew would eventually explode.

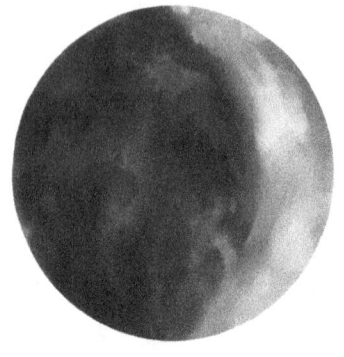

Chapter Eight

"I think you've been sitting here too long."

She jumped slightly at the sound of the soft baritone. Glancing up at Kazimir, she smiled.

He held up a wicker basket. "I have brought provisions. Check out what you must, and let us steal away together."

She looked down at the pile of books she'd been pouring over and groaned. Facts about Blackfoot traditions, sacred spaces, and genealogy swam in her mind. Rubbing her weary eyes, she leaned back. The time during her latest cleanse had done one thing right—it'd opened her mind to new venues, and helped her hone in on her meditation. There wasn't much else to do when you were given little to no food, not enough water to be fully hydrated, and constantly steamed.

"I really shouldn't." Her stomach grumbled. *Traitor.*

Kazimir smirked. "So resistant to being taken care of. I will continue to blame your less than desirable environment." He closed the books swiftly, careful to mark each one with a slip of paper. His speed stunned her. She wasn't in the habit of spending quality time with vampires. If she'd been human, she wouldn't have been able to track it.

Lifting the heavy tombs with ease, he offered his hand. She took it, still adjusting to his warmth as he helped her stand and steered her toward the checkout desk. This close, she couldn't resist the opportunity to study him. Casually dressed in a pair of dark denim jeans, a white Henley, and a black jacket with large, silver buttons and shoulders tags, he still commanded attention. Her fingers itched to touch the silken black hair that brushed the nape of his neck. He caught her staring, and she looked away, embarrassed.

"You can look all you want. I am."

She smiled. He had a way with words.

"You can also touch."

"You are presumptuous, sir."

"Merely optimistic, beautiful."

She chuckled quietly. The gray-haired woman in line turned and smiled at them.

Joss elbow him lightly. *"You're going to get me into trouble."*

"Oh, I intend to."

Anticipation made her spine tingle. His devilish voice promised adventures she'd never dreamed of. Colors were more vibrant, scents more potent, and life held infinite possibilities. Spending time with Kazimir felt like flying. It was an addictive freedom. Moving closer, she let her side rest against him. The physical touch set a glow inside of her chest. They stepped forward together, in sync.

He took her away from the darkness that threatened to surround her with nothing but a few words and his steady presence. She drew from his strength and courage. There was no use hiding her insecurities and fear when he already knew them. It allowed them to connect on a deeper level. Coasting on autopilot, she checked out her books, while her brain worked overtime.

They stepped out into the sunshine, and he pulled her to the side of the small stone building. "Enough."

She blinked. "What?"

Bending, he pressed his lips to hers. She moaned, allowing his tongue entrance. Her eyes drifted shut, and she focused on his rich flavor and masculine scent. He engulfed her in him without trying. Leaning in, she let him take her weight, trusting him to support her. Their tongues, tangled lazily. They parted, and he sighed as she took in the fresh air.

"If you continue to let your thoughts drift, I may become jealous," he said softly.

"We can't have that," she replied breathlessly.

"This is our time now. Everything else will still be waiting for us."

"How can you set it aside so easily?"

"I've lived long enough to learn the hard way; time is a creature to be respected. He waits for no one and steals things away like a thief. I've waited centuries to meet you. I won't squander a second. Because, like you, it's too precious to waste." He kissed her temple. "I thought you'd be able to recommend a place to eat away from prying eyes."

"There's a park a few towns over." She led them to her cream-colored SUV and popped the trunk. He packed her things away, and they got inside. Once she was on the road, he twined their fingers and kissed her hand. *Pull away. Don't let him think this is going to be a normal interaction.* She didn't have the heart to listen to the voice of reason screaming at her. The comfort he provided outweighed everything else.

"What happened this morning?" he inquired.

"I spoke with my mom. It didn't go well." She rested against the cool window.

"You stood up for yourself?"

"I did." She shook her head. "It was even harder than I anticipated."

"It's a lot of change. I know the responsibility you've felt toward your mother. You spoke about it often. Holding it in could turn your love to resentment."

"You don't think I'm terrible?" she asked tentatively.

"No. You are doing what needs to be done. It's not always the easiest thing. You, my sun, are loyal and kindhearted. Do not let this world make you hard. The things we're forced to do aren't who we are."

She took his words to heart. "How do you always know the right thing to say?"

"I've been around a long time. It makes one explore questions closely. I wrestled with my existence for centuries. Why was I turned, and my family perished? Dealing with the battles I'd lost to blood lust. The thing about eternal life is all of your issues come with you. Those from your previous life, and the many years that come afterward. Holding on to every mistake, incident, or misfortune would slowly drive you insane. Sometimes it does."

"What happens then?" she asked curiously.

"We take care of it before they expose us." His voice filled with steel. "We keep tabs on it. It's built in that we know when it's time to go to ground to avoid mental illness. There's mental exhaustion that comes over us after a time. Too many years gone by, loss or serious trauma can be a trigger. We keep tabs on the ones whose instincts don't work. It's how we first noticed it'd begun to happen more and more frequently."

"What happens when you're put into the ground?" she questioned, fascinated by the inside look at vampires.

"Think of it as a coma. One you go into by choice. You can come out of it voluntarily, or be woken."

"Where do you … sleep?"

"We have safe buildings equipped to hold us that are guarded fiercely."

"In a coffin?" she squeaked.

"Yes. That rumor is actually true."

Her jaw dropped. "Do you sleep there all of the time?"

He chuckled. "No. We're not that medieval."

After a few moments of silence, she broached the bone of contention between them. "What does the word mate mean to you?"

"Admitting it finally?"

"No, gathering more information."

He scowled. "Our mates are usually chosen. We don't feel the biological bond that you do. In our case, things have been different."

"Because I'm a wolf?" She snuck a glance at him.

"Yes, I think so. It's new territory for both of us. I imagine we'll learn together."

She couldn't crush the audible hope in his words. *When did I become such a pessimist?*

They made light conversation as she navigated to the park. The shock of brilliant red, burnt orange, and rich yellows were a personal invitation from fall to join in on the harvest.

She sighed as her eyes drank in the beauty. "This is one of my favorite places to go. The scenery is beautiful, and it's far enough from White Creek so I can breathe, and close enough not to raise the alarm." She turned to him. "Do you like it?"

"It's stunning," he said, never looking away from her face. Her cheeks grew heated. His intensity for her didn't waver.

"I want to show you my favorite spot."

"Allow me." He was out of the car and at her door in a heartbeat. She smiled as he opened the driver door, and held out his hand. The sincerity behind his actions changed the way she felt about the old-fashioned gesture. There was no posturing, or worry about appearances. He was just a man showing a woman how much he cherished her. Removing the wicker picnic basket, he wrapped an arm around her waist and allowed her to guide him through the park. They hiked their way to a small inlet that housed a baby waterfall.

"Perfect. Allow me to set up." He spread out a blue flannel blanket and motioned for her to sit. Kneeling beside her, he opened the basket, and she laughed when he pulled out thermoses.

"For my soup lover."

"I can't believe you remember such trivial details."

"Everything you shared with me is stored away and ready to be used."

She smiled coyly. *Was he always this smooth, or did it come from years of practice?*

"I can say the same for you."

"They say all is fair in love and—"

She placed her hand over his mouth. "Don't."

Disappointment flickered in his eyes before he gave a quick nod. "You win … for now."

He pulled out French bread, mozzarella cheesem and a bag of pine nuts.

"What are those for?" She shook the sandwich bag.

"To go with the pumpkin squash soup."

He'd brought her favorite light lunch, served exactly the way she liked it. If a way to a woman's heart was through her stomach, he had her at soup lover.

"You might be my favorite."

He frowned. "Might?"

She threw her head back and laughed. A sudden thought struck her. "*Can you eat?*"

"I don't need to or prefer to. It no longer tastes the same to me, and it holds no nutritional value for my body. I came prepared." He pulled out an all-black thermos along with silver. "This is local apple cider." He handed her the silver canister. "This is my liquid meal." He raised his black canister in a mock salute.

She wrinkled her nose. "What does it taste like?"

"Every batch varies, but think of it as wine. Some blood types are dry; others tend to be richer. I like O. Personally, it's the perfect blend of savory and sweet."

"And … Where do you get it?"

"Blood banks. We have our own now. We ship. I'm not much for taking from the source these days."

"I can't say I ever cared for the metallic tang of blood when we hunt. It's just a part of the kill. Now the innards?" She licked her lips.

"Heart?"

"And liver. Yummy."

"Heart I can understand, it's full of bloody bits."

"Anyone overhearing us would think we were serial killers," Joss said with a laugh.

"They don't know what they're missing."

She unscrewed the lid, and he joined in. It was bizarre breaking bread … er, liquids with the man who'd lived inside of her head for so many years. She busied herself preparing her soup, and he unscrewed the lid off his thermos. A metallic and slightly sweet scent hit her nostrils. Inhaling, she tried to see it from his point of view. Hints of iron and an incredibly balanced mixed of vitamins and … was that candy? Her nose twitched. "Does the food they ingest affect the taste?"

"You smell the chocolate? I have a bit of a sweet tooth. The donors don't know what we do with the blood. They are paid handsomely to donate for medical research which requires they eat certain amounts of specific foods."

"Evil geniuses." She swirled her soup, distributing the pine nuts before she began to blow on it and bring it to her lips.

"Necessity is the mother of invention," he remarked between sips.

Flavor exploded in her mouth. The rich, creamy soup sang all of the right notes. Moaning her approval, she leaned her head back and admired the blue sky. It was a sweet first date. *First date?* Here, removed from everyone else, their relationship seemed easy. But that wasn't reality.

She shook her head. "What are we doing?"

"Having lunch?" He lowered his drink.

"You know what I mean," she answered dryly.

"I'm courting you."

She cleared her throat. "You shouldn't."

"Why are you so sure this won't work out?"

"Our people have hated each other for an eternity. Where would we go and be accepted?"

"We could make our own place." He shrugged. "Things are going to change soon. Nothing will be how it used to be."

"You can't change eons of prejudice and paranoia overnight." She took a sip of the cider.

"No, but you'd be amazed what people will do to survive. The enemy of my enemy is my friend rings true every time."

"What would we do?"

"Whatever we wanted. You've been trapped here for far too long. I'd take you to see the world or find a piece of land that's ours to do as we please on. It matters not to me, as long as you're there beside me."

"And if you get sick of me, or find I'm not the person you're placing on a pedestal? I've seen what happens when someone forgets that love doesn't make the other person perfect."

"I want you just as you are, Joss."

"I'm having a hard time believing it."

"Good thing I'm a patient man, then? Hmm?" He wiggled his eyebrows. She laughed.

"There's the smile. We don't have to figure everything out in a day. All I ask is you be here with me completely. No holding back, no pretense."

"That's my usual state of existence, Kazimir." Hiding had kept her sane in a world full of odd, and not quite right.

"Not with me." He shook his head.

"I'll try."

He licked his lips, set aside his thermos, and gripped her chin gently. "You'll do more than try because what lay between us demands nothing less. We deserve this happiness. I'm not going to let you sacrifice it for some cause you think you need to champion. There's no reason for us to not have both."

Fear held her hostage, tightening its chains of doubt and anxiety around her. Pushing past them, she nodded her head and held tightly to the future she'd never imagined possible.

He rested his forehead against hers. "Let's enjoy the beautiful landscape for a bit longer. I find I'm not eager to share you with others." His nose brushed against hers.

The tip of his tongue darted out to trace her lips. They parted like petals to the sun. He plunged home, cupping her head with his large hand. He was a thorough kisser, leaving no part of her mouth untouched or untasted. She wrapped her arms around his neck and gave in to temptation, burying her fingers into his thick mane. Silky and soft, the strands caressed the pads of her fingers. Her nails scratched his scalp, and he groaned.

Moving their heads, they deepened the kiss, learning, tasting, and teasing one another as the current between them became electrified. He laid her back gently, covering her with his lithe body. Her legs parted, and he sank between her thighs. His muscles flexed, and the bulge in his jeans caused a delicious friction in the area throbbing with need. He was a wind, wild and hot, stirring her soul. She tilted her hips up, seeking more contact, and he fisted her hair. Their kiss moved from gentle to hungry and desperate as they ate at each other's lips. Grinding together like teenagers, they continued their drugging kisses between pauses for oxygen.

His lips were ambrosia, an otherworldly sweet delight, she couldn't get her fill of.

He rolled his hips, and her breath stumbled in her chest. An intense wave of pleasure flowed through her body, pushing her closer to the edge.

"Let go," he whispered, continuing his tantalizing motion.

She spread her legs wider, greedily chasing the high he was delivering. Her stomach clenched and her head swam as she drowned in the power of the handsome man above her. His dark brown pools held her future. She fell into them willingly as her body shook and he drove her to the pinnacle with the rhythmic movement of his hips. Capturing her lips, he swallowed her cry while she trembled, and the world exploded into vivid colors behind her lids.

As her heartbeat returned to normal, she realized she was cradled in his arms.

"You okay?"

"Mmhmm," she mumbled, nuzzling his neck.

"My little sun, you're every bit as dazzling as a sunrise." He ran his hand down her back. "Now I'm afraid we're reaching the end of my sun tolerance and Nakeeta's spell. She warned me to be unnoticed and protected without drawing too much attention."

His words set her into motion. She climbed out of his lap, and together they repacked their things and returned to the car.

A PRICKLING ON THE BACK of her neck, alerted her before she saw the dark-haired vampire rushing toward her in the fading light. Kazimir neutralized him with a hand clamped on his shoulder.

"You don't want to make that mistake, young one." His voice was a warning coated in the promise of violence. His eyes were narrowed crimson slits. She shivered. This was not the same man who'd taken her to have a picnic in the park. This was the vampire who survived at all costs.

"You bring a wolf here!" His heavily accented words were full of disdain, as all five-foot-seven inches of his lithe frame vibrated with anger. His cheek-bones stood out as when clenched his jaw. The cupid's bow lips and delicate facial structure made him stunning, but no less powerful.

"She is mine to do as I please with. If you ever move toward her in a threatening manner again, it will be the last thing you do."

Hackles rising, Joss growled in her throat at the threat the new vampire posed. She felt her eyes shift and her teeth elongate.

"Enculer! Look at her," the male vampire exclaimed.

"She's protecting her mate." The soft voice diverted their attention. An elfin brunette with kind eyes and a dreamy smile walked toward them. The hem of her white gown brushed the ground. Toes peeked out from the hem as she moved toward them.

"What are you doing, Rainer? It's not safe."

"Cyprian, it's okay. She's the one we've been waiting for. Can't you sense it? The feeling of puzzle pieces clicking into place?" Rainier smiled.

"Non. She nearly attacked me, like some rabid dog." He turned up his nose.

"You would've deserved it," Kazimir replied. His hand tightened, and Cyprian grunted.

"Enough." The commanding voice belonged to the curvy, brown-skinned woman in the doorway of the wooden cabin. Her slender face was surrounded by a riot of curls that tumbled down her back. Dressed head to toe in black with combat boots, she looked every inch the fierce warrior. Her magical signature was like a neon sign that flashed the words 'don't dick with me'.

Joss drew herself up, wary about the energies surrounding her.

"Nakeeta." Kazimir bowed his head in greeting.

"We're all tense. It's no reason to take it out on one another. Excuse him, his manners are poor, and we've been through a lot." The woman directed a smile her way.

Joss nodded, still not convinced, she was safe among them. A blonde vampire appeared behind Nakeeta. Shorter than Cyprian, he was solid and far more powerful.

"You always did know how to make an entrance, brother." The man wrapped an arm around Nakeeta.

"Crewe. Perhaps you'd like to collect your … *friend*." Disdain dripped from every syllable that left Kazimir's mouth. She felt his affection and trust for Crewe.

"This is not how we wanted this to go. Please come inside. We assure you, no harm will come to you. Right, Cyprian?" Nakeeta said.

Cyprian shrugged. The fight left his form as his shoulders rose and he held his head high, above all of the drama they'd caused.

"Apologize." Kazimir released him and straightened.

Cyprian's jaw tensed. "I'm sorry …"

"Joss. Her name is Joss."

"I'm sorry, Joss. I'm a little on edge, and I have my family to protect."

"I can understand that, but I'm not your enemy. This is your one and only pass," she said firmly.

He inclined his head in silent agreement.

"Now that we're all friends, it's time for introductions." The dark-haired pixie clapped her hands gleefully.

"This is Rainer. Seer, sweetheart, and peacemaker," Nakeeta drawled.

Rainer held out her hand, and Joss shook it. "It's lovely to meet you," Joss said.

"Likewise," Rainer said in her strange, lilting tone.

As they headed into the house, Kazimir kept his large frame between her and Cyprian. She squeezed his forearm, lending comfort as they gathered in the living room. The interior was rustic. Deer antlers hung on the wall, and the navy blue and green color theme screamed hunting cabin. A dark brown leather couch, sofa, and two chairs were arranged around a large table covered with a variety of mugs full of coffee and a dark red substance she knew wasn't wine.

"Well, this isn't awkward," Nakeeta muttered.

Joss snickered.

"How about we start with our names? I'm Crewe. This is my mate, Nakeeta, our friends, Cyprian and Rainer. Our companions hope to join us eventually. We didn't think it wise to be in one place together with everyone seeking us."

"Who's everyone?" Joss asked.

"Welcome to team save the world, a ragtag group of witches, vampires, and shifters trying to keep the world as we know it from ending."

Joss threw her head back and laughed. She couldn't escape cults. Leaving White Creek had only brought her to this band of questionable characters.

"Maybe you should work on that delivery," Cyprian said to Nakeeta.

"I'm sorry. You're serious?" Joss asked, catching her breath.

"Didn't you tell her?" Nakeeta directed the question at Kazimir.

"Only the bare basics."

"You know we're descended from the same vein, and that a spell enabled us to function in the world, with the stipulation that we are regulated to the night?"

"Yes."

"Well, one of my ancestors, a shaman named Seke, decided he wanted to be the most powerful being in existence, and he set about making it happen with dark magic, blood sacrifice, and manipulating nature."

Joss tensed. "How did this lead to what's happening now?"

"When he short-circuited his system, the damage he'd done to the spell only worsened over time. More than that, it's mutating."

"The insanity in the vampires?" Joss guessed.

Crewe nodded. "We believe the two are related. It's the only thing that makes sense. We think it's distorting our natural evolutionary process."

Joss turned to look at Kazimir. "This is the spell you mentioned recasting?"

"Yes."

"How do you know it's me? I'm sorry. I know you're all committed to this, but I have experience with groups who truly believe without tangible proof. It doesn't have to be true for it to have power."

"It's how we found you for one thing, and another, we have a guide." Nakeeta glanced at me nervously. "I need you to keep an open mind and try not to freak out."

Joss tensed. "What are you going to do?"

"Give you proof that we're not crazy." Closing her eyes, Nakeeta placed her hand over her chest. A green glow flickered around her hand. The power level in the room spiked. Joss shifted, unused to being in a witch's presence. Nakeeta took a deep breath and plunged her hand into her chest. Joss screamed. Kazimir's hand grasped her forearms, keeping her locked into place.

"Remain calm. She's okay."

Joss blinked away the tears threatening to gather in her eyes. When Nakeeta began to pull a brown scroll from inside of her chest cavity, Joss gasped. After the hole closed, she rested the parchment on the table between them.

"You can touch it," Nakeeta said.

"I-I'm not sure I want to," Joss admitted.

Snickers and chuckles broke the ice.

"It looks like its stored in my body, but it's really kept in an alternate dimension I'm accessing via my chest," Nakeeta explained.

"I'm not sure that's any less disturbing, but okay. What is it exactly?"

"The map that's guided us to the ancestors necessary to recast the spell. If we don't do this, the degradation will continue to all magical beings. It's about more than the ability to change at will or walk in the sunlight. Witches are experiencing a shift toward the dark as well."

How can I say no when she puts it like that?

"How would *I* be able to help?" Joss asked.

"It's all about the bloodline. We need to combine it together to recreate the spell."

"What spell?"

Nakeeta shifted in her seat. "We haven't seen the entire thing yet. We need to have all of us together to get the full script."

Joss touched the map and sparks of white magic flew. The jolt didn't hurt, but she startled.

"It's making sure you should be touching it," Nakeeta explained.

Reassured, she unrolled the map and blinked. Scrawled in what appeared to be black ink was her name along with Rainer, Crewe, and Nakeeta.

"How can this be true?"

"How can we exist?" Crewe countered.

"What do you want me to do?" Joss asked cautiously.

"We want you to look at this book."

Joss braced herself for another rummaging inside of a body.

"This is a lot simpler." Nakeeta picked up a small, worn, brown book from the table beside her and handed it to her.

She experienced the same zing of energy as she opened it. Skimming the page, her heart broke for the seer, Blythe, as she lost her family to the insanity that often came from living life in the past, present, and future. Sent to a mental facility, she learned to pretend she didn't see things. The journal was a glimpse into her life, what she saw, and her hope through it all. Tears welled in Joss's eyes. This woman had come before them, passing on a torch she could only pray would be picked up by someone else.

"Wow."

"We think she was my ancestor," Rainer said softly.

She glanced from the sprite to Cyprian who guarded her like a pit bull.

"He's not my mate," Rainer stated with a smile.

"I'm sorry." Flustered, Joss winced as her cheeks heated. "I wasn't trying to pry."

"It's okay. Sometimes I just *know* what people are thinking, so I answer." Rainer shrugged.

Cyprian leveled a stare that dared her to ask more about their relationship. Mentally raising her hand in surrender, she returned her attention to Nakeeta.

Leaning forward on the sofa, she rested her elbows on her knees. "What's our next move?" Joss asked.

"Figuring out how to find the rest of the spell. I have all of the ingredients and the first page of instructions, but I'm missing the last one." Her expression crumbled. "I'm sorry. We've been running on empty. There's an entire group of supernatural beings who don't want us to succeed. They think the time of the human is over, and we should reign. They don't care about the madness, or the fact that the imbalance in food and prey would create a desolate future where only the strong would survive, and war among ourselves would be a certainty."

"People who hunger for power seem to be experts at seeing in tunnel vision," Joss said dryly.

"You sound like you speak from experience," Crew said.

"I do. I'll help, but I can't abandon my duty to my pack. They're in danger, and like trusting children, they're too brainwashed to realize it. I helped put them into this position. I owe it them to at least try to get them out."

Kaz squeezed her hand gently. "You were a child when you were brought to White Creek."

"But when I was old enough to know better, I did nothing. I fed into the insanity."

"What's wrong with your pack?" Cyprian asked, taking an interest in what she had to say for the first time.

"It's a cult," Joss answered bluntly.

Cyprian's brow furrowed. "Surely, it can't be that bad."

"No, I mean it literally. The current Alpha has spent years preparing us for a paranormal war that pits us against each other and humans. We've been preppers long before the term was popular. He used his power and fear to manipulate them to do what he wants."

"And how do you come into this?" Crew inquired.

"I play the role of Moon Maiden. They believe I have a special link to Odin. What I see, say ... hell, how I act are all taken as signs. So, I've been coached, groomed, and directed since I was eleven."

"Why you?" Cyprian asked.

"Because of my birthmark."

He wrinkled his nose. "What?"

"You have your lore. We have ours. Mine ties in an ancient prophecy."

"And it happens to be true," Rainer said matter of factly.

Joss sighed. "Unfortunately, I've come to realize that not everything the Alpha claimed was a lie."

"She's the chosen one for her people. It has always been her destiny to bring about great change. The two will work hand in hand." Rainer's glossy, amber-colored eyes meant this was more than opinion. Joss had never been around a true Seer. The change that came over her was noticeable. It was like she had more power than her tiny frame could fully contain. "Part of a whole, the wolf will make or break the renewal. Save the wolf, save the world."

"What does that mean, Rainer?" Kazimir asked.

She jerked and shook her head. "Oh, you're different."

"What?"

"I can't see everything with you." She frowned. "This doesn't happen often."

"Her path must be linked directly to you." Cyprian stood. "How can that be?"

"We're all in this together," Nakeeta reminded him.

"I'm here to do two things. Help us win, and keep Rain safe."

"Not even you can save me from my fate, Cy," Rainer said.

"Don't talk like that," Cyprian snapped.

"I know it's not what you want to hear, but we both need to be prepared for this possibility," Rain answered gently.

"No. I'm not letting you end up in some looney bin."

"What if it's where I belong?" she asked sadly.

"It's not," Cyprian snapped, losing his cool.

"Hmmm." She peered down at the ground. "Every gift has a price."

"You didn't ask for this, Rain. There's a difference between seeking out glory, and ending up with a bad hand." He placed his arms on his shoulders. "Don't give up on me."

"Accepting my fate graciously and living in denial is not the same thing." Rainer shook her head.

Joss looked from one to the other, feeling like she was watching a rapid-fire tennis match.

"Just because you come from a family of Seers who ended up institutionalized, doesn't mean you're destined for the same path."

"No, but it's a pretty strong indicator. I'm starting to lose time and drift in and out of the tenses. Unless I find the other half to balance me out, things are only going to get worse. I want to see this through first. It's a moment in the making for my family. I want to do this for them as well as myself." She placed a hand over his. "Family is forever. Death doesn't sever that bond."

Cyprian scowled. "I'd rather have my bratty little sister alive and driving me insane. I know you're tired. It's okay. I have enough fight for the both of us. It's a big brother's job."

Watching them interact crumbled every preconceived notion she'd held about vampires. He didn't care that Rainer was a human who happened to see the future. To him, she was like blood. The range of emotions he'd run through in just the past five minutes showed they weren't the soulless, single-minded, bloodthirsty fiends the Alpha had long made them out to be. Perhaps Kazimir wasn't the exception, but the general representation. It shifted her views.

"Why isn't this changing?" Nakeeta's anxiety-ridden voice drew her attention.

"Maybe we all need to touch it?" Crewe suggested.

"Come on team, hands in," Nakeeta mumbled as she placed two fingers on the book.

"Why do I feel like I'm about to dabble with an Ouija board, and I know better?" Joss asked.

"It is a mystical portal of sorts," Rainer replied.

"Not helping," Joss said.

"Can you just put your fingers on the damn thing?" Cy asked impatiently. They exchanged a glance as they all placed fingertips on the worn and weathered bound piece of history. The ground rumbled below them.

"Is this normal?" Joss asked nervously.

"I have no idea," Nakeeta whispered.

A bright light flashed. Streaks of color exploded from the center of the book like a translucent firework display.

Nakeeta's eyes grew as round as saucers. "It's like someone murdered Rainbow Bright."

The colors darted around the room and then returned to the center to swirl together before they began to form a picture. The colors dimmed and black dominated the air above their head. Tiny dots of light became the stars. A brilliant ball of white, purple, and green streaked across the darkness.

"A comet?" Kazimir asked.

The ball burned brighter, nearly blinding them before it blinked out. The darkness swirled like a pinwheel made of black and white. Hypnotic, it changed its colors again, before disassembling to create another picture. Bodies lined the ground, pools of blood stood out starkly against the white snow.

"There's going to be another skirmish," Crewe stated.

"How do we win?" Kazimir asked.

The image shimmered, violently flashing red. They saw themselves laying on the ground.

The men hissed.

"Show us how to prevent it," Rainer commanded.

Giant black wolves with their heads tilted back in a howl appeared.

"We need the pack. The ancient pack," Joss exclaimed.

Kazimir turned to face her. "You understand this?"

"I think so." Joss nodded.

"So, we find this pack? And we win?" Nakeeta said.

The image flickered as if annoyed.

"No then," Crewe muttered dryly.

A Celtic knot, Akan symbol, wavy-lined Celtic family symbol, and infinity symbol flickered like a movie before the colors returned to the book.

"Well, that was cryptic. Ancient books. They never speak frankly," Nakeeta snarked.

"They were all about balance, unity, and family," Rainer pointed out.

"Yes, but we know we have to do this together to survive. Why would it tell us the same thing?" Crewe pondered aloud.

"Maybe it wanted to be sure we remembered that? We've already bickered amongst ourselves," Kazimir added.

"Family has nothing to do with balance though," Joss said as she mediated on the imagery they'd viewed.

"Maybe that was how it wanted us to treat each other?" Cyprian shifted his weight.

"We're not going to figure it out in one evening. The ground was covered with thick snow. We have time yet," Nakeeta remarked.

Joss leaned back and slumped against the back of the sofa, drained. More problems with no answers.

"Tell us about these wolves, Joss," Crewe said.

Conveying her experience with her father to the others, she couldn't help but hope their ratio of problems to answers would start to even out soon. It was early October. Snow could begin at any time.

"What's our next move?" Joss asked.

"Narrowing down the celestial event to give ourselves a timeline, and trying to better interpret the message," Crewe replied.

"Did we get the rest of the spell?" Rainer questioned.

"Let's see." Nakeeta thumbed through the book with speed beyond a human's capability. Joss eyed her curiously.

"*She and her mate share attributes,*" Kazimir said.

"*How?*"

"*Blood exchange near as I can tell.*"

The thought of Kazimir drinking from her nearly made her squirm in her seat. Tamping down the inappropriate images, she cleared her throat.

"It's getting late, and I'll be missed soon. I need to return to White Creek."

"Keep a tight leash on you, do they?" Cyprian taunted.

"They watch all of the members closely and monitor what they're doing. It's par for the course."

Nakeeta nodded in understanding. "I've placed 'notice me not' spells around the property, so you'll always be safe here."

"Thank you. We want to keep the element of surprise, and I have research to conduct."

Ominous thunder rumbled overhead, urging her to hasten. *Had they already run out of time?*

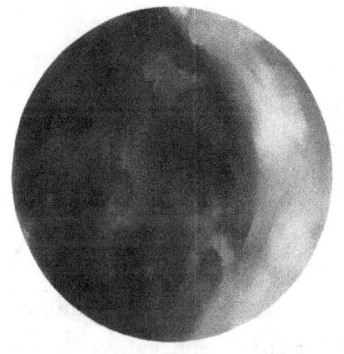

Chapter Nine

"Do you know what this is about?" Joss turned to Isiah as they walked into the meeting hall.

"Not a clue." Isiah sounded less than pleased at being left in the dark. He opened the door, allowing her to enter first. The lights were dimmed. Hundreds of candles illuminated the place.

"What's going on?" Joss asked, refusing to take another step.

The Alpha appeared, walking toward them in a black robe. "I had a prophetic dream last night. We need to have a ceremony."

"What kind of dream, Dad?" Isiah said.

"One that showed me what we need to do in order to thrive. You'll be Alpha soon, but I haven't handed over the pack yet. I will continue to do as I see fit until the day of the naming ceremony." The bass in his voice made her flinch. "We need to capitalize on the energies gathering in the universe."

"How?" Joss asked cautiously. Stepping down from Alpha appeared to be pushing him over the edge. Dark circles stood out in his paler than normal face.

"With a brand-new ceremony."

"Oh?"

"It's a throwback to our roots." He turned toward her mother. "Show them, Dorothy." Her mother walked forward with grayish brown pelts. "We've drifted too far from our origins. To prepare, we must honor the old ways and feed the wolf."

The words made her skittish. "Feed the wolf what?"

"Blood. A true sacrifice." He nodded his head and grinned, pleased with himself. "Come. We must prepare you both." While they took their cues from Viking roots, they'd never done anything this elaborate before. "Go with your mother, Joss. Isiah. You come with me."

Joss followed her mother into a back room.

"Mom?"

"We need to get you ready. Hurry. Ian's been agitated the past few days. I've never seen him like this before. He woke one evening and threw himself into research and began preparing." Her mother shook her head. "Strip down."

"How was he strange, Mom?" she asked, complying with her request.

"He mumbled to himself, barely slept or ate, and he seemed to be speaking with someone or something that wasn't there."

"What?"

"He was being guided." Her mother shook her head. "By what I can't say, but it terrified me. The cold that has taken over our home is bone-chilling and threatening. I wouldn't dare deviate from his plans purely based on my fear of what might happen. I've been held hostage by an unseen force. I'll do whatever it takes to get this thing out."

Her hands shook as she handed Joss a coarse, cream-colored dress, and a deep blue apron dress to cover it. Quickly slipping the clothes on and tying the strings on the side, she mulled over her mother's words.

"What do you think it is?"

"I don't know."

"Why didn't you tell a pack member?"

"Tell who? What can anyone do? He's the Alpha." Her mother paused and glanced around the room. "And who knows how far this entity's power extends."

"Mom, you're scaring me here." Joss's voice warbled.

She cleared her throat. "It'll be fine. Your mother is probably being silly. There's high tension and tons of pressure." She gave a fake laugh that Joss didn't buy for a second. "Sit, let me do your hair." Sinking to a chair, she studied her mother in the mirror as she finger-combed her hair, then wove two braids on either side of her hair. *I look like an extra on the set of Vikings.* Her mother completed the look, wrapping a wolf pelt around her shoulders.

"Take off your shoes."

"Mom. Has he explained why he's doing any of this?"

"No." Her lower lip trembled.

"You're worried."

Her mother bit the inside of her lip and gave a quick nod.

"And he didn't tell you anything?"

"Nothing more than what you've heard about returning to the old ways. I helped him gather everything necessary for an Old Norse ritual. I'm sure this is dedicated to Odin. He believed we need to appeal to him to ensure our future success. I was told what to do, and nothing more."

"And he got all of this from a dream?" Joss asked skeptically.

"I don't know where else he would've gotten it."

From the fortune telling lamia he's keeping on payroll under the table.

"You're ready." Her mother cleared her throat and blinked, chasing away the tears that had given her gaze extra sheen. "You look beautiful, baby. Fierce and regal, like a queen." Her mother cupped her face. "You're the best thing I've ever done, and I hope you find a way to forgive me one day for my missteps. I've only ever wanted what was best for you."

Joss covered her mother's hand. "I do realize that, Mom. It's not the mistakes, but the long-time secrecy that hurts me. I had a right to know."

Her mother sniffled. "Yes, you did."

Joss sighed. "I will always love you, and I appreciate everything you've done for me. I'm just hurt. The time I'm taking is to deal with that." She hugged her mother hard.

"It kills me. I only want to see you happy, whole, and safe. After your father died, it was my top goal. Looking at you, I see I've raised a strong, intelligent, and capable young woman. So, I didn't screw up completely." Her smile wavered.

"No, Mom, you did so much right. I'm not going to let this break us. I just need some time." She grabbed her mother's hands and squeezed.

"I can respect that." Her mother placed a sweet kiss on her forehead. It smacked of endings and good-byes. The bittersweet ritual took away some of the intense anger she'd held on to. Her mother stepped away and swiped at the tears running down her face. She cleared her throat once more. "Time to put on a show, Jossy. There won't be too many more celebrations before Ian's reign is over." Was that relief she heard in her mother's voice? Maybe her mother was tired, too? Joss straightened her spine, and lead the procession of two back into the main room. Their exchange had woken a protective instinct inside of her. *Is she safe with Ian?*

Isiah waited in front of the hearth in a long, blue, cloth tunic with a Nordic design on the trim and brown breeches. A wolf pelt was also draped over his shoulders. His hair had been clipped back and bleached a shocking blonde, just like the Vikings preferred. The process had pulled double duty back then because it also killed lice.

"Come, the others will be arriving soon. Tonight, we'll have a true blood sacrifice to Odin done in the old way. No more watered-down versions. We need to gain real favor and prevail over our foes. The pelts hold the power of our ancestors. Once pack, we'll always be pack. Even beyond the grave, they lend us their strength." The Alpha's eyes glowed, and his chest heaved. Spittle flew from his mouth. A crazed energy flowed from their usually calm leader.

She followed behind him. Outside, a massive bonfire crackled in an open field. Torches formed a circle waiting to be lit. In the center, there were two stone thrones etched with runes and symbols; she sensed latent power attached to the gray slabs.

"Go and sit in the one on the right." She walked toward the opening in the sticks for the torches and hesitated. Breeching the circle felt wrong.

"Now." The power in his voice had her legs moving despite her reluctance. Isiah grunted. The area around his eyes and mouth were strained. Drumming came from a distance. A steady rhythm accompanied by the haunting notes of a pan flute chilled her. People approached, dressed like the salt of the earth in simple cotton dresses, pants, and tunics. The sea of bleached blond locks sent her mind to *Children of the Damned*. The flickering flames of the torches distorted their faces.

Shadows created off angles and dark circles under eyes. She clutched the arms of the chair. A child led a snow-white lamb forward on a leash. The girl came to a halt in front of them as the others circled, claiming and lighting posts. The Alpha approached the center with her mother in tow.

"Today, we are here to sacrifice to Odin. What we want requires more than mere symbolism. Tonight, we spill blood in the old way." An unnatural stillness settled over the area. The Alpha began to speak in a guttural Norse dialect.

"Odin, God of Thunder, we seek your approval and power." Her mother interpreted as she lifted her arms above her head. The wind stirred, rustling the tree branches, and sending leaves skittering across the ground.

"We spill blood in your name." The Alpha stepped forward and clutched the back of the lamb's neck, pulling an old knife from a leather pouch. She was no stranger to death. As a wolf, she'd hunted her entire life. But this taking of life had nothing to do with the chase or food. He slit the lamb's throat, silencing its pitiful bleating.

Blood flowed into the silver bowl below. The lamb kicked as life slipped away. The Alpha's eyes glowed amber as he dipped his hand into the steaming blood. The thick substance splattered onto her apron and face. She flinched.

The splat echoed in her ears as the blood burned her skin. She gritted her teeth. The Alpha split the belly of the lamb and shoved his hand in, cracking bone before he began to cut out the heart.

The blood coating his hands and arms looked black in the moonlight. He held the still beating organ up. "We offer you this life's blood and take the heart inside those who will lead the pack." Her mother's voice rose above the murmurs as she continued to act as a translator. She walked over to the bowl, knelt beside the Alpha, and closed her eyes. "Fill the bowl with your intentions and hopes for the future as you taste of innocence." The Alpha drank from the bowl and handed it to her mother who did the same. "There is power in the pack. It's time we wield it."

Standing, her mother walked over to the woman closest to her and passed the bowl.

The Alpha walked up to Joss, offering the heart. "Eat and take the strength of the pack inside of you." She sank her teeth into the small muscles. Blood coated her tongue and slid down her throat. Every bite opened the pack connection up wider. He moved to Isiah, who finished the heart. A connection formed between the two of them. Her body lifted, levitating off the stone slab. Isiah floated beside her. The air around them grew charged, forming an invisible bubble. Power exploded into a cloud of purple magic that swirled around them, encasing them in a cocoon.

An uncanny knowing hit her. She'd known Isiah for longer than this lifetime. If she hadn't been floating, surely her knees would've buckled. Images of faces, empires long gone, and fingers entwined mentally pummeled her. Their gazes locked. *You.* The moment of instant recognition bound them. Lowered to the ground, they watched fuzzy imagery play across the screen of their minds. Her third eye blew wide open. A strangled scream rose in her throat as her brain hit full capacity.

A brilliant white light shot through the cocoon, snapping their connection. She slammed down her mental barriers to avoid backlash and pitched forward onto the ground. With the breath knocked out of her, she struggled to breathe. Digging her fingers into the ground, she scrambled to reorient herself. Claws easily burrowed into the soil. On the cusp of transforming, she swallowed the excess salvia and placed a mental chokehold on her wolf.

"You see the power Odin has granted us." As the Alpha preened, she tuned into Isiah's heavy breathing, in sync with her own.

"It's for this reason they will be wed in December, when the brightest comet of the year passes by."

"N—" Her protests turned into a cough as her throat swelled. The Alpha exerted his power, forcing her submission. Bucking against his control, she fought to escape his hold. Her throat constricted farther and his power pressed down on her, physically forcing her head down. The compulsion to take a submissive stance stole her breath. Wheezing, she ignored her mother's mental pleading. A throaty growl drew her attention and broke the Alpha's concentration. The pressure subsided, and a black wolf leapt in front of her, wearing down. *Isiah.*

The pleased expression on the Alpha's face threatened to make her vomit. Excitement pressed in from all sides.

"Let us celebrate this new blessing of two young, devoted cubs coming together."

"*Son of a bitch.*" Isiah's angry comment echoed in her head. He'd been just as blindsided as she. Things were spiraling, and she had no clue how to slow the descent.

They'd walked into his trap blindly, and he'd sprung it expertly, locking them into his time frame. Panting like she'd run a marathon, she tried to take air into what felt like oxygen-starved lungs. *I'm nothing more masterfully for someone else's gain.* Her stomach dropped to her feet. Her legs shook under the weight pressing onto her shoulders. Isiah nuzzled her with his muzzle. His tongue shot out and affectionately licked her. She lifted her gaze to hold his own.

"*Don't you dare give him what he wants.*"

He was right. Straightening, she lifted her head and faked the confidence she didn't feel. Isiah moved in, brushing his body against hers. Body straight, he turned into a soldier, ready to defend. Dark, sleek, and deadly, he snorted. Head held high he exuded a royal heir. The Alpha's right eye twitched. If a wolf could smirk, she would be. His Highness hadn't expected them to rally.

A blast of power forced her to stumble back. "*Kneel.*" The Alpha's voice had sounded in her head. Isiah growled low in his throat. He pressed in closer. Their powers sparkled, canceling out the Alpha's command. The Alpha blinked. His anger became a living thing as his light blue eyes glowed a bright yellow. Malevolent power oozed toward them like a wave of darkness.

"*Let's remind him that he needs our cooperation.*" Isiah fired the sentence down their mental link.

She huffed. "*How?*"

"*Follow my lead.*" He nudged her body with his own a split second before he bounded out of the circle. Bodies parted like the Red Sea. The torches flickered out, and a backlash of power hit like the recoil from a rubber band pushed past its flexibility. Ignoring the protocol pounded forcefully into her head, she followed, fully severing the connection with the power they'd amassed. High from the rush of the power leaving the group and flowing through her body and back to its source, she ran without fear of retribution or consequence.

Their paws padded over the ground as they left the ceremony site behind and reached the edge of the woods. The sounds of heavy breathing, barks, and paws on the ground, told her others had given chase.

"*He sent the betas after us. Keep up with me.*"

The bond between them rippled as he drew from the power they created together and increased his speed. Following his lead, she allowed the she-wolf to take over. Matching him jump for jump, she rejoiced in the freedom, embracing the wild, feral nature she often tempered. Plunging deeper into the forest, they left the others behind. An urgency overtook her, guiding her toward an unknown destination. She sensed the tree before she saw it. A massive trunk of a Cottonwood erupted from the soil like a mountain—wide, tall, strong, and solid as if it had always been there. They came to a stop as one.

"*We'll stay here tonight.*"

"*Yes.*" She craned her neck, peering up into the massive trunks of the tree. Lowering herself to the ground, she rested her head on her paws. Isiah took a defensive position, angling his body in front of hers. The bad blood that existed between them was absent. She felt ... safe. Exhaustion struck as the adrenaline waned, and she closed her eyes.

"*Sleep.*"

Too tired to bristle under the command, she slipped into dreamland.

A STEADY RHYTHM PULLED HER from a deep sleep. Prying her weighted lids open, she lifted her head. Her nose twitched as the scent of burning cedar, smoke, and people melded together. Night had yielded to day, and the area in front of the tree had come to life. Pitched voices cried out in song. The powerful message of praise and pride blended together as the sound floated toward the heavens. A large group of men and women shuffle danced around the fire pit. Ornate feathered headdresses adorned some of the men's heads. Ebony hair flowed down their backs, standing out against the fringed beige buckskin leggings and long-sleeved shirts.

Colorful quill work down the sides of the leggings, and in large necklaces, dated the time. She froze, terrified to move. *What will they do if they see me?* Using her peripheral vision, she searched for Isiah. Her heart knocked in her chest. She was alone in some sort of time warp. Keeping her eyes glued to the Native Americans in front of her, she took a cautious step back. A twig snapped. The group continued, unaware of her presence.

"They can't see you."

She jerked her head to the left, straining her neck. A Native American with long, black hair, black eyes, and a kind expression on his face stood a few feet away. *Where did he come from?*

"They can't see me either. We're here to observe."

She tilted her head, unable to speak in her form.

"You can change your form so we can speak. We're in a dreaming place, but it's not quite a dream."

Why?

"We have been watching White Creek you since you arrived. Tonight, you proved yourself."

Focusing, she shifted her forms, only to find herself garbed in a soft deer-skin dress with fringe and quillwork down the sides. Her hair was parted in the center and braided into two plaits.

"And how did I do that?"

"By leaving. You and the male wolf."

"Is he okay?" she asked, suddenly worried by his absence.

"He, like you, must choose his own pathway."

Shifting her weight, she questioned, "Who are you?"

"I'm Seke, and I'm here to share my story with you."

"You were the one who disrupted the balance," she whispered.

"Yes. I wanted to be the most powerful being in existence. I never stopped to think what it would cost me or my people. We live to uphold the balance. I should've known better." He shook his head. "I spent a long time paying for those poor decisions. I don't want to see you make the same mistake."

"I would never do that." She sneered at his assumptions.

"Are you sure? Hate, anger, and an unwillingness to forgive can lead us down roads we never imagined we'd travel. Don't be so sure the right path is easy. Confidence is a blessing and a curse. Too little and you'll always fall short of your goal. Too much and you'll miss the obvious, and grow deaf to the wisdom of others. It takes just the right amount to be strong, and yet humble."

Her brow furrowed as she mulled over his words. It felt like a backhanded compliment and another push toward Isiah.

He smiled. "Have you figured out that the darkness and light need one another to exist? When both play their role, day," the sky lightened, and the sun rose; heat baked into her skin, warding off the chills from the evening air, "and night are born." She watched in awe as the sun slowly sank, creating a picture-perfect array of purples, oranges, and pinks as it disappeared from the horizon. Stars came to life, like bright diamonds dotting a blue velvet canvas. "When they are in balance, they create harmony."

She gaped at the fat, round moon that appeared closer than ever. The people continued to move around their life, like phantoms of the past. She watched as the Native people gathered, cooked, and interacted with each other in accordance to the time of day. The simplicity of their lives made her ache with longing. This is how it should be when you lived on the land. Working together in a group. White Creek had twisted it. Sadness filled her heart and weighed her soul down. Turning to the man who watched her like she was a new form of reality television, she scowled.

"If you're all knowing and powerful like Oz, you'd known my step-brother and I make a job of being on the opposite ends of everything. There's no synchronization there." She shook her head and slashed the air in front of her neck with her right hand.

"Except for when there is," he drawled. "You worked together tonight."

"That's rare." She pointed with her index finger. Fury pushed aside the fear she'd felt initially.

"It wasn't always. Together what could you accomplish?" His even tone enraged her.

She opened and closed her hands, balling them into fists. "You do realize, getting along takes two people unless one is completely submissive to the other?"

"That's called balance," he said gently.

She snorted. *Because that's so easy to achieve?* People searched their entire lives for that one thing. "I haven't seen much of that in my life."

"You did. With your parents."

Did he just compare us to my parents? Theirs was the only love story she believed. "Isiah and I will never be like them."

"I wonder why *you* believe you need to be."

She paused in mid-step. "*I'm* not the one with the disillusions. Besides, isn't that what this is all about? Pushing us together? Trying to turn us into some fake Ken and Barbie?"

"The pack is not about insignificant romantic connections. It's deeper. This is a spiritual connection. You are bound by soul, blood, sweat, and tears. These are your people. Would you dismiss them over a petty misunderstanding? If so, perhaps you aren't the woman the ancestors believed you might be."

"How dare you judge me, after everything you done? If it wasn't for you, none of us would even be in this mess."

"That is the reason I was chosen for this task. I, better than most, understand what's at stake. It's a darkness that stains your soul and anchors your spirit to the worst moments of your life. Whatever's holding you back now, relinquish it."

"Holding me back from what?" she asked, thoroughly confused.

"Peace, potential, and vision. You lack the ability to see the bigger picture. You're running out of time …" He paused and glanced over her shoulder at something she couldn't see. He gave the nod and walked forward, pressing two fingers to her temple. "See." Images exploded behind her eyelids, a movie in fast forward, disappearing before she could fully grasp them. Each scene felt like a glimpse into a potential future. The visions settled into her brain, pressing down like sinus pressure. An ache began in her temples. The rollercoaster ride ended with the vision of ravens circling above her head. He removed his fingers, and she stumbled back.

"Look for the ravens." His voice faded as the world around her pitched, and she was pulled into the darkness.

Twitching, she fought through the sticky cobwebs of sleep and opened her eyes. The sun's rays trickled through the thick limbs of the trees overhead. She shook her head to clear it, and slowly eased onto her elbows. Cold, wet snow clung to her naked arms. The scenery around her had changed. *Where am I?* She craned her neck, stunned to discover she still wore the buckskin dress. Sitting up, she took in the drooping branches of the massive pines, heavy with snow. A gurgling croak drew her head up. A circle of black birds gave her pause. *Ravens?* It was a given fact ravens liked wolves. They often followed them around and alerted them to food by imitating their howls.

Look for the ravens. Was this what he meant? The inky birds swooped down, circling her head once more before flying off. Unfamiliar with her surroundings, she went against her first instinct and began to follow. Wolves ran hotter than humans, so the cold barely registered as she walked barefoot through the white frozen water. Ravens continued to cry out, keeping her on the right path. The sensation of being watched hit. Her spine tingled. Turning to look at the woods, she caught a pair of golden eyes watching her. *The wolves.*

The rustle of branches set her on edge. Her ears twitched as she guessed the numbers. The pack was big. A rush of air alerted her seconds before the large, black wolf landed in front of her. The wolf came to her chest. Stumbling back, she froze. Overly intelligent eyes pierced her own. Its lips were peeled back from massive teeth as it gave a growl of warning.

The wolf stalked forward, nose twitching as he took in her scent. She'd never seen a werewolf this big before, not even an Alpha. *This must be one of the wolves Dad mentioned.* She swallowed hard and straightened her spine. Fear would not earn respect.

The wolf expelled air through its nose. White wisps of steam curled up between them. Keen eyes studied her. Her mental walls were nudged.

Brush rustled nearby. The wolf glanced over his shoulders before bounding away. He disappeared into the trees.

"Are you okay?" Isiah asked breathlessly.

She turned. The sight of his leather leggings and matching tunic told her he'd had an experience similar to her own. "You saw him, too?"

"I saw … something. Which is why I need to leave."

"What?" Her shrill voice rang through the unfamiliar section of the forest.

"I need to arrange things."

"And in that time, we'll do what? Live like criminals on the run?"

"No." He shook his head. "I'm going to make a deal."

She scoffed. "With who?"

"My father."

She held up her hand. "I'm sorry. Were we at the same place yesterday? He's not into compromise."

"He won't have a choice."

She furrowed her brow. "What the hell is that supposed to mean?"

"We all have secrets we'd prefer not to get out. Being the owner of those dark truths gives one power."

"You're going to blackmail him?" she asked skeptically.

"Yes, and you're going to steer clear of him."

How can I trust him with this?

"We're in this together now, Joss."

"Are we? 'Cause it feels like we want two different things." She tossed her hands up in the air. "Like we always have."

"How long are you going to throw up barriers between us?" He shook his head, gesturing between them. "We've evolved into a unit."

"And that is convenient for you. This new development in line with the desires you already had," she exploded.

"You think it's easy to be linked to a person who's constantly in opposition to what I want? You'd be wrong." He took a step closer. "We have to find common ground, or we'll both lose everything. His voice lowered an octave. "There's too much at stake."

"You wield your words like a weapon, meant to force me to bend to your will."

"Are you so self-centered and paranoid?" he spat. "This is about life as we know it. As the world knows it ending."

"Yes. But why does that require me to sacrifice everything I want, and believe in?"

"Because I'm the one with the plan," he roared.

She cringed but refused to back down. "The mysterious one you've yet to share with me?"

"You want trust without giving it?"

"You owe me. You've bullied, oppressed, and stalked me for years, so don't stand here and play the victim. Don't think this thing beyond our control makes our past null and void."

"The future is coming fast, regardless. We need to put the petty issues we have aside."

"Set them aside for what? You're not giving me any choice other than blind trust."

"I'm going to do what's necessary, Joss. Unlike you, we can't all sit back and keep our hands clean while we hope for the best."

"Is that what you think I've done?" She threw her head back and laughed. "My soul is stained with the lies I've helped force-feed others. Whatever fate they meet, I helped lead them to. Don't tell me I sat back and let others do the work. I've already been a puppet for your father. How dare you expect me to do the same for you."

"Soon you won't have a choice."

"Now you threaten?"

"I'm stating facts." He sighed. "I don't have time to waste arguing with you. Come, we need to find our way back." Turning on his heel, he ended their conversation, giving her no choice but to follow him. Whatever he'd learned in his dreams had spooked him into action.

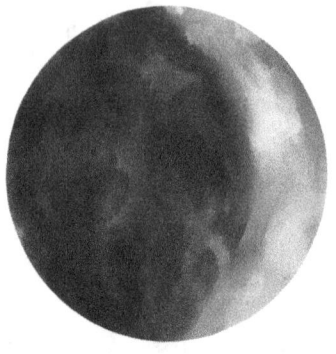

Chapter Ten

"You had no clue he was going to announce your engagement?" Brook gawked.

Joss shook her head. A week later, and she'd become quite adept at avoiding the Alpha like the plague. Not that he tried hard to find her. Whatever Isiah did kept him at bay. "He called me and Isiah out of the blue to come over. He must suspect we're hiding things. Why else would he pull this?"

"To undermine and control his son like he always has. In this instance, I think you got caught in the crosshairs."

"I wish I could buy that. I don't. Especially not with him mentioning the comet." *And all of the other things I don't dare share for fear of endangering you.*

"What does your dream man say?" Brook stirred the straw in her cola.

"Kazimir wants me to come with him." *And it gets harder and harder to tell him no.*

"What exactly happened between you and Isiah? It looked like pretty potent magic."

Her stomach bubbled. How could she explain that her enemy was an old soul she was connected to? "I wish I could tell you. We'll add it to the list of things I need to figure out." It was another lie.

"How do you plan on doing that?" Brook arched her brow.

"I'm going to see Kishi."

Frowning, Brook wrinkled her nose. "You need to be careful around her, Joss."

"I never forget who I'm dealing with," Joss assured her.

"Remember you also have people here to help you. "

They'd driven an hour and a half to escape the pack. Seated in the back booth of a restaurant they spoke in hushed tones.

"How?" Disgusted, Joss shoved her plate of fries away.

"By putting our heads together and seeing what we can come up with. How's Isiah been since the glowing incident?"

I wouldn't know. He took off out of here like a bat out of hell, and I haven't heard from him since. "I don't know. He hasn't been around lately. What happened that night scared me, Brook. It was heavy, old magic and far too personal for comfort. The things I saw confused me. It might've seemed like minutes to you, but for us it was centuries. I'm afraid of what I'll see the next time I do look him in the eyes."

"Jesus. Is it …" Brook gulped, "a romantic thing?"

"No, it's familiarity. Like he's known me longer than anyone else on the planet. God. It feels like such a lie. How can he be this important to me? We're at each other's throats constantly. We're like Batman and the Joker."

"Appropriate as one of you is extremely insane," Brook snorted. Joss rubbed her temples. "I just realized something." Brook sat up in her seat. "You're a werewolf caught between a wolf and a vampire."

"Brook. Don't you dare," Joss growled as she pointed her finger.

"You're officially Bella Swan, dude."

"I'll kill you." Joss tossed a french-fry across the table, and Brook laughed.

"Isiah is totally Jacob. Hot-headed, and into a girl who wants nothing to do with him romantically."

"I hate to burst your bubble, but Kazimir is more Jasper Hale than Edward." Joss shook her head. "I cannot believe I'm having this conversation."

"You needed a smile. Besides, there's no way in hell I was missing out on this golden opportunity to reference a favorite book. You can't avoid the men in your life forever."

"Yes, Kazimir reminds me of that daily. He likes to make sudden appearances when it's safe." Joss smirked as she sensed him near. "Like the one he's about to make now." He was an expert on walking the line between overbearing and sweet. He didn't allow her to push him away, as hard as she tried. He gave her space, even when it cost him. It was a combination of give and take mixed with communication.

"Wait," Brook sat up straight, "I get to meet Mr. Dreamy?"

Joss rolled her eyes. "He has a name." The door opened, and she smiled as Kazimir entered, drawing the gaze of every woman and a few men. Blue jeans accentuated his long legs, a black pea coat and wool hat contrasted with his pale complexion.

"How can he be out right now?"

"Magic and age," Joss answered without taking her eyes off him.

"You lucky bitch," Brook muttered. "No wonder you never looked at anyone else."

Her cheeks heated as she grinned. Kazimir strode toward her, gaze burning a hole inside of her. He was water, fluid and smooth, deceptively calm but deadly when riled. He arrived at their table and bent, kissing her sweetly.

"I missed you, little sun. Days apart are like years."

"I missed you, too." She brushed her lips over his and pulled back.

Brook watched them, a hand tucked under her chin as she sighed. "Let me live vicariously through you for a moment."

Joss shook her head with a smile. "Kazimir. This is my best friend, Brook. Brook, this is my …" She trailed off, unsure of how to categorize him. "My Kazimir." The joy at her claiming burst through their link like sun through the clouds.

He gave a slight bow at the waist. "Ms. Brook. It's a pleasure to meet you."

"The pleasure is mine. We often doubted your existence over the years. For once, I'm glad to be proven wrong."

"I apologize for taking so long to arrive. But I assure I won't be going anywhere now." The word alone was obviously implied. He took a seat beside her.

"You were discussing what happened earlier this week?" Kazimir asked.

"I'm no closer to being able to explain any of it though."

"Nakeeta would like to read your cards."

"Tarot?" Brook asked.

"She's quite skilled. People booked her months in advance in her shop," Joss said, bragging on her new friend. Her life wasn't the only one turned upside down by a mission bigger than herself.

"Yes. Nakeeta is incredibly independent and driven. She's eager to return to her business."

"How does that work? 'Cause Crewe seems like a real hard-ass to me," Joss said.

Kazimir chuckled. "Oh, he is. He's changed a fair bit, but they also challenge each other … constantly. It's entertaining to see the warrior I once knew dragged into the twentieth century."

"Pot meet kettle, I think," Brook said.

He smiled. "Perhaps. You haven't had a visit from Isiah, have you?"

"He's still gone. It's the longest I've gone without seeing him. It's not like him to drop off completely." She shouldn't worry about him, and yet, she did.

"You're concerned about him?" Kazimir frowned.

"I am. He stood up to his father for me publicly. That usually ends poorly for him." Guilt slipped in like a burglar, stealing the pieces of her happiness.

"If you've finished here, we can see the others. Perhaps Rainer or Nakeeta can help you with this?"

Joss glanced at Brook.

"Your friend is welcome," Kaz assured her.

"I'm sure Cyprian would have a field day with that."

"He's gone to meet others in our group. Silver and Reagan are in the state now."

"I suppose it's settled then."

They quickly paid the bill and headed outside. What did it say about her that after everything she still cared for Isiah? Had what happened been a spell of some sort? Even now, was the Alpha manipulating them? Unanswered questions swirled in her head, taunting her like demons.

❋ ❋

"SISTERS!" RAINER GREETED THEM GLEEFULLY in a pair of black tights and a long, black button-down covered in colorful butterflied. She looked more child than woman. Her youthful exuberance appeared to be catching. The atmosphere was lighter here, regardless of the worries that plagued Joss.

"Rainer, this is Brook."

"I know." She smiled serenely. A roguish twinkle danced in her almond-shaped amber eyes.

"What?" Brook exclaimed.

"I am a seer, and so very pleased to meet you." Rainer held out her hand and shook it exuberantly like she'd met a celebrity.

"What's this about?" Brook asked

"Your guess is as good as mine." Joss shrugged.

Crewe hung back, keeping his body between Keeta and the new wolf. He watched every move with eyes full of distrust. She could see his mind calculating as he sized her up.

"This is Crew and his better, nicer half, Nakeeta. Don't let him intimidate you. He's just a little overprotective."

Joss snickered. "That's putting it mildly."

"We don't know this new wolf. I won't take chances with Keeta."

"Yes, brother, we know Mother is essential to our mission. She's also our friend whom we'd never willingly place in danger." Kazimir walked over and placed a hand on his shoulder. "We both have precious treasures to protect."

Crewe nodded. His jaw clenched, and he fell back, in his version of relaxing. "Of course, Kaz." The bond between the two shone through.

"Brook has her role to play, too. You will treat her with kindness," Rainer said sternly.

Crewe shot her a look that would kill if it were a bullet. Clearly, he wasn't the type to take orders. The aura of power, stance, and frank words screamed Alpha. It was fascinating to watch two alpha vampires interact so casually.

"Crewe is of my blood. We shared a sire."

"Which makes you family by proxy," Nakeeta explained. "I'm still learning their ways, too. Don't let it overwhelm you."

Joss nodded, taking the words to heart. She'd gone from being on her own to being brought into the fold of a highly unlikely family. Her gut told her to accept them; nevertheless, her brain balked. When had things ever gone smoothly for her?

"Umm. What role?" Brook asked.

"If I told you, I don't think you'd believe me. There are things that we must discover on our own," Rainer insisted.

"I don't like the sound of that at all," Brook replied.

Nakeeta laughed. "I like her." It was an odd settling in. Neither of their people interacted normally. Now they had one thing in common—survival.

"Tell us what happened with your pack," Rainer said, bringing them back on track.

"I'm still trying to figure that out myself. He conjured up energy out there. Or it used him. It was a ritual for Odin, which is nothing new for us. This he called a Blot. The sacrifice was a lamb. He had us all ingest the blood, while Isiah and I ate the heart."

Keeta whistled. "Blood magic done with an innocent sacrifice. Potent. The rarer and more precious an item, the greater the magic conjured. This is why Vikings used to sacrifice children."

"Oh God," Brook gasped.

"They were brutal. How far do you think your Alpha is willing to go to immolate them?" Nakeeta asked quickly.

She thought back to the sea of blond hair. "I'm not sure."

Kazimir grasped her hand, and brought it to his lips, placing a kiss on it. "Why do you sound so anxious, Keeta?"

"Joss is looked upon as a modern-day priestess of sorts. Sacrificing you would create an immeasurable amount of power."

"Over his dead body," Kazimir growled.

"He announced my betrothal to his son. He plans for us to marry on the night the brightest comet of the year passes overhead." She dropped her head, ashamed. The nasty rumbling escaping Kazimir's chest should've been frightening. Instead, it flattered. "It won't be happening."

"Does he know that?" Brook's gaze bounced from her to Kazimir.

"Alpha or Isiah?"

"Both are going to have a problem with your change of plans," Brook said.

"I'm not springing it on Alpha until the last minute. I'm on the fence about Isiah." Lying to him felt wrong now.

"You anticipate him being a problem?" Kazimir said.

"With Isiah, you never know." She shook her head. "During the ritual things changed. We connected." She pushed her two index fingers together.

"In a display of magic that looked like a fireworks display, might I add." Brook waved her hands around.

"I saw who he once was and could be all at once. It was like the years rolled back further than we've existed in this current life. I saw all of the good and bad he'd done and was capable of doing." Her heart raced. She saw into his soul.

"People often think only a soulmate can be connected at a soul level. That's not true. Souls reincarnate together for many reasons," Nakeeta explained.

"*No!*" Joss shook he head. "How can that be true after everything he's done?"

"Perhaps this life was about testing one another. Do you challenge him? Maybe you're meant to be a catalyst for his growth."

"No. I don't do anything to him," Joss snapped.

"Yes. At every turn she does," Brook said.

"Brook."

"It's true. You're the only one he's ever let openly challenge him without retaliation or instant correction and humiliation for shirking his authority," Brook chimed in.

"Because I'm his step-sister and Moon Maiden."

"You've always been connected. Why do you think he's so drawn to you?"

"Do psychos really need logical reasons for why they do things?"

"His behavior isn't a reflection on you or your link. The darkness needs the light. One can't exist without the other." Keeta's words made sense, but accepting it felt too much like losing. All she wanted to do was escape White Creek, and yet there was another tie.

"We get what we get in this life, not what we want. You were tough enough to handle this situation. Look at how long you've already survived and held on to who you are. Don't quit on us now when the end is in sight," Keeta pleaded.

I have no choice but to see it through. "So, we're what? Old friends?"

"Think of it as a familial bond, like Remus and Romulus. Born to rule together, bring balance and change, yet too much one way or the other and the connection sours."

"Is he a danger to her?" Kazimir asked, wrapping an arm around her shoulders.

"Currently he's a danger to everyone including himself." Joss shrugged his arm off and walked the length of the room.

"You bring him away from the madness. What he senses is the fact that you're his saving grace. He doesn't know how else to process or put it into words."

"So, he assumes it's some sick version of love?" Brook whispered.

"I believe so. In the end, you both must pick a side," Rainer replied.

"What do I need to do?" Joss asked.

"Try and work on cracking this book and organizing," Keeta said.

"Well, we've figured out the celestial event now," Crewe said dryly.

"The comet? I thought that too when he announced it," Joss said.

"We have much to do and little time to accomplish it in."

Raising her hand, Brook wiggled her fingers. "Sign me up. Whatever threatens my best friend has to go."

"This could ruin your standing at White Creek," Joss said.

"The sacrifice already did that. We're a pack. We hunt, we worship, and we stay prepared for the possibility of discovery. We don't kill in cold blood and force our will on others who look to us for protection and acceptance. It's the Alpha's right to discipline disobedient pips. What he did crossed the line."

"It sounds like you left a few things out," Kazimir rumbled.

"There was no use upsetting us both."

Kazimir wrapped his cool fingers around her wrist. "If you'll excuse us."

Joss wouldn't meet his gaze as he led her through the cabin out into the night. No words were exchanged as they moved to the river bank.

"I can't protect you when you hide things from me."

"You can't be there with me every waking moment. I handled it."

"No. Isiah did."

"Is that what this is about? A pissing contest?"

"There is no competition. Do you think this is easy for me? Staying in the shadows while you deal with your pack? This goes against everything I am. You are mine, and everyone should know it."

"I'm not a possession. I'm a woman with feelings and the right to choose how I want to deal with things."

"Don't mistake my love for weakness. I won't be scolded for being concerned. Times are perilous. One secret could topple us."

"Do you want to hear how he swelled my throat to silence me? How I struggled to breathe as he forced me to the ground and tried to make me cower and submit? How fighting against his hold on me did next to nothing?" He stepped forward, and she pushed him away. "No. This is what you wanted, and I'm going to finish." Her voice cracked. "I was at his mercy. And the only thing that kept me from complete humiliation was my few fries short of a Happy Meal creeper of a step-brother who I'm currently promised to marry. I owe him now, and I fucking hate it." Her voice was shrill, and her chest grew tight. She hiccupped. Her vision blurred as she battled against tears.

"I should have been there, little sun. I'm sorry."

"All of this time I told myself I was choosing to stay. That I could leave any time I was ready. It was a lie. I'm just as trapped as everyone else." Anger, sadness, and shame clashed. "I've been so damn stupid."

"Naïve perhaps. You have to realize you were stunted by proxy. Yes, you resisted, but you've been hidden in the middle of nowhere, surrounded by believers, rules, and impossible expectations. All of these things have affected you. Hold on just a little longer for me, and I will show you the world." He framed her face with his hands.

She closed her eyes, allowing herself to envision a future away from White Creek. One that was no longer a dream, but a reality. *All I have to do it survive.* The time for sorrow would come. Packing her emotions away, she inhaled. "I'm sorry. I'm normally made of sterner stuff."

"Never apologize to me for being human. Holding on to the pain will slowly kill you from he inside." His eyes bled from brown to red. "Do not ask me to have mercy for those people should we meet."

She squeezed his forearms, allowing herself the small intimacy. The feeling of helplessness she'd experienced still woke her from her sleep in the early hours. Control was an illusion she'd bought into like everyone else. *No more.*

"Take that indignation and channel it. Remember this moment when you hesitate, or second guess yourself. Do whatever it takes to be ruthless, Joss, because these people will stop at nothing to see the empire they've worked so hard to build come to pass. You have to play things their way."

She nodded, taking his words to heart. She'd underestimate the Alpha once. It wouldn't happen again.

"I always thought of myself as separate from everyone else in White Creek. I'm a member of a cult. The hows and whys don't matter. I obey the same rules, live in the same compound, and I keep the same secrets." Raw and exposed, she wrapped her arms around his waist.

Winding his fingers in her hair, he pulled her close, sheltering her from the wind. "You are more than your title and circumstances. They've tried to strip you down, steal your individuality, and tell you who you're going to be. It's a familiar method launched over and over again to control. You're no longer alone."

Her life was breaking apart and reforming at an alarming rate. Inhaling his scent, she cleared her mind, using the breathing techniques an intense focus she'd been learning. Settling her nerves, she gathered her thoughts. *I've never been weak. This won't break me.*

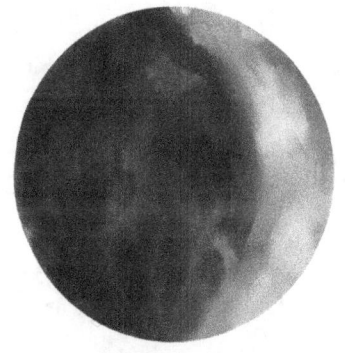

Chapter Eleven

SHE SWAM TO AWARENESS COVERED in sweat and tangled in her sheets. Fighting with the sticky cloth prison, she managed to kick herself free. Heat burned her from the inside out. Fatigue made her limbs heavy. Her tongue was swollen and clumsy. She struggled to swallow. Forcing her eyelids open took most of the energy left after her battle with the bedding. Salivating, she moved out of the bed and stumbled to the bathroom just in time to empty her stomach in the toilet. Her gut exploded in pain. Cramps hit her like a sledge-hammer. This was unlike any sickness she'd ever encountered before. Trembling she collapsed onto the cool tile, grateful for the reprieve from the raging inferno occurring inside of her.

Her temples throbbed. She shut her eyes against the light, which inten-sified the threatening migraine. Curled into a ball, she weathered the illness hammering against her immune sickness. Wolves weren't ill often. Even colds tended to be cured in a day or so, which made this sudden onslaught of symp-toms suspicious. *What did I eat?* Fighting to get her mind off the pain wracking her body, and the fog of sickness clouding her mind, she attempted to retrace her steps the night before. She'd had dinner with the others in the cabin after an afternoon spent trying to coax the book into spilling its secrets to them.

The simple fare of fresh bread and spaghetti couldn't be responsible for this violent reaction. She hadn't tried anything new or come into contact with something that could come from a questionable source. Struggling to her knees, she grabbed the cup on the sink and filled it with water. Her hand shook as she brought the rim of the plastic cylinder to her lips. The cool water coated her bone-dry mouth and slid down her throat. Closing her eyes, she savored the temporary bliss.

Her heart raced, and her head spun like a merry-go-round. Slumping over, she rested her back against the bathroom cupboard. She wiped a hand over her brow, took a deep breath, and pulled herself into a standing position. Bracing her hand against the wall, she inched her way to the showers stall. Fumbling with the tap, she turned the knobs and pushed off the wall. After she stripped down, she climbed under the lukewarm spray and tilted her head back. The beads of water cooled her hot head and washed away the grime the sweat left behind. Grabbing her turquoise body scrubber, she created a lather, and slowly soaped her body.

Every action took concentration and effort. Satisfied with her cleanliness, she cut the water and stepped out onto the light blue, fluffy rug. Grabbing her oversized towel, she dried off, ignoring the ache, and made her way to the bedroom. She slipped on flannel pants and a white T-shirt, then tussled with the sheets on the bed. Grunting, she tugged them free, dragging them to her hamper. Tossing a flat sheet onto the cushioned mattress, she collapsed face first, devoid of energy.

Sharp pain in her side doubled her over. Curling into a fetal position, her muscles locked, as her body twitched like a live wire. Visions slammed into her brain, overloading her circuit. Isiah stood, supported by chains that led down to heavy silver manacles clamped onto his wrists.

"This is what happens when you get in over your head," a gravelly voice barked. Male laughter rose around him, taking pleasure in his torture. The liquid burned his flesh, and he screamed. Their connection burst wide open, and she shared his pain. *Wolfsbane.* She opened her mouth to scream, and choked on the sound. Flesh bubbled, sizzled, and peeled back. The stink of burning charcoal and sulfur made her gag. Panting, she tried to distance herself from his reality.

Locked on like a heat-seeking missile, Isiah clung to her. Hyperventilating, she suffocated from lack of air. She arched off her bed. Skin split on his back, a deep burn encased her in a crisscrossing pattern. The whip whistled as it flew through the air. Flinching in anticipation, her scream melded with Isiah's in her head. A mental cloak fell over her, bringing calm and the numbness of nothing. Latching on to Kazimir like a drowning victim, she said a silent prayer for the vampire's methodical stillness.

"*What's happening? I'm outside of your compound,*" Kazimir said.

"*They're torturing Isiah,*" she replied shakily.

"*Who?*"

"*I don't know.*" Her chest heaved. Opening her eyes, she re-acclimated herself with the powder blue walls of her own room to combat the cold dampness of the stone prison.

"*And you feel it so strongly?*"

"*Yes.*" Even now she felt him, muffled, and just beyond her range. "*He's reaching out to me.*"

"*Block him.*"

The truth rolled in like the scent of garbage on the wind. "*I don't think I can.*" Muscles in her stomach clenched. Isiah burst through once more, blowing her mind wide open.

The metallic scent of blood and rice pudding engulfed her. Kneeling, Isiah gritted his teeth.

"How much can you take? The little prince isn't so tough away from White Creek." The vision of a square-faced giant with wheat-colored hair cut close to his scalp, and yellowed-eyes bright with blood lust danced in front of her eyes. His thin lips were curved up into a cruel jack-o-lanterns smile. *He's another wolf.* Isiah hadn't been kidnapped; his contacts betrayed him.

"When the life leaves your body, your failings will guarantee our victory. Is the knowledge more painful than this?" A red-hot poker slid through the skin on his belly like it was melted butter. His mouth opened in a silent scream as he strained against his chains.

"Where's your pack now? Who's coming to save you?" a male baritone mocked cruelly. He lost consciousness and she knew peace.

"I will not allow you to continue this way."

"What choice is there?" she asked tiredly.

"Whatever it takes. You have two choices. You come to us, or we come to you."

"I'm not in any shape—"

"Those are the terms, Joss."

Clenching her teeth, she balled her hands into a fist as the lingering tremors rocked her.

"I won't trade one jailer or another."

"I will always do what's necessary to protect you."

"Even I end up hating you or it?" she challenged.

"Yes, even then."

Angry, she pulled away from their connection. Unanswered questions filtered in. When he woke would she experience the same symptoms again? How could she hide this from the others? Should she? Isiah was in trouble. What would that information do to the pack? The Alpha had been on his best behavior so far. Could she handle him solo if he decided to go rogue? It'd be the perfect time to resume his leadership and remain a hero in the community's eyes. *I can't let that happen.*

Moving gingerly, she found herself free of the pain that had first woken her. Peering out of the window at the skyline just bleeding from deep blue to purple, she rose, hefting the weight of uncertainty on her shoulders. She'd spent the majority of her lifetime ignoring the situation that existed before her. The time of avoidance had passed. She needed answers and strategies in place. Lifting her chin, she retraced her steps to the shower, determined to be on the road before the sun rose. A true soldier didn't admit defeat before the battle.

Slipping the moon necklace that had once belonged to her father over her neck, she slipped the good luck talisman into her black sweater. He felt closer today. Winding the old, black scarf he'd given her years earlier around her neck for comfort, she slipped her feet into combat boots and tucked the dark jeans into her shoes. She laced them tight and wrapped the belief of her father and herself around her like armor. The blood of powerful wolves pumped through her veins and the mark of the fates declared her chosen.

It did no good to cower. Biting her tongue until it bled, remaining still and soft so she blended into the crowd had never stopped anything from happening. Destiny had declared her a moving cog in the wheel of change. It demanded her participation by any means necessary. Today she took up her sword and shield, bared her teeth and claws, and faced the war head-on. Slipping on her waist-length leather jacket, she grabbed her purse, and left the house, ignoring the eyes she could feel fixed on her.

She climbed into her car, and turned the key. *If you want me, you'll have to catch me first.* Slamming the car into reverse, she gunned the engine, letting her superior senses take over as she shot out of the driveway. As she wove along the dirt road, she opened up her engine. The scenery sped by, blurring as she barreled toward the front gate. She laughed as the guard on duty scrambled to start the opening mechanism on the gates when she didn't so much as slow down. The team assigned to trail her gave up on stealth. Their eyes glowed in the reflection of her taillights.

Clearing the half-open gate, she made a sharp right, taking the backroads that cut close to the human dwellings. They wouldn't risk discovery with daybreak so close. Laughing, she rolled down the windows and let the air flood in and remind her she was a child of the wild never meant to be tamed. They'd clipped her wings, placed her in a cage, bullied and pushed her to the breaking point, and yet still, she remained. Blurred vision alerted her to the tears slowly rolling down her face.

Allowing the saline to flow, she mourned for all of the things she'd lost and the person she'd never had a chance to be.

When she reached the cabin, her tears were dry, and the sun was high in the sky. Kazimir waited on the porch, leaned against a beam in a deceptively casual pose. The anger simmered inside of him like a boiled pot ready to spill over. Throwing her car into park, she unbuckled her seat belt and took a deep breath. She wouldn't be a pushover. There was far too much at stake. Bending to the will of another would be jumping from the frying pan and into the fire.

Squaring her shoulders, she held her head high as she slipped from the car and walked toward him with purpose. His eyebrows arched. He straightened to his full height and glided to the edge of the wooden deck.

They stopped inches from one another. Unsure how to begin the conversation, she froze.

"You have things you wish to say to me?"

Nodding her head, she cleared her throat. "We may be mated, but we do not own one another. There are no absolutes. Love should not be about control. I've seen what that does to people. I won't have any part of it."

His eyes bled red, and he growled in his throat. "You think you can escape me? You choose to deliver your Dear John in person?"

"I'm laying down my terms, vampire." She remained firm against the hurt battering against their bond. "It may go against your nature to temper emotions, but you're on new territory now. I'm a wolf. I'm wild and never to be tamed. If you try, you'll only push me further away."

Kazimir balled his fists at his side. "What is it you expect me to do?" His jaw twitched. "This is who I am."

"No. You've said yourself things are changing."

"You have no concept of how hard I work to keep my behavior acceptable for you. Every day that you return to a home where you're in danger goes against all of my instincts. I've lost a bit more of myself and my control as we wait in this ridiculous holding pattern. You finally admit to yourself that I am your mate, the one soul destined to accompany you for the rest of our lives, and in the same breath you lay down rules? Stipulations to what forces greater than us have crafted?"

His fangs elongated. Peeking from between his lips, they altered his speech. "Please tell me how? What must I do to please you, little sun? How should I ignore instincts bred into my very DNA?" The wave of angst and madness that swept over her made her gasp. "This is what I protect you from. The insanity I stave off because we are not properly connected. And yet it's not enough for you. You want me to comprise? What about you?"

Her lower lip trembled, and her legs weakened as she wilted under the onslaught of emotions battering her like a boat caught in a tropical storm. She clutched her heart and stumbled. His hand shot out, steadying her, and a mental wall rose, sealing her off from the chaos.

"I'm old. I can withstand a lot. I'm willing to give you the time you need to adjust and become comfortable with me. But I refuse to do this. To live out a bastardized version of what we're meant to be."

"I-I didn't know," she whispered. "Why wouldn't you tell me?"

"I know your past. I did not want you to feel pressured or pushed into making choices you might later regret."

"What are we going to do?"

He shook his head. "I don't have an answer for that yet."

"I can't let you continue like this."

He held up his hand. "I am fine. I've dealt with far worse. My intention was to protect you, but I see it's only led to misinformation." He shook his head.

"What else are you keeping from me?"

He glanced away.

"Kazimir."

"Our bond is unusual. Neither of us seem to have a choice in the matter. Normally we can choose to … sever the contract with the person."

"But not us?"

"I do not believe so."

"Which means?"

"It's possible I'd succumb to the blood lust." He paused. "Eventually."

She closed her eyes. Another complication she could little afford. "That's not happening," she stated bluntly.

"I cannot give you the reassurances you require because I myself am uncertain of the effects our mating will have on each of us."

"What about Nakeeta and Crewe?"

"We could speak with them, but she's a witch, and he's a vampire. It's not the same biology."

Biting the inside of her cheek, she nodded. "It's a risk I'm willing to take after my people are safe."

"You love them so much when they made your life a living hell?"

"I let my life become one. They're innocent bystanders, buying into a false prophet I help keep in power. By my calculations, I owe them a debt I can never fully repay."

"They're a funny thing, debts, or markers as we called them. One never knows when they'll be called in or the price they'll ask for. You should be careful you don't end up left with nothing to sustain you."

"What are you trying to say?"

"I am suggesting you examine your motivations. Saving them at any cost won't make up for all that was done for you. The hole inside will remain as dark and cavernous as it was before. The only way to fix it is from the inside out."

"Suddenly you're an expert on psychology?" she said skeptically, crossing her arms beneath her chest.

"No. But I know the darkness intimately." He frowned. "We'll find no resolution here. Let us relocate inside of the house. Nakeeta wishes to examine you." He stepped back and offered his hand, letting the disagreement disappear into the background. His smooth transition shocked her. She took his hand, and he helped her up the stairs. Studying the wood beneath their feet, she realized she had expected him to belittle and bully her into agreeing to his plan. *I have to stop waiting for him to act like those in White Creek.*

They entered the house, and Nakeeta strolled into the living room in black and red checkered flannel pajamas. Joss looked behind her for Crewe.

"He's still sleeping. Despite the recent changes, this isn't their usual time to be up."

"I will leave you ladies here for now. If you need me, I will be in my room." Kazimir bowed before he slunk away.

Too often, she forgot what it meant to be a vampire. All the times he appeared to her during the day was unnatural for him. He'd used magic, and his age to do that. *It must take a toll on him.*

"It's easy to forget what they are, but we shouldn't," Nakeeta said softly. "They sacrifice for us. Both of them are from a time before our own. When men were providers, fierce warriors, and the heads of their family. The phrase 'cut off your own nose to spite your face' comes to mind. They will always strive to give us what we need. It's our job to recognize what it costs them. In this way, we balance one another." Nakeeta sank down beside her on the couch. "I won't sit here and tell you a relationship between you will be easy. We're wired differently, and raised in different times that cause many of our beliefs to clash. It's a lot of work and compromise. I can say, it's one-hundred percent worth it. With Crewe, I'm becoming the best version of myself, and I know I can trust him with my life. It's not an experience I'm used to. I lived a solitary life the past few years before Crewe. I made some poor choices, and found myself mixed with dark magic."

Joss's jaw drop. "But you exude light."

"Now. It took me a long time to get here, and I'm sure this journey I was placed on and my bond with Crewe had a lot to do with it. Once the darkness is let in, it never fully goes away. It's like being a drug addict. You have a craving. It calls to you, seeks you out, and tempts you." Nakeeta shuddered. "The best way to fight that darkness is love. I'm surrounded by that now. We are a family, even if it's odd and at times slightly dysfunctional."

"Why are you telling me this?"

"We've all watched Kazimir struggle. Crewe and I share a familial bond, we feel his struggle and anguish. I told him to tell you. Stubborn ass," Nakeeta huffed.

"I've been doing this to him?"

"He did it to himself. The real question is now that you know, what do you plan to do about it?"

She shook her head. "I-I don't know." Sweat broke out on her brow and upper lip. Heat engulfed her face. She removed the scarf around her neck.

"Joss?" Nakeeta said softly.

"Is it suddenly hot in here?"

"No." Nakeeta's brown eyes narrowed. "This is not a human sickness. This is magical."

"What?" She smacked her lips, searching for moisture.

"Lay down." Nakeeta rose and hurried off, and Joss complied, suddenly weary. The room grew fuzzy, and her breathing grew labored. Her skin prickled as she was slowly submerged by the bond reaching out for her.

Her body jolted. Her vision blurred and refocused. The hard, cold slab of stone pressed against her bare back. She jerked in an attempt to free herself from the heavy manacles burning her skin and weighing her arms down at her side.

"All of this can end if you tell me what I want to know." The witch stood above Isiah like a Sith Lord, shocking him with a blast of green energy.

"Don't pay attention to what's happening with my body."

The masculine voice was thready and weak.

"*Isiah!*"

"*I hide here in our bond to find relief. I don't mean to keep pulling you in, but my mental walls are slowly eroding away. Eventually, my control will fail.*"

"*Where are you?*" she asked.

"*I don't know. They shoved a black bag over my head and encased me in a magical prison. I couldn't sense anything.*"

"*What do you want me to do?*"

Static erupted in her brain.

"*Get. Wooolves.*"

"*What? I don't understand what you mean.*"

"*Go now!*" He shoved her away from their bond. Twitching, she came back to herself in the tiny cabin, surrounded by familiar faces, along with a few new ones.

Nakeeta wiped her brow with a cool washcloth. "I think she's back with us."

"Get wolves," she croaked.

"What are you talking about, solynshka?" Kaz knelt beside her, brushing her damp hair back from her face.

"Isiah said I needed to get wolves. I'm not sure what he meant." She shook her head.

"Rest."

"No, there's no time for that." She shook her head furiously.

"How do we stop this, Keeta?" Kaz asked.

"No." Joss sat up. "This is a way to get an advantage over our enemies. We can't afford to lose that. We're still trying to figure out the nuances of the spell. We're not ready. An edge is exactly what we need."

"She's right," Cyprian said.

"Words I never thought I'd hear from you," Joss mumbled.

"Count yourself lucky then, hmm?" he drawled.

She snorted.

"How long can she withstand this?" Kazimir asked, words clipped.

"I'm not sure. I can do things to help sustain her, but she will grow weaker."

"Give me the time to find out something we can use against them," Joss pleaded.

"Do what you can, Keeta. I need air." He stood smoothly and flashed away.

"I'm going to check on him," Crewe said softly before following his brother out of the cabin.

"How long was I out?" Joss asked softly.

"Hours."

"My pack is going to kill me."

Nakeeta pressed a staying hand on her shoulder. "You can't leave. We have much to do yet. Everyone else, give us space."

She watched curiously as the purple-haired vampire, brunette man, and blond mohawked man who felt like witches slipped away.

"You'll meet Cian, Silver, and Reagan later. For now, I need you to close your eyes and block out everything else. I need to get you in tune with your body again. Isiah may borrow your strength and your headspace, but it's yours. Your bond is wild and ungrounded. It's why neither of you can control it. The two of you don't see eye to eye."

"That's putting it mildly. Even now, the only thing that keeps me from turning my back on him is our past and the fact that this is bigger than my vendetta."

"This is why you were chosen. You can see past the surface. Breathe with me."

She listened to Nakeeta's deep breaths in and out for counts of three. Following her example, she slipped into a meditative state.

"Now I want you to visualize the energy flowing through your body, from your crown on down. See the blood flowing through your veins, and the muscles that do the heavy lifting and the joints that flex. Imagine that powerful energy flowing into every part of you that makes you strong, increasing their size and efficiency." Nakeeta's voice held an almost hypnotic quality as she spoke. Joss's body tingled as the magic the witch wove begin to flow into her body, restoring and strengthening. Her blood fizzled like champagne as peace and joy spread up to her heart and mind. It took her a few moments to realize Nakeeta had finished casting.

Clear-minded for the first time in days, she opened her eyes.

"How do you feel?"

"Like I slept for a month."

Nakeeta chuckled. "That's good. Are you up for meeting the others I know are lurking just around the corner?" she asked, rolling her eyes.

"Should we wait for Kaz?"

Nakeeta paused. "No, let's give the two of them time to decompress. They understand each other after all of this time as brothers. Some days we need to hear harsh truths from those who've known us longest."

Pop. Pop. Tiny explosions sounded. Little balls of light appeared in the air, like mystical popcorn. They danced above their heads.

"What is this?" Joss whispered.

"Old magic. The book."

"It finally has more to say, non?" Cyprian asked.

Crewe appeared at Nakeeta's side. "Is it safe?"

"Yes."

"The book has a message to deliver. It wanted to get our attention," Rainer said as she swept in from the hallway. Her pixie haircut was wilder than usual, and her eyes glowed in an almost cat-like manner.

"How do you know?" Cyprian asked.

"My ancestor, Blythe, came to me in a dream. The powers that be are displeased with us. We're wasting time we don't have."

"Opposed to doing what, Rain?" Kaz asked as he perched on the side of the couch in the spot Nakeeta vacated.

"Learning how to come together as one," Rainier said.

"How do you propose we do that, petite?" Cyprian asked.

"Wait and see."

The popping continued, and the small lights filled the room, growing brighter and brighter, as they moved faster and faster, turning from gold to red to a brilliant blue. A loud boom sounded. The room shook when the lights exploded. Her stomach bottomed out as air rushed past her face. She landed in a heap of limbs on a firm surface.

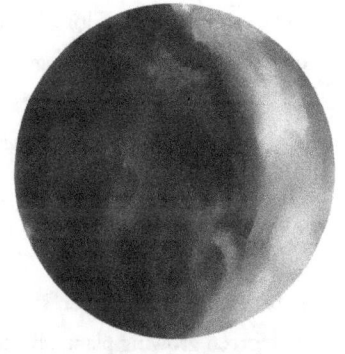

Chapter Twelve

A PURPLE LIGHT THE SIZE of a soccer ball flickered to life, illuminating their surroundings. She lay beneath Kazimir who rested heavily on top of her, far too still and cool. The light grew brighter. Joss flinched and braced herself for another assault by light.

"It's okay. I'm controlling this one." Joss turned her head and found Nakeeta in a similar situation with Crewe. Their men protected them with their own bodies.

"Where are we?"

"I have no clue." Nakeeta carefully eased Crewe off her smaller frame, and Joss did the same with Kaz.

"Are they okay?" Joss asked shakily.

"Yes, this is the state they used to assume once the sun rose. It's a sort of death, but it's not permanent."

"Are you sure?" Joss croaked.

"Reach out for him with your mind."

Tugging at their bond, she felt him, muffled as though he were in a deep sleep. Exhaling, she slowed her racing heart. Tilting her head back she sniffed. The overpowering scent of earth, damp, and the lingering scent of decay gave no hint to their whereabouts.

"What do you smell?" Nakeeta asked as she slowly spun, taking in the large cavern.

"Earth, dampness, and people, though they're long passed away."

"You are in the Ciur-Izbuc Cave in Romania, where all of your people originated at one point." A brown-skinned woman strolled toward them. Her long hair was an array of rich green growing plants. Butterflies perched on the hair at her temples and along her arms. A gentle white glow surrounded her long gown. Joss couldn't help but believe she was in the presence of royalty.

Nakeeta knelt. "Earth Mother."

"You know who this is?" Joss whispered.

"She's the mother of all life."

"I have been known by many names: Earth Woman. Mother Nature. Crow Mother. From the beginning, I've been by your side as you struggled into being, and began to grow. You've done wondrous, terrible things to each other." She shook her head sadly. The maternal voice made Joss want to weep.

"We're sorry, Mother. We know that we aren't worthy to be in your presence."

"Rise. I don't require subservience. I need you to fight. This world wasn't meant to be encased in darkness. The dark needs the light, like the masculine needs the feminine. It's the way of things. Have you not noticed I placed you in pairs?" She gestured toward Crewe and Kaz who lay on the ground.

"Rainer is alone," Nakeeta stated.

"For now," Earth Mother answered cryptically.

"Where is she?" Joss asked.

"Where she needs to be," Earth Mother said with a smile.

Nakeeta shook her head, her brow furrowed. "I don't understand, why have you brought us here, Mother?"

"To make you understand. It's about the whole. The group. The pack. Do you see?" She cupped her brown hands together, and large, vibrant magenta blooms sprung forth, giving off an exotic scent. "Little things must all come together to produce a blossom. Rain, sun, soil, and temperature. There's a delicate balance to maintain a healthy life. Your balance was broken long ago, and what you see is decay." The flower withered, falling in onto itself as it turned brown. "Mutated." The slimy brown lump struggled to reform, sprouting crooked leaves, and a sickly green petal as it became a mockery of its original form. "You've been sick for so long. You trust it's the proper way to be." Tiny rivers ran down her face. "All of you were once attuned to the earth, and part of a bigger family. Returning to that system in this modern age is the only option for continued survival."

"After all of the harm we've done to one another, do you really believe this is possible?" Joss asked, astounded.

"I've seen the world ravaged and reinvented many times. There's little that isn't possible."

"How, Mother?" Nakeeta asked.

"With the one thing everyone understands. Power. Inside each of you resides the power of creation." She walked toward Nakeeta. "I will fix what's been warped inside of you. Rise, daughter, and receive your birthright." Nakeeta stood, and Earth Mother kissed her forehead. Tulips sprung up from the ground beneath Nakeeta's feet. A cocoon of violet power surrounded her, blocking her body from view.

Whining in the back of her throat, Joss shifted her weight. Attacking this powerful being would mean certain death.

"Relax, little wolf. She is merely changing like a caterpillar does before it becomes a butterfly. You are not yet whole. There are fragmented pieces inside of you that need to be joined."

Joss grimaced.

"Do you know of what I speak?"

"I think so?" she whispered, glancing down at Kaz.

"No, daughter. Both."

"Both?" Her words were stolen as Earth Mother delivered a swift kiss to her forehead. The world spun around her "When you are whole, you will know what to do."

Joy bubbled up inside of her. Peaceful, she closed her eyes and surrendered. *Surely, death could never feel so good.*

THE COLD WEATHER SEEPED IN through her wet clothes, and she opened her eyes. Sitting up, she found herself alone in the midst of a snowstorm. White flakes drifted down, obscuring her vision. Blinking, she shook the clumped, frozen water from her lashes. She sniffed, detecting the scent of freshly fallen snow, pine needles, and the wild. *Where am I?* Standing, she shook her body like a wet dog and noted the stiffness of her limbs. *I've been here for a while.* As she scanned the white landscape lined with trees for signs of the others, she came up empty-handed. Stepping forward, she sank into three-inches of snow.

Plodding forward, she felt her senses tingle. There was something out there in the distance, watching her. She didn't recognize this part of the forest. Craning her neck, she took in the night sky. She found Polaris and re-oriented herself, drawing a line to the horizon. *North, south, east, west.* Trusting her gut, she walked north. The undeniable feeling of eyes increased as she walked. Her ears twitched, as she strained to hear.

Caw. The unnatural cry of a bird broke through the stillness. Increasing her speed, she searched out the sound. Lifting her gaze, she saw a large raven. Understanding struck.

"Are you my guide?"

Caw.

"I'm taking that as a yes."

The bird launched itself from the branch, and she followed the black streak through the night. Wolves and ravens had a special relationship in the wild. They could even mimic wolves to alert them to meals. Jumping over a fallen log, she trusted in the knowledge she gained as the woods closed in around her, and she lost her sense of direction. A low snarl came from the right. Increasing her speed, she continued to follow the raven. The sounds of paws on snow alerted her to trackers. Unsure if they were a friend or foe, she moved in a zig-zag pattern, becoming a more difficult target to capture.

Magic prickled along her nerves. Howls broke out around her. *I'm surrounded.* Breathing heavily, she planted her feet. Desperate, her eyes searched for leverage. She could go up into the trees. In human form, she could climb higher than a wolf. But it would leave her a sitting a duck. Yellow eyes glowed in the distance, moving closer. A massive wolf stalked forward, flanked by eight followers, four on either side. The intensity of the Alpha stole her breath. She'd never felt such raw power. Their midnight coats marked them as the wolves of legend.

Outnumbered, and in need of their help, she made the choice to kneel. Bowing her head in submission, she spoke. "The ancestors have sent me here in search of assistance. You know well what's gone on in White Creek. I'm doing everything to stop them, and repair the damage done long ago by Seke. There are many of us who've joined forces to right the wrongs, and return the natural balance."

The smaller wolf to the Alpha's right huffed in disbelief. The wolf shimmered and shifted to reveal an Amazon with a riot of bone-straight, black hair plaited in one braid, high cheekbones, and a slender nose that boasted her Native American ancestry. A doeskin dress with fringe and high moccasins adorned her feet.

"You come to ask us for help?" She scowled, baring her teeth. "We've watched you and your people make a mockery of our beliefs, desecrating our land with your rituals, and poisoning other wolves with your lies."

"I didn't have a choice—"

"There is always a choice," she snapped.

Joss bowed her head, shamed by the truth in the woman's words. "What would you do to save the life of one you loved?" Joss asked hoarsely. The conviction in the beautiful warrior's words made her feel small and near-sighted.

"We all return to the great spirit eventually. I would never sell my soul for them. You want to speak with the elders of my pack? Then you must earn the right in combat."

Caw. Caw. Ravens flew in, circling overhead, watchers to the unfolding events.

"So be it." Joss shifted, ignoring the fact that the woman dwarfed her. This must be what her kind had once looked like, more Dire Wolf than anything else. The woman circled her, eyes burning with anger. Her ears went back, and she lunged. Using her size to her advantage, Joss dodged her and ran away, nipping at her flank. The wolf's paw caught Joss's side, tossing her across the circle created by the Native pack like a rag doll. Her flesh stung where the claws had raked into her. The she-wolf licked her lips, pleased at the taste of Joss's blood. Furious, Joss focused in on the bigger wolf. Running toward her, she zig-zagged, forcing her to move her heavier bulk to keep Joss in her sight. Rising onto her hind legs, Joss rocketed up, raking her claws across the bigger wolf's face. The she-wolf brought her large paw down on her neck, pinning Joss to the ground. Her teeth snapped a hair's breadth from her face.

Freed from the heavy heaviness, Joss blinked, stunned to find herself protected by Kaz and Cyprian of all people. Staring down the Alpha, Kaz crouched down, ready to defend his position. The she-wolf grunted. Rising on all fours, she shook her head, clearly dazed. Three ravens descended, perching on Joss, Cyprian, and Kaz's shoulders. The Alpha morphed into a tall brown-skinned man, with sleek black hair adorned with a feathered headpiece.

"Enough." The Alpha raised his hand. "Clearly the ancestors have spoken. We must listen."

He stared down the she-wolf who dropped her head. "I am Mingan, Alpha of this pack. I grant you safe passage into our village."

"You doubt him?" Koko asked, offended.

"You will forgive me if I'm cautious. We're clearly outnumbered," Kaz said calmly as he helped Joss to her feet.

"You have my word, vampire. You'll forgive the less than hospitable welcome. Others have come seeking our power," Mingan explained.

Kaz mulled the words over. "I'm Kazimir, and this is my mate, Joss, and brother, Cyprian."

"Why are we different?" Cyprian asked.

"None have had the raven's approval, nor have they shared the lifemate bond. I've never seen one between a wolf and a vampire before," Mingan marveled. "This is my mate and second Alpha, Koko." The woman nodded curtly. "I'll introduce the others around the fire."

"Allow me to tend to my mate first," Kaz demanded.

Mingan nodded. "Of course."

Joss watched as Kaz bit into his wrist and held it up. The thought of drinking his blood squeed her out, but her body ached, and the wound on her side continued to dribble blood. Determined to create a united front, she accepted his wrist and brought it to her lips. He tasted like caramel and … butterscotch? Sweet, savory, and warm, he slid down her throat, chasing away the cold. Her body temperature rose, and her skin began to knit itself back together. After a few more pulls from his wrist, his bites healed, and she pulled away, licking her lips. The intimate exchange had been oddly pleasant.

"*Not so bad, was it, little sun?*"

"*No.*"

"We're ready. Cyprian? Tell the others we're fine?" Kaz asked.

Cyprian bowed and darted off, quickly swallowed up by the snow and lost to the white landscape. He was our backup plan. The assurance that the cavalry would be ready and waiting.

"I must ask, how did you manage to find this place? It's sacred, and heavily protected by magic," Mingan stated.

"Oh. I-I don't know. I woke up here after being transported here by … well, the Earth Mother."

The pack tensed. "Lies," Koko hissed. "She'd never show herself to one such as you."

"And yet she did." Kaz's blood unlocked a door inside of her. Her fingertips tingled. Wiggling them, she gasped when the ground thawed, and flowers bloomed.

"She speaks the truth," a pack member whispered.

"Why you?" Koko said.

"Because she is the wolf we've been waiting for, Koko. Show her the respect she's due," the Alpha cautioned.

"We all know where she's from," Koko muttered.

"But you don't know *me*," Joss said quietly. "I didn't want to be in that compound, but my mother brought me when I was nine after my father died, and the rest is history. The pack magic keeps her cancer at bay. It's kept me there far longer than I care to admit. Now I understand, what we're facing is bigger than one person. Than all of us. I saw the future if we don't fix this. It's not one any of us want."

The words lingered between them as they walked deeper into the woods. They came to a frozen lake.

"This will require trust," Mingan cautioned. Holding Koko's hands, he stepped onto the icy surface. Halfway across, they disappeared.

"Magic," Joss whispered, remembering Earth Woman's words. *We all come from magic.* These wolves maintained more of what was lost. Clasping hands, Kaz and Joss stood tall as they followed in the Alpha and his mate's footsteps. Pressure surrounded them when they walked through to a tiny village, bustling with life. A grouping of teepees were arranged, spread out to provide privacy, but keep safety in numbers. Cooking fires were lit. Women roasted meat on them or boiled it in a bowl made of stone. It as a living history lesson. Once the people caught sight of them, they moved into their teepees. A few children stared in awe, before being hurried inside of the relative safety of their buckskin.

"*I'm assuming they do not receive many visitors.*"

Joss smiled at Kaz's wry response.

"*I guess not. Especially ones with our skin tone.*" The history that existed between them saddened her. They'd learned nothing. Even among the supernatural they warred over differences.

"*I do not blame them for being afraid of outsiders. Too many times we fear what we cannot understand.*"

"*But we have a chance to change that now, right? That's what all this is about?*"

"*I hope so, Joss.*"

They paused in front of a large teepee with markings on it.

"This is our meeting lodge. Please enter, and join us in smoking the peace pipe as we ask the ancestors to join us and help guide our decisions." Mingan lifted the flap on the dwelling and allowed them to enter. The scent of sage and sweet grass greeted them in the warm space. Directed to sit on a pile of soft furs, they were joined by Mingan, Koko, and two other warriors.

"There are my betas, Rowtag and Apisi."

Rowtag grabbed a hide drum, and Apisi handed Mingan a beautifully carved wooden pipe. Bleached white buckskin decorated with a blue white and yellow beaded design wrapped around the front and back ends. Fringe hung down from each decorative piece. Rowtag began to drum and Apisi joined him in singing in their native language.

"First I'll fill the pipe with tobacco, and we offer them to Mother Earth and Father Sky, acknowledging the four directions." We watched as he retrieved a small, brown bag and pulled out raw tobacco. He filled the pipe and began to offer it up in the directions, speaking in his native tongue. A feeling of reverence and energy began to fill the space.

"We ask that you come to us, ancestors, and guide us in the way we should go. Help us form bonds of trust that will last a lifetime and help us return to the way things were meant to be." Mingan placed the pipe to his lips and drew the smoke in. He blew the smoke out slowly, and it curled up in the air wildly. The space became smaller as if it was filling up with people who could not be seen. Her eyes darted around wildly.

"*Do you feel that?*" Joss asked Kaz.

"*Yes.*"

He handed the pipe over to Koko who did the same. With every person who held the pipe, a greater sense of peace and rightness settled over Joss. She closed her eyes, relaxing as a feeling of oneness settled in. Apisi handed her the pipe. Taking the smoke into her mouth, she exhaled and passed it on to Kaz. The rhythmic drumming placed her in a semi-trance.

A flash of Isiah being submerged in wolfsbane-laden water made her cringe. Gritting his teeth, he refused to agree to lead them back into the compound. They wanted him to be a Trojan Horse.

"If you won't lead us, you will tell us the secrets to your boundaries." They dunked his head again. He struggled. They pulled him up, and he gasped for breath. Red welts and boils covered his face.

Her heart ached.

"I don't know how you're managing to hold out, but rest assured, I will break you," the man snarled.

Isiah was placed back under water. Diving into their connection, she fed him the peace generated during the ceremony.

The break from the pain allowed Isiah to focus in on her. "*They're coming soon, Joss. I can't hold them here much longer. They want the advantage of surprise, but they'll settle with using brute strength if they have to. Patience is wearing thin.*"

"How long do we have?" she asked.

"*A few days at most.*"

She shook her head. They weren't ready. "Where are you? We need to get you out."

His sorrow assaulted her like a pungent order. "*No, this is my burden to bare. She showed me how wrong I was.*"

"Who?"

His pain leaked into their bond.

"You have to go now. Tell the others to be ready."

Their link cut out and she blinked.

"Where were you just now?" Koko asked suspiciously.

"With my brother, we share a bond." The half-lie rolled off her tongue with ease. "He's been captured. He says the enemy will be coming in a few days."

"You speak of the Alpha's son? He's not to be trusted," Koko snarled.

"And yet, he continues to be tortured because he won't lead them to our pack."

"Everyone has their breaking point," Koko sniffed.

"This is a place for peace," Mingan reminded them.

Returning to their respective corners, the women shut their mouths.

"We have to complete the spell," Joss said. "That's why we came. We haven't been able to figure it out on our own, and the spirits showed me this pack could help."

The four pack members exchanged a look.

"We know what you need." Mingan stood and walked to the corner of the te-pee, and reached beneath a pile of blankets. A yellowed leather bag that had once been brown was brought back to the fire. Reaching inside, he took out a stone carving of a wolf. The black stone was speckled with splashes of white and splotches of tan.

"The pack stone has been passed down from generation to generation as we waited for the wolf who walked the path between all. That is you, Joss."

"Are you sure?" she asked shakily.

"Hold it in your palm, and we'll see," Koko challenged.

Joss turned to Kaz who nodded his head.

Controlling her fear, she held out her hand, palm up, and met Koko's gaze. Mingan placed the smooth stone in her hand, and she held her breath. Her heart plummeted. Nothing. Panicked, she glanced at Kaz. He placed a hand on her shoulder, and the stone glowed a brilliant amber. It pulsed, reminding her of the book's light display.

"What do we do with it, Mingan?" she whispered.

"That is up to you to decide, She Who Walks Between," he replied with a smile.

"Will you fight with us?" Kaz asked.

"Yes. When the time comes. We've remained silent for long enough. This is our world we fight for, too, but you must agree to honor our privacy."

"We will do everything in our power to maintain your pack's way of life," Kaz said, as Joss nodded her agreement.

"Then it is settled. We prepare our people for war."

"We can't make battle decisions without speaking with the rest of our group. There are many of us who fight together … witches, wolves, and vampires. We understand the delicate balance must be kept," Kazimir said.

"She says they plan to come in a matter of days. You must rally as many as poss—"

Joss screamed and flopped onto the ground. A piece of her heart shattered as her link with her mother sent up an S.O.S. signal. Fear made her nauseous. She'd never experienced terror like that from her mother. Their bond remained, weakened and strained.

"Block him out, Joss," Kaz demanded.

"T-that wasn't from him. It's my mom." The blood drained from her face. *What would feel like that? Had they already invaded White Creek?*

"What's happening?" Mingan asked.

"I have to go. My mother's in trouble."

"Perhaps the war has already come to us. My pack will accompany you," Mingan announced.

"We have to get the others."

"I'm not waiting, Kaz. Call them, because I'm going." She took off from the teepee, transforming into a wolf without a thought. Her mother's anguished emotions echoed in her head with every mile she covered.

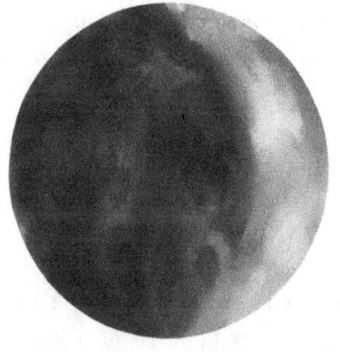

Chapter Thirteen

"Come out, come out, wherever you are!" The crazed screams from the Alpha pierced the night. She could sense her mother's pain increasing as she grew closer to the compound. The smell of burnt wood assaulted her. Plumes of smoke rose up into the sky. *What the hell is going on in there?* Rational thought escaped her. There was no hiding from the pack. They sensed her presence as she did theirs. Terror filled the air, sickening her. They didn't approve of the Alpha's choices. That scared her more than anything else. Skidding to a halt in front of the compound door, she waited for the others.

"This is your pack, Joss. What do you want us to do?" Mingan asked.

Standing tall, she gathered the pack magic inside of her. "We're going to overthrow that sadistic motherfucker."

She balled her fists, letting the energy flow to her hands. Thrusting them in front of her, a white stream of power flew forward, blowing the doors off the compound entrance. Joss walked over the twisted metal and surveyed the wasteland before her. Smoldering patches of burned grass littered the area. Bonfires rose high, turning faces sinister as they flickered. The dilated eyes of her people begged her silently for help. White robes were soaked red with blood. Her back tensed in sympathy as she recognized the whip marks used in the cleansing process.

"There she is. See how long she allowed you to suffer before she showed her treacherous face?" The mass of people blocked her view. Walking forward, they split down the middle. Her heart rose and stuck in her throat. Her mother lay on the ground, legs and arms tied down to stakes. Her back was a shredded red ribbon. The Alpha stood above her, with a maniacal gleam in his eyes.

"You have sullied us all. And now I must cleanse!" He held the whip up high and brought it down on her mother's back once more. She screamed, and the others cried out in sympathy

"You will stop this now." Joss ground the words out through her teeth.

"She's forgotten her place." He held the whip out toward her. "Look what she brings amongst our midst. And yet where is my son?" Spittle flew from his lips as he raved.

"Kidnapped!"

The crowd gasped.

"He contacted me through our link. I'm the only chance you have of finding him alive, so I suggest you put down the fucking whip."

"You think to threaten me?" His eyes bled to amber.

She allowed her eyes to glow in response. "No, I'm promising."

"Abomination!" he roared.

"Look at her eyes. They're purple."

Well, that's new.

"You've destroyed us all," the Alpha roared. "I won't allow it. One last sacrifice to Odin, one he won't ignore."

Is this where he finally offs himself? He reached into his robe and pulled out a dagger. The blade glinted in the moonlight. Surging forward, she changed her shape. The world moved in slow motion as he brought the blade down on her mother's tailbone. She leapt, aimed for his throat. A beta pummeled her side, knocking her off course, and her mother's screams rent the air. Shaking her head to clear her daze, she squared off with the light gray wolf with silver hairs. *John.* Snarling, she snapped her jaws. Lunging forward, another beta head-butted her side, blocking her from the Alpha. Their mission was to contain her.

Her mother's anguish increased. She glanced up to see the Alpha raise an ax.

"Kaz!"

John went flying, followed by his beta counterpart, Malcolm. Kaz crouched beside her, eyes red, and fangs distended.

"I need to get to my mother."

"Then you shall." They sped forward, pausing to battle wolves, dog-piling on top of Kazimir and trying to block her from the Alpha. She slashed with her claws, bit deeply with her fangs, and used her body to bulldoze through, backing Kaz every step of the way. The sickening sound of metal on skin, bone, and her mother's cries drove her to the brink of insanity. The moment her mother stopped moving, her brain broke. Her vision blurred, and her conscience receded to the background as power flowed into her body. The stone around her neck in a pouch grew hot. Her body changed once more, increasing in size. Muscles swelled and bulged, tearing as they reformed. Bones grew longer and heavier. She howled as anger, sorrow, and pain hit at once. Wolves joined in, echoing her. The Blackfoot pack was accepting her.

She stumbled forward, standing heads above the rest of her pack. This new form dwarfed the betas, who backed off, whimpering as they fell to their bellies. They were loyal, not stupid. This wasn't a battle they could win, and they knew the Alpha had gone too far. Blocking out her humanity, she walked forward, staring down the man whose hands were still red and slick from her mother's blood.

"I challenge you for the leadership of the White Creek pack."

Kaz moved to stand beside her.

"You can't interfere in this, Kaz."

"I understand." He battled with the warrior inside of him as the Blackfoot pack closed ranks around them.

Tension spread as the wolves waited for a response. The Alpha brought his ax down one last time, severing the backbone completely to create a blood eagle. Kicking her mother's body over, he exposed her organs. Her nostrils flared. Rage exploded inside of her, turning her vision red. Kaz's hand on her shoulder pinned her in place, keeping her from charging him.

"Win this for your mother."

Holding herself in check, she watched horrified as he dipped his fingers in the blood pooling around her body and painted a solid line across his face and around his eyes and two lines down his face on either side, bisecting his eyes. She pawed the ground, eager to draw blood for blood.

"I accept your challenge, Moon Maiden." As Alpha, he was already bigger than most in the pack, but he couldn't touch her new size. He changed into a fierce silver wolf, still coated in the markings of her mother's blood. The scent muddled her brain, making it hard to think straight.

"He's doing everything he can to distract you. Don't let him. Fight smart, and when you see your opening, show him no mercy."

Kaz's level-headed voice kept her from losing herself to grief.

"Do not let him control this fight. Make the first move."

Trotting over, she reared onto her back legs. The Alpha met her as they batted each other with their powerful paws. She sank her claws into his face, and he returned the favor, grazing her shoulder before they returned to all fours. Their mouths nipped at each other's neck. She flung her larger arm over his neck and sank her teeth into his flesh. His blood flooded into her mouth. He bucked her off, snarling. His breath puffed into clouds, and his eyes flashed a dark gold. She licked her lips, mocking him.

Body stiffening, he prepared to jump to her left. She feigned to the right, and he faked her out, pinning her to the ground. His claws dug into her shoulders. She yelped, scrambling to get her legs underneath her. Delivering a blow to his under belly, she thrust him off her. He ripped free from her, taking flesh. Blood sprayed through the air and settled on the white layer covering the ground. Ignoring the pain, she circled him, hungry for her pound of flesh.

The Alpha reared up on his hind legs, and she struck, clamping down on his left leg. Her teeth bit through to the bone. She jerked. *Crack.* His leg snapped. He dug his razor-sharp claws into her flank and dragged them up her body as he went down. Yelping, she shook him off. Blood welled up from her wounds, and exhaustion threatened. Hobbling, he continued to track her slowed movements. They were both injured, but neither planned to give up. The wolves howled. Kaz opened their link, infusing her with his energy. She stood taller, preparing for the last strike.

Watching the Alpha's every move like a snake charmer, she waited. Driving forward, he came at her. One-hundred and fifty pounds of silver furred muscle pounded. She remained still, waiting, waiting. At the last moment, she launched herself up and locked onto his neck. Sinking her teeth in, she set her jaw. He bucked, pummeling her body, and sinking his nails into her flesh. She hung on like a bull rider. His spicy, hot blood flowed into her mouth and onto her skin. Closing her eyes, she remembered the way her mother looked, life seeping out of her, the bite of the whip as he cleansed her growing up, and the way he broke Isiah. They collapsed together on the ground in a heap. Days could've passed by as she drifted in and out of consciousness.

"Let go. He's gone, Joss."

She pried her jaws apart and rose shakily to her feet. A wave of movement swept through the crowd as the community shifted and lay on their bellies in submission. Limping over to her mother, she licked her face, threw back her head, and released a mournful howl. *I'm an orphan.* Dropping her head, she swayed as the blood loss caught up with her.

"And yet, you will never be alone." Kazimir appeared beside her. The wolves growled. Eyes gleamed in the darkness. An unsettling mix of confusion, mistrust, and anger filled her nostrils. The betas stood together, uncertain. Ignoring the exhaustion setting into her battered and bleeding body, she waited. The betas didn't disappoint. John rocketed toward her, a gray missile intent on harm. Malcolm followed suit. Kazimir caught Malcolm by the throat, and she knocked John down with a well-aimed blow to the face. Landing in the snow, hard, he whimpered. Lumbering to his feet, he shook his head back and forth and crouched.

Malcolm lost consciousness from lack of oxygen and dangled in Kaz's hold like a limp rag.

The crowd shifted restlessly.

"Let Malcolm go."

Kazimir dumped the wolf unceremoniously onto the ground.

Forcing her body to shift, she stood.

"This is my mate. You will show him the respect due to that of the Alpha's chosen. If anyone wishes to challenge me for my position, come forth now. I'll show you as much compassion as I did Ian." Her voice boomed over the crowd. Lightning cracked in the sky. The wind stirred as snow began to fall. Her hair whipped in the wind, flying out behind her like a banner.

"I am Joss Weber. Your Moon Maid, and the new Alpha of this pack. Obey me or suffer my wrath. I will rule justly. There will be many changes, but I promise, they'll be for the better. The wolves you see before me are allies. The legendary Blackfoot pack has agreed to stand beside us in the upcoming battle. Ian had one thing right. We are facing a time of change. I intend to do what I was born to—make sure we're on the right side. The White Creek pack is done being out here isolated like sitting ducks. I plan to lead the charge on our enemies and rescue Isiah."

Grumblings rose through the crowd. Sending forth her power, she called them all to change. Furry shapes burst forth as they hit their knees. She couldn't afford to be timid.

"Go back to your homes, treat your wounds, rest, and be ready. I will prepare my mother's body for a proper funeral. You all owe her a debt of gratitude. One I will never allow any of you to forget." She balled her fist and fought down the urge to sway. "Leave me." They scurried away like the lemmings they'd become under Ian's rule. *I can't fix everything in one day. Right now, my mind must be set on survival.*

Leaning heavily on Kazimir she blinked, seeing spots.

"You need to take my blood before you pass out."

She allowed him to bite into his wrist and feed her. The minute his life-giving elixir hit her system, the wounds began to repair themselves from within. His caramel-like taste coated her tongue and throat, and she knew peace amidst the storm. With the Blackfoot pack on guard around them, Kazimir's people on scout outside, and the other part of her soul nourishing her, she was safe.

"How do we complete our bond?" Her mother's death blew a cavernous hole in her soul. Willingly walking around missing another piece wasn't a viable option.

"I must drink from you as well."

"Do it."

"I do not think now is the ideal time."

"I refuse to lose anyone else I love, Kazimir."

He blinked. *"When you've had your fill."*

She continued to drink, basking in his endless well of love and comfort. Full, she pulled back, licking her lips, and bared her neck. Swiftly he bit. A quick sting gave way to intense pleasure. Closing her eyes, she slipped away from the present and into him. The door between their minds was thrown open, and she knew all that he was. In the blink of an eye, she traversed his life, seeing things from his perspective, gaining his knowledge and knowing the full extent of his love. For him, she was color and light. He lived to see to her well-being and happiness. It was overwhelming and completely endearing.

They breathed as one—mind, body, and soul—as they became more than vampire and wolf.

A throat cleared.

"I know this moment was a long time coming, but I needed to see for myself you were okay."

"Brook." Turning, she threw herself into her friend's arms.

"I am so sorry, Joss."

Burying her face in her friend's neck, she inhaled the scent of a true packmate.

"There are no words I could say, so I won't even attempt it. I just wanted you to know I'm here. It's not much, but I'm here."

She hiccupped. "It's everything, Brook." They pulled apart, and she swiped at her face. Crying would come later; she couldn't afford to lose it now.

A male throat cleared.

Joss pulled back to a smiling Mingan.

"What would you have us do next, White Creek Alpha?"

"I have to take care of my mother. She deserves to be sent back to our ancestors." *At least now, you can be with father again.* Her gut churned. They'd been on abysmal terms, and she'd never get to apologize for her harsh words. Her vision wavered. *Did she know how much I loved her?* A lump of guilt sat heavily in her stomach.

"He deserves nothing. Leave his body to rot and become carrion devoured by predators."

"You will make a fine leader," Koko said.

The unexpected compliment stunned her.

"It'll be our honor to do this for you," Mingan promised.

"Somewhere he won't be found?"

"Take care of your mother. We will find you when this is finished, and we'll regroup," Mingan assured her.

"We thank you," Kaz said.

Forcing her stiff legs to move, she walked over to her mother who lay in the snow, a fallen angel, encircled by her own blood. Kneeling beside her, she closed her eyes and brushed the hair from her face. True to her word, Brook remained by her, silently lending support on her right side as Kaz did the same from her left.

Even in death, her mother's face held the horror she'd experienced in her final moments. Bowing her head, she bent down to her mother's ear. "I'm sorry, Mom. I thought we had more time to fix things between us. I know you did the best you were able to do. Rest well."

Shoving the crippling grief that threatened to crash over her like a wave to the back of her mind, she slid her arms under her mother's slight weight and lifted her up. The pack power made a task that would've been nearly impossible as easy as breathing.

A solemn silence fell over the somber group as they walked from the compound, deeper into the woods. They came to a stop beside the Sacred Dancing Lake where Joss and Brook gathered wood. The Blackfoot Pack stood a distance away, and Crew and Nakeeta approached.

"Please allow me to help you with this task."

Joss paused. "Okay." Her voice wavered. Nakeeta helped them arrange the wood for a bonfire.

"I want her to be free, distributed into the wind, the water, and the earth," Joss whispered. Her mother had been caught in a cage alongside her.

"I think it's beautiful. We are dust, and to dust we return," Nakeeta replied.

"After this, we'll finish the spell. I think I understand why it didn't work before. I hadn't reached my full potential." She turned to Brook. "I won't make you leave, but I'll warn you that this is incredibly dangerous."

"I learned tonight that everywhere is." Brook glanced down.

Joss reached out and grabbed her hand. "I promise you nothing like that will ever happen again."

"Why are you rescuing Isiah?" Brook questioned.

"Because I know he's a part of this. You were right. We're meant to do this together." Earth Mother had given her clarity and strength. Becoming Alpha had given her knowledge. All that the wolves before her knew, so did she.

Arranging her mother's body on top of the wood, Joss stepped back.

"Would you like me to do it with magic? I can make it … faster than the normal means," Nakeeta stated. They shared a unique sisterly bond since the cave.

"Please." Stepping back, she stood between the two women, three female warriors bidding their sister good-bye.

A brilliant violet streak came down, swallowing her mother's frame. Closing her eyes, she listened to the crackle of the wood as the empty shell that once housed her mother's spirit. *Be free, Mama.* The grief she'd held in broke over her like a dam, giving way, and she choked on her sobs as her shoulders shook. Her legs gave away, and she hit her knees. Covering her face, she purged. Kaz's strong arms wrapped around her, and he pulled her into his lap. Wrapping her arms around his broad chest, she burrowed her face into his neck.

"If I could take this pain from you, I would, my love." He rocked her back and forth, stroking her back until she was spent.

"Where did the others go?" she asked shakily.

"Back to the cabin." He kissed her forehead. "Do you need more time?"

"There will be time later." She sniffled. "We have other things to tend to." Leading meant setting personal issues aside. Ian had shown her everything she didn't want to be.

He brushed his thumb over her cheeks, clearing away the tears. "My beautiful mate, so strong even as her heart is breaking."

"I'm faking it until I make it, Kaz."

"No." He kissed her lips softly. "You underestimate your abilities."

"I feel like a child playing dress up. I never intended to be the pack Alpha." She shook her head, disgusted by the things she'd done. "I have blood on my hands and in my belly, and I forced them all to change, stealing away their will—"

He placed a finger against her lips. "All of which was necessary."

Her voice shook. "How can you be so sure?"

He placed a hand over her chest. "Your heart is pure, Joss. The strongest desire you have is for the betterment of your pack. Every choice you make reflects that. Don't let fear make you believe otherwise."

His words penetrated the slow creeping self-doubt that had begun to bind her like vines. Nodding, she pressed her forehead to his. "What would I do without you, Kaz?"

"You'll never have to find out. We should finish up here. The others are waiting at the cabin."

"What about the pack?"

Kaz paused. "Nakeeta has adjusted her magic to include them to our location."

Rising, she walked over to the pit of ashes. She bent, gripping a fistful. A gentle breeze blew through as the sky turned from deep blue to purple. The wind took the dust from her hand, and it danced on the current, carried away. Repeating the process until there was nothing left, and the magnificence of the sky resembled a watercolor, she knew she'd done the right thing. Moving to the lake, she rinsed her hands in the sacred waters. *Tell Daddy I said hi, Mom.*

"I'm ready." Lifting her, he used his speed to bring them to the cabin. The door opened, and a sleepy Rainer greeted them.

"Where are the others?" Kaz asked.

"They all sought out their beds. We settled Brook into the spare room. We plan to reconvene after a few hours of rest. You need time to recuperate."

"But they're coming."

"They won't arrive tomorrow. I'm certain of it." Rainer smiled and disappeared from the doorframe.

She'd never get used to the woman's uncanny knack of knowing.

"I need a shower." She sighed, too tired to contemplate it longer. Pausing in front of the door, she tilted her head. "You coming?"

Kaz grinned and nodded.

Turning on the shower, they stripped down like their clothes were on fire and stepped into the steamy stall. Soaping up her hands with the sandalwood body wash, she slowly learned the width of his shoulders and the breadth of his chest. His muscles twitched in response. Her knees grew weaker as he returned the favor, thumbing the rigid peaks of her breast. The water beat down on her back, easing the ache that had settled in as it warmed her from the inside out. Everything that happened left her cold. Her blood heated as he skimmed over her flesh, teasing as he cleansed and massaged tension from her body.

"I have to make sure you're clean."

"Yes, I can see you're very thorough."

His eyes flashed red, and his fans distended. "Your eyes are amethyst. You must like my attention to detail."

"I could say the same for you," she whispered, quivering as he knelt in front of her, kneading her calves, inches away from the aching core that demanded his attention. His nostrils flared, and he smirked up at her. The wicked vampire knew exactly what he was doing. She crooked her finger, and he complied, rising.

She cupped his face and brought his head down. Tracing his lips, she sought entrance to his mouth. He parted the perfectly formed lips, and she slipped her tongue inside.

"Remind me that good still exists, Kaz."

"As my mate requests."

Skimming his hand down her back, he cupped her thick globes as he took a breast into his mouth and sucked. She arched, seeking more. She buried her fingers in his hair, trying to force him closer. Chuckling, he pulled back, releasing her breast with a pop.

"No," she whimpered. He gently nipped her nipple, and she pressed her thighs together as her womb clenched. Soothing the sting with a swipe of his tongue, he gave its twin the same treatment. Molten lava simmered inside of her as he built her up. He spread her legs with his knee, brushing her slick core in the process. Her muscles flexed, and she trembled. Pausing, he tilted his head and repeated the move, pressing his knee into her. Her thighs came together, and her hips rocked as she sought friction.

"You smell so sweet, my little sun. I think it's time I experience how hot you burn." He eased her legs open. "Wrap your legs around me." He lifted her with one hand, and locked his gaze on hers. His hard length rubbed against her slick center. The pulse at the heart of her throbbed painfully in response.

"Are you ready?" he rasped.

"Yes," she replied shakily.

He eased inside and she gripped his shoulder as he worked his way deeper, devouring her lips. She could taste his desire and the sinfully addictive flavor that was his alone as her inner walls wrapped around his thick length. She flexed, and he moaned as filled her inch by inch. Fully seated, he nipped at her neck, and circled the rapid pulse in her neck with the tip of her tongue as he gave her time to adjust to him.

Burying her fingers in his thick hair, she shifted her hips. Taking the hint, he moved inside of her, increasing his speed.

"Oh, Jesus." They found a steady rhythm and the pressure built inside of her. His fangs brushed against her neck and she shuddered.

"Please," she whimpered, wanting to feel all of him at once.

He pierced her neck. The burst of pain, followed my intense pressure sent her over the edge. She screamed as she shook, tightening around him as he quickened his thrust. He swallowed her down, removing his fangs and licking the sensitive pinpricks to heal them shut. Launched headlong into a second peak, waves of bliss washed over her. He thrust once, twice, and exploded inside of her, shaking as he moaned her name. The beats of their hearts synched and she rested her head on his shoulders, basking in the peace that came with being one.

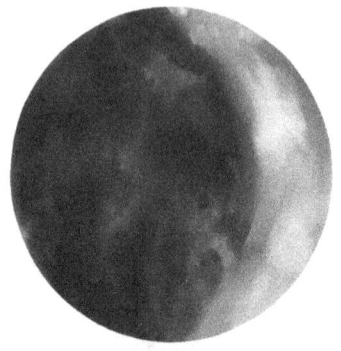

Chapter Fourteen

"THIS IS IT?" JOSS ASKED skeptically as they looked over the spell revealed by the stone. Scrawled in black ink on the back of the map taken from Nakeeta's chest, the simple four-line verse seemed incredibly underwhelming.

"Don't judge the spell by its content. This is blood magic," Nakeeta whispered reverently as she trailed her fingertips over the aged leather.

"Wait. We need to do a blood sacrifice?" Joss asked, disgusted as she thought back to the innocent lamb Ian slaughtered.

"No." Nakeeta clicked her tongue. "It requires the blood of the lines that were wronged. This is why we all had to be together and agree on how to proceed." Nakeeta looked up at the others. "I'm willing to conduct this, but I can't tell you what will happen as a result."

"I don't like the sound of that," Joss said.

Crewe scowled. "What other choice do we have?" he asked.

"None," Rainer replied.

The six of them gathered in a room they'd set up like a study with books and spell ingredients lining large oak shelves.

"The comet approaches swiftly. Our enemies plan to attack the final day. If we want to get the jump on them, we need to do this now." Rainer seemed more aware than she had previously. Her time with Earth Mother healed some of the damage her power had done over the years.

"None of us like this," Cyprian sighed. "But we are out of time."

Joss tilted her head and peered up at Kaz, who stood behind her chair. Meeting her gaze, he gave a curt nod. "I concede. We're out of options."

"What do we need to do?" Joss asked, throwing her lot in with the others.

Nakeeta walked over to the bookshelf and plucked a silver chalice. "We'll combine our blood, say the verses, and pray for the best."

Joss nodded her head. *In for a penny, in for a pound.*

The three women gathered in a circle, holding their wrists out to their vampire companions. A second later, their blood dripped together into the chalice.

> *By my own blood, I swear*
> *Fire, Earth, Water, Air*
> *Restore your children born of night*
> *Help make what is wrong right*

The ground moved beneath the floor. Pictures rattled against the walls, and books fell from shelves. Joss struggled to stand.

"Get outside," Nakeeta cried.

Kaz picked her up and rushed her to the back. The sky turned gray as clouds rolled in, blocking out the sun. Yellow streaks of lightning lit up the sky.

My God. What did we do? Snow fell in fat flurries that obscured her vision and stung her skin on contact. The miniature earthquake continued, and the wind whipped, tugging her hair. A round ball of ice made her flinch. The hail hit the ground with a heavy thud.

"It's the elements. Water, air, earth," Nakeeta yelled over the howling.

"What about—" Rainer began

A vicious flame burst through the circle, preceded by a scaly, black dragon with slit neon yellow eyes. Joss's jaw dropped. An elongated snout and the spikes along its spine gave it a sleek, wicked look. The form was translucent but no less dangerous as it circled them.

"The sky people are sending your guardians." They turned to see the Blackfoot pack walking toward them.

"We did a vision quest, and the ancestors spoke to us," Koko explained.

"The Above People were the first beings created, similar to the Christian's angels. They live in the sky, watching. It is rare that they become involved in what goes down below. If we can prove our worth, I believe they will join our fight. Being given such powerful spirit guides is an honor not many are granted," Mingan said as he bowed his head.

The dragon dove down, landing in the snow. It bowed its head, and Rainer walked forward. Cyprian grabbed her wrist. "It just breathed fire, petite."

"*Imig* won't hurt me." She smiled and tapped her temple. "He told me." She pressed her hand on to his shoulder. "You've spent years taking care of me. Let me return the favor now."

The dragon huffed impatiently, blowing smoke from its nostrils. Fearless, Cyprian stared down the golden-eyed beast.

"So, you've come to keep her safe then?" The dragon appeared to nod. "If you do not, I will find a way to kill you."

Its wide mouth opened in what looked like amusement.

Rainer walked over and stroked its snout. "We're going to be good friends. I can tell."

"Of course. The dragon symbolizes coming into power and magic."

A rumbling purr drew their gaze to the woods where a sleek black panther stalked forward. Its coat glistened in the sun. The dark eyes locked with Nakeeta's and it came to kneel before her.

"The panther is a symbol of feminine power and magic," Nakeeta whispered as she knelt. "Hello, my friend. Thank you for coming." She petted the large head gently, and the cat leaned into her caresses.

"And we have our final guardian," Kaz said, nudging Joss. She followed his gaze to the woods where a large gray and brown Dire Wolf padded toward them. Head held high, he was regal and muscular. She felt peace and protection flowing from him. Kneeling in the snow, she waited as he approached. The overwhelming sense of pack washed over her. She smiled as he nudged her shoulder with his muzzle. Lifting her hand, she giggled when his long tongue shot out to lick her. Like a powerful ghost, he had a foot in the spiritual world and one in the present. Almost solid, but not quite, he had an indescribable feeling.

"How are we supposed to prove our worth, Mingan? We need their help if we're going to win this." Joss scowled.

Mingan shook his head. "It's not for us to question the wisdom of the ancient ones."

The dragon flapped its wings and puffed smoke.

"What's wrong with it?" Cyprian asked.

"Him. He knows where the enemy is, and where Isiah is being held. He wants us to bring the fight to them."

The way she said Isiah's name gave Joss pause. It was as if she *knew* him. Frowning, she studied the elfin girl. Her amber eyes were clear and focused. She stood tall and sure. The look was new.

"Why does *he* care so much, Rainier?"

"Oui, please sure, Rain," Cyprian said suspiciously.

"For the same reason Cian avoids Brook," Rainer said softly.

"Don't drag me into your sibling drama," the blond, mohawked man crowed.

Joss turned to eye her friend. Brook's checks had turned suspiciously red, and she refused to meet her gaze. *What have I missed?*

"Surely not! A dog, Rain?"

"Do not call him that," Rain snapped, amber eyes flashing.

The puzzle pieces clicked to form an image that turned her stomach.

Mates? "You and Isiah?" Joss choked on the sentence, horrified. He'd eat her alive and still be hungry for more.

"Where do you think I went with Earth Mother? Have you heard him lately?"

"No." Joss shook her head.

"Because he has a new link now. The burden is shared, the way it was always meant to be." Rainer jutted out her chin, proudly. A tiny warrior, ready to stand her ground, and defend her beliefs. "You two are bound by pack and spirit. Nothing will change that. This is all that bond should have been. He understands that now."

"Does he?" Joss challenged. She'd seen the wolf fool people far savvier than this naïve seer.

"If this *wolf* keeps Rain from descending into madness, I don't care about much else," Cyprian said coolly, reminding her of what was at stake.

"You will," Brook promised.

"Soon no one will be what they once were. Holding on to the past will only lead to pain and confusion," Rainier said sadly.

"What do you see, Rain?" Nakeeta asked gently.

Rainer smiled. "I see many possibilities, but it's up to us to choose the final outcome."

"More mystery." Crewe spat the words out.

"If we're to leave soon, we must gather our forces," Kaz said. "Where are we going, Rainier?"

"To the Vortex. They're using a leyline to draw power for their own spell for power not too far from here."

"Jesus." Joss closed her eyes. "When do we leave?"

"Tonight. We'll need the power of the moon on our side," Rainer replied.

"I need to gather my pack," Joss said.

"You're not going alone," Kaz said.

She smiled wryly. "I wasn't planning to." They were a team.

"We meet back here before nightfall," Crewe said.

"I'll work on a spell for protection and strength," Nakeeta said with a nod.

"Be sure you rest, too," Joss said.

"I think we've all grown weary of the wait. I've rested long enough."

One way or another, this would all end soon. The words were unspoken but felt by everyone.

"We'll rally our people on this end as well. The groups have been scatted, but moving closer each day to remain safe," Crewe said.

"Until we meet again, brother." Kaz walked over, and they clasped forearms.

She turned to Brook. "Will you be one of my betas?"

Brook gasped. "I'd be honored."

"There's no one I'd trust more at my back," Joss admitted.

They clutched hands, resting their foreheads against one another as the took a deep breath.

"I always knew you would be the leader we needed." Brook's voice shook as her eyes grew glossy.

"Hold that thought." Pulling away, Joss wiped at her eyes with the back of her hand. "I have to see if I still have a pack."

Brook arched an eyebrow. "They're followers. Where else would they be?"

"Halfway to anywhere else by now?" Joss replied.

"No. They witnessed your power. If the last Alpha held them with little more than threats, prophecy, and brute force, you are already respected for your show of actions," Kaz said.

"I hope you're right. Because if not, I don't have much time to win them over."

❧ ❧

THE LINGERING STENCH OF BLOOD, death, terror, and pain tainted the air as she entered the main courtyard of the compound. Someone had rigged the gates, but no sentry stood guard. Patches of burned ground and red flecks of blood remained visible. The silence and lack of people gave the impression of a ghost town, abandoned and haunted by bad memories. The snow crunched beneath her boots as she walked, observing the area. She could sense her people in their homes, waiting for a sign or traveling as far away as fast as they could.

There was no anger toward those who fled. Once, she'd dreamed of being one of them. She paused in front of the grand home that had housed Ian and her mother. Her stomach soured at the bitter memories. She and Isiah had suffered here. Anger tore through her like a wild horse. The need to do something to distance herself from her past sparked her into action. Stalking up to the house, she picked up one of the rocks along the path and pitched it into the main window. It caused a small dent. Choosing another, she repeated the process like a pitcher practicing at spring camp. Each throw harder than the last.

The window gave. Holes in the perfect window into their lives. The stage set where lies played out. It crashed inward, falling into the snow and onto the gleaming wooden floors. Ignoring the curiosity and alarm from Kaz and Brook, she walked over to the mess, stepped inside, and continued to the kitchen. Turning on the gas stove, she moved to the fridge, took out a chilled bottle of wine, and dumped out the contents.

"Are you going to do what I think you are?" Brook asked.

"Burn this motherfucker down? Yes." She tossed the 'bless our home' tea towel in the sink and hurried to the wood carving station where she unearthed two full cans of turpentine.

"Are you sure you won't regret this later?" Brook asked.

Joss laughed. "Trust me. There's not a damn thing I want from this house. If I never returned to it, it would've been too soon. Not having to see it will be a relief." Memories of hours spent on her knees on the cold concrete basement floor beneath her feet beside Isiah when they were punished flickered in her mind. Not everything that sparkled was gold. Beneath his beautiful museum dedicated to Ian, awful things occurred. Ripping the tea towel in half, she dumped the can of turpentine onto the strip and filled the bottle. Shoving it into the bottle as a wick, she grabbed a lighter from beside the candles on the counter and walked out the way she came, trailing the remainder of the can onto the ground.

"For my first act as the new Alpha, I will topple the patriarchy … literally." She tossed the bottle into the house and watched as it exploded into a puddle of fire, spreading like a hungry beast as it lapped up the trail of accelerant she'd left behind.

"Well, that's one way to ensure your turn in office is fire," Brook croaked.

"Stay with me, girl. I haven't lost it yet."

Kaz squeezed her shoulder in support as they walked away. The loud boom and the crackling of wood as it burned signaled it was time to move onto her next phase. Throwing back her head, she howled. Opening her link to the pack for the second time, she called them to meet at the Alpha's house.

They showed up slowly, trickling in with huge eyes.

"If you want to leave, you know where the door is. I will not rule with fear or hold anyone against their will. That died with the old Alpha. His reign of terror, pain, and blood are over. It perishes in these flames." She gestured at the house behind her. "To protect what we've built here, a place to be ourselves, free and unburdened, we will have to fight. The world is nowhere near ready to know of our existence. If they did, this peaceful place we have the ability to create would be destroyed."

"How do you know?" a voice in the crowd shouted.

"Because I've seen what's coming. A supergroup of witches, werewolves, and vampires with one goal, ending the time of humans."

"Would it be so bad?"

"The magic they wield would change us on a molecular level. They are the ones responsible for the change in our shifting patterns, vampires who can walk in the day and a new biological disorder that slowly drives the most powerful of vampires insane. What they offer is chaos. A bleak existence where we'd struggle to survive, and ruin the world we're expected to live in during that process."

She ignored the conversations going on around them. "The only way we can win is to come together, not only with different packs, but witches, vampires, and any other manner of magical beings willing to fight beside us. The resistance has been forming, and they've asked us to join them. I plan to be there. You must choose for yourself."

"You come here with vampires and wolves we've never heard of, kill our old Alpha, and expect us to trust in you?" John asked. His dark gaze burned into us.

Her tattoo tingled in response to his aggression. "Have you all forgotten who I am? I am the Moon Maiden. I am meant to usher in change. Would you punish me because you don't like that transformation?" Her voice grew louder. "I have given my entire life to this pack. If you've ever held any faith or belief in me, trust me now."

"They need a sign to believe in, my love. Show them."

"How?"

"Can you feel the power inside of you? Use it."

"What I if I can't control it?"

"I will help you."

Releasing the power built up in her body, she gasped as the sky opened and a torrential downpour fell onto the house, contained to the area.

The pack gasped, taking a step away from her.

"You did this?" she asked Kaz.

"You did it. I simply distributed the power to the proper place."

"Jesus, Joss. You're glowing," Brook murmured, awed.

Joss glanced down to see her body engulfed in the same white light her tattoo had begun to give off.

"She's still the Moon Maiden. Look! What proof do you need?" Brook barked.

"I will do everything in my power to keep White Creek safe and build a pack we can all be proud of. But none of that can happen if we don't win the fight coming. They seek to harness the power of the comet to bring their will into existence. We can't let that happen. You have been trained for this from the moment White Creek came into existence. You're ready. Who will be brave enough to join me in this fight?'

A deafening roar spread through her pack, and her light shone brighter in response. This wasn't what she imagined. In a way, they'd all been wrong about what being Moon Maiden meant. This was a kind of change she could get behind. Perusing the crowd, she spotted the old Alpha, James. He'd always been trustworthy, kind, and level-headed. He'd also refrained from rising against her when she took on Ian.

"James," she barked.

"Yes, Alpha." He jogged over to her.

"Show Brook the ropes, and help organize our people to travel. I have a final task I need to attend to."

"Alone, Alpha?" he asked carefully.

She glanced at Kaz. "I won't be."

A war was fought and won in his expressions. "As you wish."

They needed every advantage they could get. Leaving without speaking to Kishi and reworking their agreement was a loose end she couldn't afford to leave untied. Taking off for the secluded cave, she gasped at the extra speed she's acquired. This was vampire speed, not wolf.

"What is this, Kaz?"

"You've picked up some of my qualities."

"What did you get?" she asked curiously.

"Other than a craving for rare meat, I'm uncertain."

The corners of her mouth tugged up at his dry humor. This must be the 'laugh to keep from crying' stage. Hesitating when she reached the entrance, she studied Kaz.

"I'm not sure how she'll respond to you."

"Knock, and we'll find out together." His tone told her he'd be staying put.

Tapping on the round wooden door, she waited. It swung inward, and the bronze goddess appeared in a silken black dress.

"You've been bussy." Her tongue drew out the s's.

"You know why I've come," Joss said, all business.

"I have a few thoughts. Vampire. You may enter my lair, but I caution you to be respectful."

Kaz inclined his head, and they stepped inside of the entryway.

"I'm not on a social visit, let's skip the tea and niceties."

Kishi gave a husky laugh. "Blunt. I appreciate that trait in a leader. Ask your questions."

"Do you plan to honor the previous agreement with the old Alpha?"

"Yes. Though I prefer a more cordial exchange."

"I would as well," Joss agreed. "Can you help us with this?"

"For a price," Kishi said.

"Name your price, enchantress." Kaz moved closer protectively.

Kishi's tongue flickered out, and the buttons on her tail rattled. "Freeeedom." She lingered on the e's.

"Define that word."

"To leave this accursed cave and move about the compound." It was a small price to pay for her help.

"In exchange for what?" Joss asked, keeping her face blank.

Kishi's spine stiffened, like a snake ready to strike. Kaz tensed beside her, nudging her body to the side as he placed his body between them.

"How could you help? I've encountered your kind before. You weave lies as easily as a spider spins a web."

Kishi hissed, revealing fangs dripping with venom.

"She and I have an understanding I would not jeopardize." Kish focused her gaze on Joss. "Even from here. I can lend my power to your cause should I so choose."

Ignoring the fight brewing, Joss swallowed hard. "Can we win this?"

Kishi's gaze grew unfocused. "Yesss. But you could lose it just as easily. The outcome is still too close to call."

Joss sighed. "Do what you can from your end. We'll rework the details of our agreement when I return."

"Wait." Kishi slithered off to a room beyond their vision.

"*You trust this one?*" Kaz asked, perplexed.

"*Yes. To a point.*"

Kishi returned with a glass vial of cloudy, white liquid. "This is my venom. You'll know what to do with it." She didn't dare think about why she might need such a deadly ingredient.

"Thank you, Kishi."

"I hope to see you soon, Alpha."

Me too. The sadness prevalent in Kishi's tone, haunted her as they retreated from the cave and raced back to the wolves waiting to be directed. She could not fail. It would render all of the sacrifices made on her behalf worthless. Her lower lip quivered as she thought of her mother.

Not now.

Beating back the distraction, she locked in on the next step, traveling back to the cabin with her pack and finding a temporary peace between the different factions that would arrive.

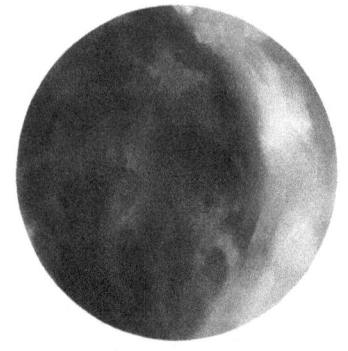

Chapter Fifteen

This is straight out of a horror movie. Joss watched as Nakeeta stirred the bubbling potion in the large, black cauldron they'd set over a fire. Steam crept over the sides and onto the ground, thinning into nothing as it flowed toward the massive crowd gathered around the cabin.

"Tonight, we will all become one pack. The potion I've made will connect us for the next forty-eight hours or so, combining the best of our powers. You'll be faster, stronger, and see into the spirit world. We have one mission. One purpose fuels us, and until we win or lose this battle, our loyalty belongs to each other." Nakeeta straightened. Purple energy crackled around her. "I am the one you've heard whispers about. The mother who houses wolf, witch, and vampire blood in my veins." Her panther paced in front of her, a semi-translucent behemoth with a wicked snarl. "Before clans, covens, packs, and grudges and grievances, we all come from one magical source. The bastardization, hate, and purposeful isolation that separated us have led us here on the cusp of a civil war, fighting for life as we know it. If we survive this, we have to do better moving forward." Nakeeta turned toward Joss, giving her the stage.

Clearing her throat, Joss gathered her courage. "I'm the Moon Maiden. The pack member of prophecy." Lifting her shirt, she bared her glowing tattoo. The wolves in the crowd murmured among themselves. "They've captured my pack mate, the other half of this prophecy. We need him back. The time for change has arrived." Letting the power wash over her, she transformed into her new form. Resurfacing as a Dire Wolf, she watched her counterpart spirit guide stalk in from the woods to stand beside her. She remained in her form for effect as Crew and Kaz took center stage.

"We've all lost loved ones to the virus ravaging our people. It all stems from the magical corruption. If we don't stop this now, we will die out." Crewe stared down the vampires in the crowd.

"I was infected with this virus. If it weren't for a dedicated group of witches and my mate," Kaz placed a hand on her shoulder, and the shock from the crowd nearly made her recoil, "I would not have survived. If for no other reason than self-preservation, we must join forces tonight. We're out of time and options."

Joss regained her shape and twined her fingers with Kaz. Nakeeta and Crewe mirrored them.

"If you're with us, come and drink. This is your final chance to retreat." Nakeeta's voice echoed like a loud clap of thunder.

A heartbeat passed as a few stragglers slunk into the night. Cian, Cyprian, and Rainer stepped forward, first in line to drink. Silver, Regan, and Brook followed them, with her pack close behind. Pride swelled the fast-pumping organ in her chest. Joss lifted her head and jutted out her chin. The others had the power of the vortex behind them. It'd take a miracle to gain the upper hand in the face of that. Still, her wolves came one by one to drink from the metal ladle. Her *pack* expanded rapidly, growing to encompass all who were assembled. The hairs on the back of her neck stood on end in response to the potent energy brewing.

A scream sliced through the air. The crowd dispersed as people stumbled back to get away from the vampire seizing on the ground. The pale man's face was a nauseating purple. Blood ran from the corners of his mouth and trailed down from his eyes like tears. Another body fell, this time a female witch, joining him in flailing, foaming at the mouth and bleeding.

Nakeeta offered the ladle to Crewe, who drank it himself. "Did I forget to mention the spell for traitors I slipped into this brew?" she asked innocently. Lifting the ladle, she smiled. "To your health." Joss and Kaz quickly drank their potion.

"You'd do well not to underestimate us," Joss drawled, smiling at Nakeeta who'd become her sister in arms connected by ancestry and camaraderie. More bodies fell. Their varying cries formed a symphony of pain and regret. When it grew silent, Nakeeta nodded her head.

"Now we're ready. Scouts, it's time.

"*Go with them.*" Joss spoke to her swiftest wolves who belonged to the small scouting party that trailed Imig, who led the group.

"Will they be discovered?" Joss asked.

"No. The spell I did is powerful, and Imig works on a spiritual plane. I think the Above People are protecting them. They are unlike anything I've ever encountered before," Nakeeta marveled.

"You're mated?" a gentle voice asked.

They turned to see an older, olive-skinned woman with stick-straight black hair threaded with silver. The hem of her colorful skirt dragged the ground as she approached them. Her aura announced her as a rather powerful witch.

"Yes, sister," Nakeeta said kindly, elbowing Crewe out of the way gently. "What's your name?"

"Zelda. I felt a pull to this area, and I came. I sensed things were off for some time. But I never imagined us all coming together this way. It's a sight for these old eyes. Brings me hope."

"You have no idea how much I needed to hear that right now, Zelda." Nakeeta squeezed her arm gently.

"How can you be mated?" The tow-haired youth with jade eyes eyed them suspiciously. He sniffed, inhaling their scents in an attempt to detect a lie.

Kaz growled. The youth flinched, stepping back.

"Kaz! He's just a kid."

"He's a punk who needs to learn a lesson."

"We can't explain it any more than the other odd things that have happened recently, but he's no stranger to me. I've dreamt of Kazimir since I was a small girl," Joss said kindly. Naturally, they were all going to be curious about the unusual pairings.

"Silly. We don't dream," a haughty brunette female vampire said. She stalked forward with a gentle sway of her full hips. The voluptuous, brown-skinned woman eyed them with disdain. "This is fanciful imaginings."

"No, Monica. I, too, shared this dream. Although, I didn't remember them consciously until after my run-in with the virus. It was all occurring in my subconscious."

Her brown eyes threatened to bulge out of her head. "You are saying we dream, but don't remember?"

Kaz shrug. "I can only share my own experience. Is it so odd to find we don't know everything?"

"I suppose not," she said quietly. "This has given me a lot to think on."

"Joss. Monica is one of our great minds. She helps record our evolution and history."

"I wonder if this phenomenon has occurred in others. It would bring so much hope to those of us who have yet to find mates. Perhaps we're simply looking in the wrong places." Her eyes gleamed with excitement.

"Monica, you help us get through this, and you can study us to your heart's content," Joss said.

"I believe I will hold you to that," Monica said as they forged a tentative step toward friendship.

The potential for new bridges to be built existed. It was a vast departure from the belief system she'd had pounded in her head growing up. Shaking her head to clear her scrambled brain, she continued to greet people with Kaz.

"Do you truly believe this camaraderie will remain after everything is said and done?" a bitter voice asked.

Joss turned to see almond-shaped brown eyes full of loathing aimed at her from underneath straight bangs. "I think it could be an excellent starting point."

"We weren't meant to live in harmony. Predators living too close will devour the prey. People go hungry, and everything starts to go downhill."

"Predator?" Joss tilted her head. "Correct me if I'm wrong, but aren't you a witch? What exactly do you hunt and eat?"

"Stupid people who bite off more than they can chew." She grinned maliciously.

"Sounds like a personal issue. Be us witches, vampires, wolves, or other, we choose the path we follow."

The woman snorted, crossing her arms under her leather vest-clad chest. "Are these the lies you're selling to get everyone to jump on your bandwagon?"

Who pissed in her Wheaties?

"I'm not a salesman, so I don't follow you." Joss squared her shoulders.

"I know your type … Alpha, arrogant, aggressive. You think you're the queen of the jungle and we're all your servants."

"You're mistaking me for a different Alpha," she said calmly.

"You might have all of these people fooled, but not me. I'll be watching you."

"How about you help instead?" Joss challenged.

"I don't think you want my kind of help." The wind whipped around her body.

"I don't even know your name, why would I want anything from someone who runs their mouth about things that show their ignorance? If you want a piece of me, find me when this is all over, and I'll be waiting. As of now, I don't have the energy to spare on an insignificant altercation."

"Bitch." The witch moved to strike, and Joss's spirit guide appeared before her, crouched and snarling.

"You're right, I am a female pack leader, but I prefer the term Alpha."

The witch stumbled back, startled. Despite their collaboration, old attitudes tended to die hard.

"*You were magnificent, little sun.*"

"*Is that attraction I hear?*" she teased.

"*I admire a strong woman.*"

"They've arrived," Rainer said.

Kaz wrapped an arm around her waist, and they moved toward the Seer.

"The guards are lined up around the perimeter of the Vortex. They have Isiah chained to a pole in the center of the Vortex. Witches ate chanting." Her voice shook. "He's wrapped in chains that burn his skin."

"Silver," Joss snarled.

Rainer's jaw quivered. "They're draining his life force, and feeding it into some sort of spell."

"My God, they mean to use him as a sacrifice to the leyline," Nakeeta said.

"Non. That will not be happening," Cyprian growled. He might not care about the *dog*, but his love for his surrogate sister, Rainer, was unparalleled.

"Tell us more about security," Crewe said.

Peering through the eyes of her pack, Joss looked on to the sight from a distance. Large wolves sat sentry beside bulk witches and others shifters. She was using her strength to hold the line.

"Do they sense you?" Nakeeta asked.

"No. I don't think they anticipate an aerial assault, and Imig isn't quite of this world."

"We're altering our plan of attack. I need all who can fly," Crewe barked the order, setting everyone into motion.

Tense, she watched from a distance while their aerial warriors lined up, ready for flight, as the rest of them stood downwind, anxious and ready for the signal to attack. In their claws, birds of prey clutched bottles full of magical warfare, a magical concoction set to ignite upon impact. She brushed shoulders with powerful vampires with the gift of flight and shapeshifting. Their aura made Joss's senses tingle. Kaz stood at her back, lending silent support and strength. Together, they'd changed each other on a cellular level. They were still learning the aftereffects. Already her senses were keener. Large hawks, eagles, falcons, and bats pushed up off the ground and followed Imig as he glided away.

Shifting her weight, restlessly, her muscles tensed as she waited. Everything hinged on the outcome tonight. The ground shook. Flashes of green lit up in the distance. The vampires took to the air. Her jaw dropped as she watched them float up into the air like superheroes. They followed just behind on foot. Chaos greeted them. The perimeter line was broken as guards swathed in green fire dropped to the ground, and ran. Chartreuse flames licked the ground. Witches surrounded the flares-ups, combating them with rain and spell work as they rushed forward through the weakened shields and spread out.

The five witches surrounding Isiah chanted faster. He hung from the pole limply. Their connection flickered. *We're losing him.* Dodging the two bear shifters locked in combat, she continued forward. Bodies dropped to the ground as vampires slashed throats. Blood sprayed over her black shirt when a vampire sank her teeth into the carotid artery of her enemy. Her wicked fangs gleamed in the moonlight. She shot toward Joss, who countered with equal speed.

Her red eyes narrowed. "Freak." She gurgled. A hand burst through her chest, holding her heart.

"Mate," Kazimir growled, pulling free. The woman's body slumped to the ground. Tackled from the side, Kaz hit the ground.

"You were the last person I expected to betray us," the stout man with dark hair and eyes snarled, snapping his teeth.

Kaz head-butted the man and kicked him in the stomach, sending him flying. "Piotr. This has been coming for a long time. I'm not surprised to see you on the wrong side."

"Why should we continue to hide when we're at the top of the food chain? Humans have had their time. It's ours now." Piotr climbed to his feet and crouched. He sped forward, and they came together, bodies unyielding and hard. The thunder-like crack made her flinch.

"*Go, little sun. I'll handle this.*" Kaz delivered a bone-crunching kick to Piotr's face. Piotr's body spun as he hit the ground. Recovering quickly, he lunged at Kaz, nails lengthened.

Going against her instincts, she pressed forward. Everywhere she looked, beings were locked in combat. Jumping over a bloody frame, she kept Isiah in her sight. A scaly, tan and brown lizard man with a distended snout jumped in her path. Sharp claws slashed at the air where she'd been standing milli-seconds before. His tail whipped out and caught her leg. She brought the heel off her opposite leg down sharply on his thick tail. He hissed, showing rows of sharp teeth as he released her. She'd heard of Komodo dragon shifters, but this was her first time seeing one.

Rolling away into a crouch, she extended a leg, balancing herself as she waited for his move. His tongue flicked out, tasting the air. Shifting into her form, she stood on her hind legs and swiped with her paw. The Komodo man returned the favor, slashing at her shoulder pad. The fur and skin split. She sank her teeth into his arm, and shook her head, jerking his arm from the socket. His tail caught her with a heavy thud. Pain exploded in her side. Backing up, she shook harder, bringing him onto the ground. She pounced, landing on his back and crushing his throat with her jaws. He bucked, throwing her off. Red blood flowed from his throat. Holding a hand to the wound, he backed away, retreating.

Once she lost him to the mayhem, she bounded forward. Her spirit guide appeared at her side, joining her as she made her way across the battlefield. A sharp, stabbing pain sliced through her head. She stumbled sideways. The crushing pressure in her head increased. Vision blurring, she tripped over her own paws, feeling drunk. Whimpering, she lowered her heavy head. She struggled against the stranglehold placed on her mind, as she tried to find the source. A pale blonde with icy blue eyes that glowed with power and sharp features stood in the middle of the ground untouched as she chanted. *The witch is doing it.* Her fists balled, showing off slender fingers in her fingerless black gloves. Bright red nails stood out against the flickering blue flames.

Stomach rolling, she arched her back and dug her paws into the ground, resisting. The witch stumbled, and the pain paused. Her spirit guardian lunged from the right, breaking her focus. The witch threw a blue sphere of power. Her spirit guardian disappeared and reappeared behind the witch. Taking advantage of the distraction, she sprinted forward toward the dilapidated, old church where an orangish-red glow emanated. The broken-down walls allowed her to see Isiah. A cauldron boiled over the fire. White energy flowed from Isiah into the metal container. Deep purple bruises stood out against his ashen gray skin and under his sunken in eyes. Emaciated, his collarbones and ribs stood out in his chest.

They leyline thrummed, hungry and eager to be directed. The electrified atmosphere made her fur stand on end. The witches' voices rose higher. Isiah cried out, tugging against his chains. A chasm formed in the earth, black smoke began to seep up, thick and disturbing. Her gut protested in response to the wrongness it gave off. It crept on the ground, like a monster on a quest. It wound around its first victim, tightening like a boa constrictor, crushing the life from them as they screamed and their eyes bulged.

"It's time for the sacrifice, sisters," the lead witch called. Shifting her form, she landed outside of the church, desperately seeking a way to stop the spell. Imig swooped down over the witches' heads, breaking their concentration. They threw out a bright green bolt of power, which Imig dodged. Circling, the dragon came down and opened his mouth. Yellow flames shot out of his nostrils. A second witch joined the fight, helping shield from the magical flames being rained down on their heads. Placing a hand over the pocket of her vest, Joss remembered the vial of Kishi's venom. Powerful spells were complicated. One wrong chant or ingredient could ruin everything. She spotted Rainer creeping up from behind the building. Their eyes locked. She nodded her head.

Removing the vial, she jumped into the remains of the building and pitched the glass case into the cauldron. Bolts of power hit her in the chest, throwing her out of the building. Fire raced through her veins, and she convulsed. Kaz knelt beside her, and he placed his wrist to her mouth.

"Drink, little sun."

Opening her mouth, she swallowed. The blood soothed the burning and restored her strength. Licking her lips, she sat up. The cauldron rattled angrily, hopping around like a tantrum-throwing toddler, before the contents exploded. Inky darkness burst forth and flowed into the chasm that grew wider.

"It's been promised a meal, and it plans to collect. You can't stop what's been started here," one of the witches inside cackled. A tentacle-like tendril of darkness wrapped around her and yanked her toward the opening. Tilting her head up, she went to her earthbound grave, with her head held high. Her body disappeared inside of the crack, and the wind began to howl.

"Joss." Rainer's desperate cry drew her attention to her brother. His chest rose and fell slowly as he fought to breathe.

Standing, she flashed herself to his side. As she knelt over him, she met his gaze.

"The Alpha's dead, Isiah. You can't leave me here to rule alone."

His lips quirked up. "Good," he rasped.

"This is going to hurt," she warned him. Placing her hands on his chest, she forced the power of the pack into his body. He grunted, arching off the stone ground he'd slid to as he received it. Eyes rolling into the back of his head, he shook violently as the wolf took over. Fur sprouted, bones popped and shifted, as he changed. He stood on shaky legs, a bigger, heartier wolf. Shock colored his expression at his new Dire Wolf form. The final puzzle clicked into place with his recovery. The pack magic hummed happily.

"Look," Kaz cried.

She turned to watch as the members of her pack shifted, taking on their new forms one by one.

"Looks like we leveled up." Isiah's mental voice lacked its usual strength, but he was there.

"Just in time." The fight was nowhere near done, and the slithering thing from the chasm continued to capture and devour at will.

"We need Nakeeta," Kaz said.

"Where is she?" Joss scanned the area and found the witch surrounded by her loyal band of vampires and witches as she cast spells.

"It's time. She needs us," Rainer said.

"Time for what?" Joss asked.

"To do what we were chosen to do," Rainer replied cryptically.

"Help us get to Nakeeta." Joss sent the command to her pack.

They advanced, with the help of the pack and Kaz. Joss worked with Isiah, keeping the waif Seer between them.

Cyprian and Cian moved to allow them to enter.

"You got him." Nakeeta panted. Sweat dotted her brow, and her shoulders drooped.

"We did. What are we going to do about the Loch Ness Monster coming out of the ground?" Joss gestured toward the terrifying darkness creeping closer.

"We have to seal the vortex. They ripped it open, and something nasty is trying to come through," Nakeeta answered.

"And how do we do that?" Kazimir asked.

"I'm still working on that," Nakeeta said..

"It's a wound. It must be healed," Rainer explained. "When we were chosen, we were given that power. It's in our blood."

"That's a massive *wound*, Rain," Joss said skeptically.

"But we're harnessing the power of the comet tonight," Nakeeta whispered excitedly. Her eyes glowed. She dug a black-handled, silver knife out of a holster she wore on her hip. "This is a ceremonial blade. We're going to call on nature to heal this blight. It's unnatural, and the universe wants to regain its balance." Nakeeta slashed her right hand. "We'll do the spell palm to palm." She handed the dagger to Rainer who cut a line on both palms and handed the blade to Joss.

"The spell chant will be 'Spirits of nature, we are one, heal this wound, and make there none.' Do you have it?" Nakeeta asked.

"Yes," Rainer and Joss replied.

They stood in the center of chaos, palm to palm, arms held high.

"Spirits of nature, we are one, heal this wound, and make there none," they chanted, scanning the area for signs of change.

"Don't stop," Kaz cried.

"God's bones. Look up," Crewe said in a hushed tone.

Above them, a whirlpool of light had begun to form in the sky.

"Spirits of nature, we are one, heal this wound and make there none." They put more power behind their words as their blood continued to flow, mingle, and drip onto the ground below them. The whirlpool began to churn violently. Thunder rumbled, and the air grew charged. Her body tingled while energy flowed from the soles of her feet through the crown of her head. She squinted as Rainer and Nakeeta began to have a luminous glow. Light burst from the vortex above them. She blinked, blinded momentarily.

Her jaw dropped, and she faltered in her chant as she spotted the beings floating down. Made of pure light that pulsed, they stood tall and slender. She stuttered. "S-Spirts," resuming her recitation.

The beings worked together, flying down to the chasm in pairs. The creature of darkness fled from them, quickly slithering away from the light and back down into its hole. The glowing beings sealed the earth, like surgeons repairing a tear. Joss's heart pounded in her chest. *What are they?*

"For centuries the Above People have watched you destroy the land and one another. Today, you cry out for healing and come to us as a united force.

We've heard you, and choose to honor your request as you usher in a great time of change." They pulsed, growing too bright to look upon.

She closed her eyes and felt the heat and light through her lids. A hot gust of air blew over her. The light dimmed, and she opened her eyes. Scorched spots of earth were all that remained of their enemies. The power the beings wielded frightened her.

"We have begun the process, but it is up to you to complete it." Their voices were sexless and pleasant to the ear. But there was no mistaking the raw power behind them. The Blackfoot pack bowed their heads, and Joss followed their example.

"You honor us today, Above People. We thank you." Nakeeta's voice shook. They lowered their hands and watched as the mysterious beings returned to the sky in a final flash of brilliant white light.

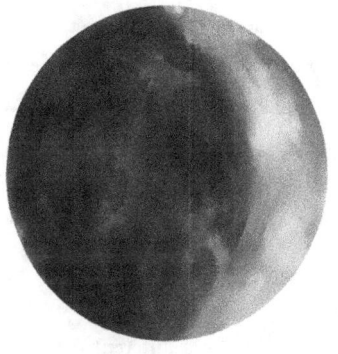

Epilogue

Joss WALKED BESIDE NAKEETA AS the private jet the vampire council sent for Crewe was loaded with their bags. Rebuilding and negotiating had been a painfully slow process, but they'd managed to form an interspecies council. The trust and communication between them remained a work in progress.

"Where will you go?" Joss asked, already missing her.

"Back to my store. I've missed it, and Crewe has been granted permission to live and operate from my city." Nakeeta gave her a shy smile.

"Yeah, being the savior of life as we know it will give you some serious pull," Joss replied sarcastically.

"You'd know all about that wouldn't you, co-Alpha?" Nakeeta nudged her side with her elbow.

Joss smiled. "Maybe a little." It would've been inconceivable to have a vampire live among them just a few months ago, but now everything had changed. Joss placed a hand over her gently rounding belly. *The impossible has become almost normal these days.*

"When they said they expected us to usher in healing, I hadn't expected this side effect," Joss admitted dryly.

"But what a lovely miracle," Kazimir drawled.

"You're next." Joss gestured from Nakeeta to Crewe who smiled.

"I think you mean to say Rainer will be next," Crewe said.

"Wait. Are you?" Joss asked.

Nakeeta nodded happily, and Joss squealed and hugged her. "Congratulations."

"Thank you. Apparently, the Above People wasted no time."

"They are showing us we're more compatible than we ever believed," Rainer said calmly. Isiah stood beside her, a different man. The time being tortured, freedom from his father, and the discovery of his mate changed him. She'd begun to see glimpses of the boy she'd once been close to.

Running the pack together had been the most viable answer, but they were still working through their personal issues. Forgiving didn't mean forgetting. Little by little, they were overcoming hurdles, and airing out the septic wounds, so they could function as a healthy pack. Each of them bore wounds. She'd brought in counselors and opened a voting system up to the others as they tried to piece together a new way of life and rules everyone could get behind. It wouldn't happen in a season, or even two, but she felt confident eventually they'd get there. Releasing her friend, she watched as Kazimir gave Crew a manly hug before he came to stand beside her, placing a hand over her belly. Leaning against his side, she watched their friends board.

It had taken twenty-five years, but her life had finally begun, and it was worth every hurdle she'd had to overcome to find happiness and true freedom. Together they would build a legacy to be proud of.

THE END

About the Author

Shyla Colt is the sassy USA Today Bestselling author of the popular series Kings of Chaos and Dueling Devils M.C. This genre-hoppers stories feature three of her favorite things: strong females, pop culture, and alternate routes to happy ever after. Listening to her Romani soul, she pens from the heart, allowing the dynamic characters, eccentric interests, and travels as a former flight attendant to take her down untraveled roads. Born and raised in Cincinnati, Ohio, this mid-west girl is proud of her roots. She used her hometown and the surrounding areas as a backdrop for a number of books. So, if you're a Buckeye, keep an eye out for familiar places.

As a full-time writer, stay at home mother, and wife, there's never a dull moment in her household. She weaves her tales in spare moments and the evenings with a cup of coffee or tea at her side and the characters in her head for company.

You can interact with Shyla Colt online:
www.shylacolt.net
Facebook: www.facebook.com/authorshyla.colt
Twitter: @shylacolt
Instagram: https://www.instagram.com/shylacolt

Previous Works

Bad Duology
Bad Blood

Witch for Hire Series
Witch for Hire
Hail to the Queen